For my girls,

BLOOD MONEY

A SAM POPE NOVEL

ROBERT ENRIGHT

CHAPTER ONE

For years, Simon Grant had been looking over his shoulder.

Some of the more experienced board members of Apex had told him, when he ascended to CEO a few months after his forty-second birthday, that a man of his position would always have enemies. As the market leader in bio-chemical production in the UK, Apex had certainly experienced its fair share of controversy. From a litany of sexual misconduct charges against a number of previous authority figures, to the usual environmental campaigns painting them as the enemy, the company was shrouded in villainy.

It was, on the other hand, one of the most profitable organisations in the country.

In the near two decades Grant had been at the wheel, the company had expanded beyond anyone's imagination, and the board members who were still in their seats worked tirelessly to keep the wolves from the door. Their bank accounts were full to the brim, thanks to impressive growth under Grant's tutelage, and the majority of them didn't want to know the finer details.

Chemical weapons.

That had been the game changer for Grant, and when he assigned an elite team of scientists and engineers to begin work on world-changing weapons, it opened more doors than he could walk through. Every warmonger in the world was soon in contact, and through a well-designed and impenetrable network, Apex soon became the dominant force in the world of chemical warfare. For a while, Grant had struggled with his conscience. The thought of being the hand that built the weapons that mutilated cities and killed thousands of innocent women and children often visited him in his sleep. But as with all things, when the money came rolling in, those deaths became a necessary outcome of the business he was a part of.

It wasn't his kids being murdered.

It wasn't his country under siege.

But something changed four years ago when Sam Pope took down the notorious gangster, Frank Jackson.

Grant never regarded the gangster as a friend, but as an associate and he'd experienced the offerings of Jackson's High Rise a number of times. When he turned fifty, Grant discovered his wife's affair and sent her packing, ensuring that she never saw a penny of his vast wealth. She'd tried to take him to court, but when money talks, it's those with an endless supply who speak loudest. In the decade since then, he'd kept to himself, paying for his physical needs to be met and Jackson had been the man with the greatest selection.

Until Sam Pope took it away.

Then other dominos began to fall.

Grant had never been in the same room as the Kovalenkos, but any major player in the UK was aware of who they were. Once touted as an untouchable force in the underbelly of London, the family and their sex trafficking operation were eradicated from the earth by Pope.

One by one, the elite and the powerful were soon taken down.

General Ervin Wallace.

Harry Chapman.

Slaven Kovac.

Dale Munroe.

Hell, even Pierre Ducard, the man who was destined to become the prime minister of France, found himself in Pope's crosshairs.

But all the while, Grant's confidants assured him that their secrets and their dealings would remain so deep in the shadows, not even someone as ruthless as Sam Pope would be able to find them. It was an assurance that had kept Grant sane for the past few years, but as he stepped out onto the street from his luxury apartment block in Chelsea to the Rolls Royce, he looked over his shoulder.

His chauffeur, who was always armed, would assure him that they were safe, but every day, Grant wondered if it would be his last.

Wondered if a man as deadly and as relentless as Sam Pope would finally draw his sniper rifle up, see Grant in the scope, and squeeze the trigger.

There had been an avalanche of articles written about Pope in the years since he'd begun his crusade. Depending on which side of the political divide the outlet sat, they were either admonishing him for breaking the law and painting him as a serial killer or heralding him as the saviour of the people. The reality was that Pope existed somewhere between the two of them, and Grant respected and loathed the man in equal measure.

Men like Munroe and Ducard were supposed to be untouchable. They were supposed to have amassed such power and wealth that even the governments put in place to manage them would buckle before they would.

That was what was expected.

That was the status quo.

It was what Grant had been promised and for years had become accustomed to.

Then came the news that Vladimir Balikov had been arrested.

The morning the news broke, Grant had rushed to the toilet in his five-bedroomed penthouse and chucked up his breakfast.

Balikov *was* untouchable.

That was what had been promised to him when he'd been approached by *Poslednyaya Nadezhda*, with Balikov's right-hand man Artem Alenichev courting Grant for months to finalise their partnership. The courtship consisted of a luxury yacht, the finest women and cuisine the world could offer, and the promise of a prominent seat at the table when their vision became a reality. The wheels had been turning on the operation for years, with Balikov insistent on changing the world for the better.

Of burning it all down and rebuilding it on a different set of principles.

A sterner, harsher world.

One that made people earn their status and not just be handed what they expected.

Grant had been impressed and even found himself to be a guest of honour at the inaugural *Boytsovskaya Yama* tournament, along with three other men from the same social circle. The relationship between Russia and the United Kingdom had gone beyond breaking point over the past few years, yet Balikov could see the intelligence in rebuilding that bridge. But in the world he envisioned, that relationship wasn't upheld by the puny governments which had allowed the world to go soft.

It would be based on the respect held between the rich and powerful who took what they wanted and were willing to make the hard calls to stay on top.

It was a new world, a potential nirvana for the elite, and Grant soon found himself supplying *Poslednyaya Nadezhda* with the required shipments to begin the construction of their nuclear weapons. His conscience had long since evaporated, and while he knew he'd be responsible for an historic change to the world as they knew it, it would all be worth it.

He, along with a few others, would mould the United Kingdom into a better place.

Now, he lived in fear.

The reports of Balikov's arrest were limited, with several high-ranking officials, who Grant considered personal friends, only recounting hearsay.

An *off-the-books* mission.

A secret arm of the government.

Sam Pope.

These were the whispers.

And they were the reasons why now, on a brisk autumnal evening, his chauffeur was navigating through the busy streets of London with Grant anxiously sitting in the back seat. Although the windows to the Rolls Royce had always been tinted, Grant had spared no expense to bulletproof them, along with the rest of the car. What had once been his luxurious transport was now a safe haven, and with the rumours of Sam Pope taking down *Poslednyaya Nadezhda* swirling, he and his cohorts needed to take steps.

That was why Grant had called the meeting.

And he hoped the other three men had already arrived.

With zero regard to the restrictions outside the building, his chauffeur parked the car across the double yellow lines. Whatever ticket the local council would pin to the window, Grant would have one of his finance team take care of. A small price to pay if they needed to make a speedy exit.

The chauffeur stepped out and made his way around the car and then pulled open Grant's door.

'We're here, sir.'

Grant nodded his appreciation. Having recently turned sixty, Grant's life of excess had begun to take its toll, and the chauffeur offered his hand to help Grant guide his portly physique out of the car. Once standing, Grant pulled his expensive overcoat tight as the wind blew through his thinning, white hair.

'Keep your eyes open,' Grant said firmly. The chauffeur nodded and then adjusted the holster within his jacket, which housed a Glock 17.

Loaded and ready to be used at a moment's notice.

Bakku was one of the most exclusive restaurants in the city, with a small and wealthy membership list. Grant had insisted upon being one of the first members and laughed off the five-figure annual membership fee. The restaurant was on the eleventh floor of the building, which loomed large over Kensington, mockingly basking in the affluence of the area. Such exclusivity enabled the restaurant to limit its capacity to just ten tables, but it's ever-changing menu and extravagant wine list was so grotesquely priced that it would give the housing market a run for its money. The entire experience of Bakku was to feel elite.

Above the common man.

It was owned by an Albanian man called Omar Kelmendi, who had ties to the Albanian royal family. Not only did it ensure the authenticity of the produce, but it also meant that the security within the restaurant was of a similar calibre. Every night, there were six armed guards standing strategically throughout the establishment, each one plucked from paid mercenary work after long stints in the Albanian Armed Forces and each one trained to eliminate a threat without hesitation.

With the right amount of money, anything was possible, and Grant was grateful for the 'no expense spared' policy that Kelmendi had implemented. Bakku offered a safe haven to men of power, or for those, like Grant and his associates, who needed to meet in private.

To feel safe.

As they stepped out of the elevator onto the eleventh floor, Grant signalled his chauffeur to head back to the car, while he was greeted by the maître d', who smiled from behind his podium.

'Ah, Mr Grant. Some of your party is already here.'

Grant was shuffling himself free of his coat, and the maître d' helped ease it from his arms.

'Thank you.' Grant offered a forced smiled. 'Usual table?'

'As always, sir.'

'Has Mr Stokely arrived yet?'

The maître d' checked the reservation book and shook his head.

'Not yet, sir. Shall I bring him through as soon as he does?'

'Please.'

Grant strode into the restaurant, which was full to capacity. A few heads turned his way, some of them nodding respectfully. Grant had no need to mingle with the clientele, knowing most of them knew who he was and would no doubt try to use him to climb the social ladder. If people wanted to succeed, they could do it off their own work, not his. A few young, rich men were entertaining strikingly beautiful women at one table, and on the far side of the room, a couple of lone people were dotted across the bar. As he approached his table, his guests turned and stood.

'Please. Sit.'

He waved them off, and Colin Hutchins and Piers Bloom sat back down. Grant took his seat, lifted the bottle of wine that was already on the table and tutted.

'Have you no taste?' he asked, and then motioned to one of the waiters standing around the room like well-dressed statues.

'Apologies, Simon,' Bloom said. 'Although I am learning.'

'Yes, but not fast enough.' Grant smirked, and the waiter approached. Grant ordered the most obnoxious sounding wine from the menu and was applauded for his tastes. Once the waiter scuttled away, he turned back to his guests. 'So, I take it you've read the proposal?'

The two men looked at each other. Like Grant, they were on the wrong side of sixty and were in varying stages of their decline. Bloom's hair had long since departed, but unlike Grant, hadn't allowed his wealth to dictate his eating habits. A wealth that had been amassed over thirty years as CEO of the leading engineering firm in the UK. The man was as fit as a forty-year-old, and he made up for his hair loss with a thick, neat grey beard. Hutchins was the polar opposite. A meek, frail man who'd amassed his fortune through the crypto currency market. They, like Grant, had been absorbed in *Poslednyaya Nadezhda*, with their companies and skill sets already working towards the brave new world Balikov had promised.

It made them complicit.

Which now made them targets.

As Grant waited for his answer, the waiter returned with the bottle and presented it to the cantankerous man like it was a trophy. Grant waved off the notion of tasting it, knowing that every bottle was pulled from the most expensively assembled wine collection in the UK. As the waiter poured the wine into three fresh glasses, Bloom sighed.

'I think it's too risky.'

Grant's thick, white eyebrows arched as he regarded Bloom, and then he swirled his glass. After a generous swig, Grant placed his drink down and responded.

'So, what do you propose we do instead, then? Hmm?' Grant never broke eye contact when he spoke. 'Balikov is out. That means *everything* he built will come crumbling down and all three of us were pillars of his operation.'

'He's got a point,' Hutchins said, as he pushed his glasses up his nose.

'Of course, I have a point. Look, Stokely is a man who I've relied on a few times over the years to handle certain situations for myself and my business.' Grant paused for a moment, as if the ghosts of the past had just run through him. 'If what we are hearing is true, and Sam Pope was involved, then there's a high chance that he'll be coming for us as well.'

'And this…this Stokely chap. He's what? Going to take him out?' Bloom asked with clear irritation.

'Exactly. He'll be providing a service that I'm sure we'll all agree with.'

'Not me.' The interruption caused all three men to snap their heads to the left, their eyes widened and faces dropped, as Sam Pope pulled back the fourth chair around the table and plonked himself down in it. An expensive jacket clung to his muscular frame, and he loosened the tie that hung around his neck. 'That's better.'

'What the fuck is this…' Bloom stammered as he looked around the room for security.

'Stokely isn't coming, by the way,' Sam informed them politely, but the threat was ominous. Casually, he rested his hands on the table and drummed his fingers. 'We need to have a little chat, don't you think?'

Before any of them could answer, Sam had already clocked the three security guards thundering towards them.

He sighed, rolled his shoulders to loosen them, and resigned himself to the fact that he'd have to do this the hard way.

CHAPTER TWO

For a brief moment, Sam Pope had thought about walking away.

From all of it.

The sobering thought crossed his mind as he sat on the flight back to Gatwick, less than an hour after saying goodbye to Amara Singh and Director Blake. As he sat in his seat, he could feel people shooting glances in his direction. He didn't blame them. The stitches that held his eyebrow together dominated his forehead, and one of his eyes was swollen shut. What they couldn't see were the bruises that dominated his body having survived *Boytsovskaya Yama*, which culminated in his brutal fight to the death with Balikov's son.

As he cast his one good eye out over the clouds, he thought about walking away. He already had a new identity, and with his previous fortune having been transferred across to it, he could simply disappear.

But the USB stick in his pocket had kept him on course.

Vladimir Balikov was in custody, and most likely, would

be executed for the crimes he committed, whether the death penalty was still legal or not. Russia wouldn't take kindly to one of their own threatening to topple the regime and ignite a new world order across Europe, and Sam knew that he and the rest of Directive One had stopped an international disaster.

But Balikov hadn't acted alone, and the sickening feeling in the pit of Sam's stomach was that within his own country, there were those who supported the cause. Powerful people who'd believed in the vision of tyranny that Balikov had painted, and those people needed to be brought to justice as well.

Blake hadn't just given him a USB stick with their names on.

He'd given him permission to act upon it.

For the weeks that followed, Sam rested up and allowed his body to recuperate. When he was feeling ready to step back into the fight, he began working his way through the list. Powerful and influential people who were held up as cornerstones of the British economy had invested in Balikov's plans. It sickened Sam how far the man had infiltrated the UK, and Sam did his best to investigate some of the more well-known names on the list.

Simon Grant had been a titan of British industry for almost two decades and when Sam saw the name on the list, he felt his stomach flip. Grant was a billionaire, but one whom ensured his public image was so squeaky clean you could eat your dinner off it. Charity drives that raised millions for orphanages and childhood cancer research. Sponsorship schemes that had benefitted thousands of under-privileged children and put many young adults into work.

The man was a virtual saint.

Yet, as Sam combed through the data, the man had

donated more than fifty million to *Poslednyaya Nadezhda* and was the supply chain for Balikov's dreams of chemical warfare.

Grant was a traitor.

He had to be stopped.

For the next few weeks, Sam had studied Grant. His movements. His means of transportation. Everything. With London has busy as ever, it wasn't hard for him to effortlessly follow the business mogul into restaurants or bars, nor was it tricky to hop into a rented car and follow the multiple routes the chauffeur would take to return him to his penthouse in Chelsea.

What Sam needed, however, was the right moment to strike. The plan was never to put the man in the ground, as much as he'd have liked to. It was to expose the corruption and treachery and to show the government what was happening under their noses. They'd allowed these powerful people to exist on a different plane to the rest of the country, as long as they donated when the time was right and showed their support during the elections.

Sam needed more.

It took less than half an hour to draw up a list of workers who were employed by Apex in their IT department using LinkedIn. The platform was a treasure trove of information, and all Sam needed was to find an employee who'd been there long enough to be overlooked, and easy enough to be swayed.

Josh Lowton.

Seven years working on the Support Team and no progression of any kind. It was worth a shot.

Sam accosted Josh on his lunch break, as the man queued at his favourite stall in the local food market and Sam quickly made his proposal. He would pay Josh ten thousand pounds if he could provide Sam with access to

Grant's calendar, which Josh explained could land him in prison.

Sam upped it to fifteen, and the deal was done.

Not only that, Josh threw in access to Grant's email account too, with the access being provided across a secure, undetectable network. It gave Sam the opportunity to read through Grant's prior correspondence, where he stumbled across the plans Grant was putting in place with a man known as Stokely.

A fixer.

What was most interesting was that their discussions were about Sam himself, and the thinly-veiled threat that Grant wanted Sam taken out as a means of protection.

They set a time and place.

Bakku.

Within ten minutes, Sam had once again dipped into the generous war fund his good friend, Paul Etheridge had left him, and acquired a membership to the outrageously expensive venue. Then, posing as Grant, he made contact with Stokely and asked for a pre-meeting catch-up to brief Stokely on the other people who'd be joining them.

Names that had appeared on Sam's list.

Stokely agreed, and on the way to surprise Grant, Bloom, and Hutchins, Sam had made a detour to the car park just outside Hammersmith where he'd directed Stokely. He'd parked his rental car in one of the spaces and then waited.

Promptly, Stokely arrived, looking as inconspicuous as he possibly could but to the trained eye, was clearly an ex-military man.

Strong posture.

Purposeful.

Clearly trained.

As the man stood patiently, Sam stepped out of the vehicle and walked nonchalantly across the car park.

Stokely's eyes fell upon him, and as Sam moved within range, Stokely had barked at him to move along. Sam pretended he couldn't hear, and as Stokely took an aggressive step towards him, Sam struck a hard blow to the man's throat, and then drove his elbow into Stokely's temple and shut his lights out. Quickly, Sam took the man's keys, unlocked the car he'd arrived in, and dumped him in the boot. Then, he sped off through London to Bakku, signed in as Ben Carter and took his seat at the bar.

It had all gone to plan.

But now, as the three men stared at him in panic, he noticed the security guards closing in on the table. He sighed, cracked his neck slightly and waited for the first hand to land on his shoulder. Sam had done his research, and he knew the security detail that patrolled Bakku were not only highly trained, but they were once mercenaries who sold their skills to the highest bidder. Not many people were as cash rich as Kelmendi, and not only could he offer them the easiest work for the highest pay, he ensured they could do so with a Glock 17 strapped to their ribs. Sam had ventured into the bar for the past few evenings, just so he became a familiar face, but also to scope out the venue itself.

How many guards were on shift at any one time?

Where the exits were.

All that information flowed through him as he took a breath, and as the guard tried to lock his grip on Sam's pressure point, Sam dropped his shoulder. The man's hand slipped forward across Sam's leather jacket, and Sam yanked it down by the wrist, drilling the man's face into the dinner table. As the man's head snapped back, and the blood burst from his shattered nose, Sam locked on with his grip and stood, wrenching the arm backwards and driving his other elbow into the man's jaw. As the mandible shattered, Sam wrenched the Glock 17 from the guard's holster, lifted it up into the air, and pulled the trigger.

The gunshot echoed in the confined space and sent the entire room into a panic, as customers and staff succumbed to the panic and began racing towards the door. The other two guards who were rushing towards Sam drew their own guns from their jackets and without hesitation or concern for the terrified civilians, pulled the trigger.

Sam spun behind the injured guard, and the bullets rattled into the unfortunate man's back. Having felt the force of a bullet one too many times over the past few years, Sam was thankful for the man's unwilling sacrifice. Before the dead body could slump onto him, Sam side-stepped and allowed him to crash to the floor. As he did so, he drew the gun up into his expert eyeline and squeezed the trigger twice and planted two bullets between two sets of eyes.

The two guards dropped dead.

The entire restaurant was rocking with terror, as people fought among each other to filter through the single door towards the stairwell. As they unknowingly formed a blockade that kept two of the other guards out of the restaurant, Sam turned and pointed the gun directly at the three rich, old men who were still glued to their seats.

'It's a bad night to be a bad guy, huh?'

'Fuck you!' Bloom spat through clenched teeth.

Sam turned the gun on him and pulled the trigger. The bullet ripped through the man's shoulder, sending him spinning out of his chair and into a howling ball of pain. He turned to Hutchins, who whimpered and begged for his life.

Then he turned to Grant.

'Turn yourself in,' Sam ordered. 'Admit to everything. Balikov. *Poslednyaya Nadezhda*. Every last detail.'

'Just kill me,' Grant muttered feebly.

'Excuse me?'

'Just fucking kill me,' Grant begged. Sam stepped forward and pressed the gun to Grant's wrinkled forehead. As fear jolted through Grant's body, he closed his eyes and took a breath.

Accepting his fate.

Sam withdrew the gun and Grant's eyes opened in confusion.

'The world deserves to know what you had planned. And you deserve to rot in prison.'

Before Grant could respond, Sam turned as a foot crunched on a felled wine glass, and before he could pull the Glock around with him, the fourth security guard charged forward. Driving his shoulder into Sam's recently repaired ribs, he lifted Sam off the ground and slammed him down on the table. The impact drove the air out of Sam's lungs, and the guard showed no signs of relenting. The guards' eyes were crazed, clearly fuelled by vengeance for his fallen colleagues. He wrapped his hands around Sam's throat and pressed his thumbs down on Sam's jugular. As he did, Grant and Hutchins left their seats and rushed to Bloom, who cursed wildly in Sam's direction as they tried to help him to his feet. Sam threw a few brutal strikes up at the guard, but the man's adrenaline absorbed the strikes and he pushed down harder, closing Sam's windpipe and pushing Sam closer to death.

Sam fought.

He punched and punched, but as the air seeped from his body, the strikes he threw grew weaker. His hand fumbled on the table blindly, and he knocked over a wine glass. Sam wrapped his fingers around it and shattered it against the table. Then, with his fingers wrapped around the base, he drove the broken shard up into the man's armpit.

The guard roared with pain and loosened his grip, and as soon as the air flooded back into Sam's lungs, he swung the broken glass into the man's neck. The jagged edge punctured the man's skin and Sam drove it as deeply into the man's throat as possible.

The guard relinquished his hold and stumbled backwards, lamely pressing his hand to the glass as the blood began to pump through his fingers. He gurgled as he choked on his own blood, and Sam rolled back on the table and then drove a boot into the man's chest, sending him stumbling backwards into another table.

The man hit the deck, coughed up a large spatter of blood and then went limp.

As Sam sat up and glared at Grant, the final two guards burst through the final few stragglers of the panicked crowd and aimed their guns at Sam. As they fired, Sam rolled off the table and hit the ground hard. He ignored the pain of the impact and lifted the gun he'd already used to send two men to the grave.

A few more bullets hit the table, and Sam closed his eyes, took a breath and zeroed in on the footsteps. It was a skill he'd learnt nearly two decades ago, when he first joined the Sniper Division of the British Armed Forces.

Push out the noise.

Use his senses to map out the situation.

Execute.

As one of the guards bumped into a table to the left, Sam spun to his feet, the weapon already drawn, and he unleashed two bullets that thudded into the man's torso. As the guard hit the ground for his final breaths, Sam locked in on the final guard, who was a millisecond behind.

Sam pulled the trigger first.

The bullet snapped the man's head backwards and blew out the back of his skull, sending him flopping to the bloodstained floor and painting the tablecloth behind him in a violent shade of red.

All six men had been killed.

The police were most likely on their way.

With the seconds escaping him, Sam worked the pain out of his hip and stepped towards the three men, who were huddled fearfully on the floor. The only one with any real fight, Bloom, was turning a sinister shade of pale as the shock and blood loss were kicking in. Sam bent down and took Hutchins' hands and guided them to the bullet wound he'd administered.

'Press down here. Both sides,' Sam instructed. 'He'll live.'

Knowing the game was up, Grant lifted himself to his feet with considerable difficulty as Sam turned to leave.

'You're a dead man, you hear me, Pope.' Grant spat as he realised defiance was his final card left to play. 'You've made some dangerous enemies.'

'I'll just add you to the list,' Sam replied, and then he stopped and turned back. 'Like I said. Every detail. Otherwise, everything you men have built, everything you believe to be your legacy. I'll burn it to the ground.'

Grant's bravery dissipated as the realisation set in, and he slumped down next to his acquaintances, who'd all accepted their fate. Sam strode past the carnage he'd left in his wake, and as he approached the doorway, Omar Kelmendi confronted him.

'What the fuck do you think...'

THUD!

Sam drove the butt of the Glock into the man's skull, sending him slumping against the podium and its contents crashing to the floor alongside his unconscious body.

As Sam pushed open the door to the stairwell and began to descend the building, he could hear the sirens wailing in the distance.

The boys in blue would be there in the next few minutes, armed to the teeth and ready to take Sam down.

All they would find was the bloody aftermath and three of the most influential businessmen in the country and their biggest arrest in years.

Sam would be long gone and ready to check another name off his list.

CHAPTER THREE

The past few years had felt like a whirlwind for Detective Sergeant Jess Sutton.

Growing up in Harrow, she'd always felt on the outskirts of London itself, with the town existing in the borough of Middlesex and bordering Hertfordshire, it never felt like she was a "city kid". Although it was situated within the dreaded M25 motorway that looped around London itself, Harrow lacked the hustle and bustle of the inner city, as well as the claustrophobic feel. In fact, despite clear evidence to the contrary, Harrow was seen as an affluent haven full of rich kids and private schools. The famous Harrow School had much to do with that, sitting at the top of the hill and existing in a world so different from the rest of the town. Whereas the Harrow that DS Sutton grew up in was like any other town, complete with an average high street, the hill itself was a monument to wealth and status. The large houses were gated, situated along winding, private roads and scattered around the grounds of the school, which had separate buildings dotted throughout. Renowned for educating a number of Nobel Prize winners, along with national icons such as Winston

Churchill and Lord Byron, the school's place in the fabric of Britain was well known. Its extortionate term fees were well into the five figures, and those attending the school had to take it as seriously as their parents' bank balances did. There were a few pubs and restaurants that Sutton had ventured up to during her late teens, to experience the world atop the hill, but again, it was nothing that could compare to the capital itself. Growing up, she'd watched her two older brothers excel at school and head off to university, but it was a path that had never excited her. She found more thrills in the possibilities of police work, especially when her uncle regaled her with stories of his time serving as a copper.

'It was a different time back then.'

He would often end his stories with that line, as if it would justify the actions he'd taken.

'The world's gone soft now.'

That was another favourite. But it had stoked a passion within her, and when she passed out as a twenty-year-old police officer, she was proud that he'd accompanied her parents to watch her. For a decade, she'd lived and breathed the life of a police constable, throwing herself into the hard life it forced upon the brave people who took up the mantle and juggled the impact it had on her socially. It wasn't until she'd turned twenty-eight that she'd settled into a serious relationship with a man called Matt, but after a few years and a failed engagement, they parted ways when he told her she put the job before him.

She couldn't correct him.

She did, and she knew she always would.

The ten years had flown by, and Sutton had managed to get on the property ladder as well as forge a career as one of the most reliable police constables in the Met.

Then everything changed.

Nearly four years ago, she was handpicked to join the

dedicated Sam Pope Taskforce, which had been put in place by the then Assistant Commissioner Ruth Ashton to hunt down the known vigilante. It was one of the most exciting times in Sutton's career, and had culminated in her ushering Adrian Hill and his daughter, Jasmine, into the back of a police car after a daring raid of the Port of Tilbury. Detective Inspector Amara Singh was an inspiration, not just to Sutton, but to a host of others and it was her dedication to bringing down Sam Pope that pushed Sutton to take, and ace, the detective's exam. For three years, she'd been working a number of cases that had links towards Sam Pope's apparent return from the dead, including the assault of Sean Wiseman and the death of Olivier Chavet. Such stellar work had seen her rise quickly and now, six months into her role as a detective sergeant working out of Charing Cross Police Station, she was working her way through the mud of another case.

Six men killed in Bakku, the fancy restaurant that overlooked Kensington and the riches below. But more newsworthy was that three of the most powerful businessmen in the country had been present and were in the midst of speaking with their legal teams about preparing a statement. Speculation was rife, with many linking it to the fall of the Russian Oligarch, Vladimir Balikov, but as always, Sutton would wait for the truth.

It meant taking an extra step, or pushing herself through hell. The truth was always worth it.

Innocent until proven guilty. That was the foundation the British justice system was built upon, and she thought the court of public opinion, as well as the rumour infested slog that comprised social media, never helped anyone. And, for all the excitement, she'd been strapped to her desk for hours working through the endless avalanche of paperwork. A voice drew her attention from her desk.

'Is it your boy?'

The voice belonged to DS Connor Vokes. The two of them had been working together for over a year now, and they'd built up a strong bond. Vokes, at thirty-six, was two years older than her, but had an extra three years of detective experience. Although they were the same rank, they understood what that seniority meant and Sutton both respected and trusted Vokes entirely. He was a good man, classically handsome, with dark hair that was cut into a short parting and green eyes that pierced through their target. As dedicated to the job as he was to his wonderful wife, Laura, and his two kids, Vokes didn't share Sutton's disdain for Sam Pope.

'It looks like it,' Sutton said as she rocked back in her chair and stretched her back. 'Another six on the list.'

'Going by the records kept on those men, that's another six bad guys.' Vokes shrugged. 'You'd think he'd charge us for the service by now.'

'Ha,' Sutton said dryly. 'It doesn't matter if he's knocking off bad guys, Connor. He's still just walking around handing out his own form of justice.'

'Fair point.' Vokes nodded. 'Coffee?'

'If you're buying.' She smiled. Although she never felt it herself, Sutton was strikingly beautiful, with shimmering brown hair that was cut into a short bob, and brown eyes so dark it looked like she had no pupils. Combined with her sharp cheekbones, Sutton had a number of fans within the Met, although she was too focused and shy to notice. 'But I've got to get through this shit before—'

'Before we get to speak to the bigwigs? Yeah, that's not happening.' Vokes shook his head.

'What the hell do you mean that's not happening?' Sutton's entire face shifted to a scowl. 'They were clearly targeted by Sam Pope, and we need to know why.'

Vokes broke out into a condescending chuckle, a rarity in their relationship, but Sutton knew the reason.

It was when she was being naïve.

'Come on, Jess.' He rested his hands on his hips. 'The second these guys started throwing their weight around, you knew for a fact it was going to be swept under the rug. Whatever the reason, and I actually believe you're right. This goes way above our pay grade.'

'How is that right?'

Vokes shrugged and looked around the office, where a few constables were working at their desks.

'It ain't right. But money talks. Come on, you know that. You grew up in Harrow, right?'

The jibe drew a smile from Sutton. Vokes was born and bred East London and had the upbringing to match his cockney swagger. He was fully aware of the reality of what Jess's upbringing truly was, but throwing out the lazy stereotype usually lightened the situation.

'Not rich enough to buy my own coffee,' she replied and waved him away. 'Off you pop.'

With another chuckle, Vokes turned and headed back across the office, and Sutton slumped back in her seat. It wasn't a shock that barriers had been put up, especially when the elite were involved, but it still turned her stomach. As much as she despised Sam Pope's one-man crusade against crime, she knew that those who ended up in his crosshairs were usually there on merit. Which meant that Simon Grant, Colin Hutchins and Piers Bloom were likely involved in something that they didn't want to become public.

That they wanted to handle it off-record and with the way the legal system usually bent to the weight of wealth, meant they'd get away with it and if she kept pushing the envelope, she'd be one of the names who would be swept under the rug with their crimes.

It happened more than the public knew. Assistant Commissioner Ruth Ashton was given a golden handshake after her links to General Ervin Wallace were discovered. Her inspiration, DI Amara Singh, fell off the radar after the incident at UCL. The much maligned DI Adrian Pearce gave up his crusade against corruption when he rattled too many cages. Even Commissioner Bruce McEwen, esteemed and beloved by the majority of the Met, tangled with both the Munroe family and the political clusterfuck that was the Ducard incident and was then pushed into early retirement.

The wealth dictated the power, and the law was only there to ensure it stayed that way.

As a worthy successor to McEwen, Commissioner Henrietta Sarrett had said all the right words with regards to protecting the city, and along with the Mayor of London, Dipti Patel, they put forward a united front of culture and diversity. As the first Black woman to take the top job, Sarratt threw her conviction behind everything she said, but in the months since she ascended from her role as assistant commissioner to the throne itself, little had changed.

An initiative here.

A by-law change there.

Nothing that told Sutton the imbalance of power would ever truly change.

With a heavy sigh, she checked her watch. It was nearly eight, but the outside world had been dark since four. Winter was falling across London with a vengeance, and the brisk winds carried a bone tingling chill on them. The city was already covered in festive lights, even with it being over fifty days until Christmas. But the capitalist nature of the world meant that the pressure to be ready for the Christmas holidays was thrust upon the public as early as possible. Sutton should have clocked off an hour before, but with the case still lost among the paperwork, she knew she'd be sitting there long after the night shift had started.

A coffee would help, and then, when Vokes headed home to his family, she'd probably nip out and pick up the nearest takeaway she could find.

She wanted to get into the depths of the case before higher brass took it from her, and she wanted to understand why three powerful men were targeted by Pope.

If she wasn't able to catch him, she wanted to at least keep building a picture of the man. If, as reported, he took down the French presidential candidate in his own estate or turned a Scottish haulage yard into a war zone, that was their problems to deal with. But leaving six dead bodies a few miles from her doorstep didn't sit well with Sutton, and if the timeframe to figure out why was dwindling, then there wasn't any reason in the world strong enough to pull her away from her desk.

With a deep sigh, she began shuffling through the paperwork once more, certain it was going to be a long night.

And she was right.

But not for the reasons she thought, and as Vokes returned with the coffee, neither of them was ready for the chaos that was about to unfold.

Another night of death in London.

Only this time, it would shake the Metropolitan Police Service to its very core.

CHAPTER FOUR

When the first call came in, Commissioner Henrietta Sarratt was beginning to wind down another delightful evening at home. The temperature had once again dropped, coating most of the wet country roads in a potentially hazardous sheen of ice. Thankfully, her journey back through the winding roads to the small village just outside of Woking wasn't too treacherous and her train journey from London to Woking Rail Station had allowed her to catch-up on the emails she'd missed during her afternoon of meetings.

As always, she was greeted at the door by Lance, her German Shepherd, who, despite technically still being a puppy, leapt up and placed his paw on her chest.

'Hello, boy,' she said eagerly, ruffling the dog's ears and squeezing his thick, fluffy body. 'Where's your daddy?'

She didn't expect an answer, nor did she need one. The rich smells that wafted through from the kitchen told her that Jordan was in the final stages of preparing their dinner. When Bruce McEwen informed her of his immediate departure from the Met, Sarratt had dreaded the impact it would have on her life. Already working tirelessly as the assistant commissioner, she knew McEwen had been grooming her to take the reins when he stepped away. It just came a few years earlier than either of them anticipated, and right in the middle of Jordan's launch of his own restaurant. As one of the most highly regarded chefs in Surrey, her husband had spent years honing his craft in London before branching out and lifting one of Surrey's most popular restaurants to a Michelin star. It gave him not only the confidence, but the vindication in his own ability and the launch of Sarratt's in Horsell was supposed to be their focus for the next few years.

But the chance to become the first Black Commissioner of the Metropolitan Police was an opportunity they both said was too big to turn down, and Jordan had leant heavily on his friend and business partner to carry more of the burden as he helped her adjust to her new position of power.

She stepped into the kitchen, was greeted with a kiss and a glass of wine, and as they enjoyed the fantastic prawn linguine he'd prepared, they discussed the ongoing issues she faced. As always, he listened intently, offered a few words of support, but when it came down to it, it was her decision that was important.

'Henny…end of the day, you need to do what's right.' He wrapped up the conversation. 'You might want to drag them all over the coals, but if that's going to bring down a shitstorm on you and the Met…then maybe you need to find another solution?'

More annoying than him calling her Henny, was the fact he was right. Her loyalty to McEwen during his tenure had made her privy to his dealings with the 'elite' and it was ultimately his refusal to bend over for the Munroe family that put him in the firing line. Then, when he held his ground against his own government who were placating a French politician, it cost him his career.

Henrietta Sarratt had worked too hard to get to her position to throw it away, but she was starting to resent the fact that she'd have to compromise her principles to keep it.

As Jordan went to work on cleaning the kitchen and clearing away the dishes, she threw on her wellies, strapped Lance's leash to his collar and ventured out for her much-needed walk. The brisk air and bitter chill was enough to waken her senses, and as she meandered around the twenty-minute loop that was their village, she indulged herself in a couple of cigarettes. Jordan had long since given up smoking, which had been a cornerstone of his career at one point, but he never judged his wife for the occasional puff.

She just didn't like doing it near the house.

As she trudged through the muddy paths that comprised her village, she nodded to a few other late evening dog walkers, but the bitter cold meant nobody was stopping for an idle exchange of small talk. As she lit her second cigarette of the walk, she contemplated calling McEwen and asking him for his steer on the whole Bakku situation. The man had a wealth of experience, not just in handling the politics of being the most powerful person in the Met, but also in dealing with Sam Pope himself. Eventually, she decided against intruding on the man's retirement and pulled her coat tight and picked up the pace. As she approached her house, the kitchen light was off, meaning Jordan had already retired to their room and a small rush of excitement tingled through Sarratt's body at the thought of joining him for an early night.

But the vibration came from her pocket, and as she eased open the front door to their detached house, she pulled her phone from her pocket and answered the call.

Two minutes later, she was headed back to her car, and

this time, she was heading straight for the city of London itself.

New Scotland Yard was in a state of shock.

The building sat on the London South Bank, overlooking the iconic River Thames. Compared to most police stations in the city, which were run down and effectively held together by tape, the New Scotland Yard building was a shining example of modern architecture. With its glass windows and doors, along with state of the art security systems, the building was a fortress that sat behind the iconic, twirling sign that stood outside.

A usual hive of excitement and activity, the entire building was already grieving the sickening news that had pulled Commissioner Sarratt back to her office and was already spreading throughout the Met.

Despite their best efforts, there was nothing they could do to stop the media machine going into full cycle as the death of PC James Harrington became public. Commissioner Sarratt was locked in a meeting room with some of the most senior figures of the organisation, as well as the Minister of State, Graham Henshaw. As one of the most despised men in the Met, Henshaw had been the one who'd approved single officer patrols, something which Sarratt and both her predecessors had fought valiantly against. But as with all things to do with the government, it was about the money, and Henshaw had a reputation for being able to cost cut just enough for it to have an impact on a few, but not on many.

It was now blowing up in his face.

PC Harrington had attended a call from a concerned resident about a group of teenagers lurking in the alleyway behind their house in Hackney. Usually, these calls resulted in a few stern words and a quick scattering of the youths.

Not this time.

They listened back to the radio recording of Harrington informing control that there were no teenagers in sight. Seconds later, the panic button on his radio was hit. As many available officers as possible rushed to the scene, only to find Harrington alone and motionless in the dank, wet alleyway, with a clean slice across his throat.

His eyes were wide open, and a young man who'd only just passed his twenty-seventh birthday had been murdered in cold blood.

The mood was one of anger, and Sarratt was aware that housing the man her officers held responsible was a potentially volatile move. But as always, Henshaw was steadfast in his belief that something else must have been a factor in the senseless death of a young officer.

An agenda?

An unfortunate accident?

Anything to cover his tracks and keep the blame from the government's door.

Before the meeting could escalate further, the unthinkable happened.

Another death.

The room was shocked into silence as Chief Inspector Mary Dummett burst into the room; her face a ghastly shade of pale as she announced another PC had been found dead in Willesden. PC Melanie Dyer had been found motionless in an alleyway that ran alongside an abandoned building just outside of the estate. Willesden was one of the more notorious crime hotspots in the London Borough of Brent, with drug use rising at a worrying rate. Dummett didn't have all the facts, but the on-scene uniform was telling her that due to the fatal injuries sustained by the young officer, it seemed like she'd fallen from the top floor of the adjacent building.

Two officers reported dead within ninety minutes of each other.

The Met Police were being targeted.

Sarratt put the word out for the PR team to contact every major news outlet immediately, demanding that they hold back on the story they would no doubt sensationalise. It would likely do two things – illicit fear among the citizens who relied on the police to keep them safe and stoke the fury of those who hated the badge with a passion. If word got out that someone was killing police officers, it could inspire those with a grudge to do similar.

A mandate was also put out across every radio and to every police inbox that, for the time being, any call-outs must be attended by two officers. Henshaw, despite his usual penchant for cost cutting, agreed wholeheartedly. Beyond all the political nonsense that would usually be thrown around such a meeting, the core issue overpowered everything.

Two police constables had been murdered on the same night.

It was unprecedented, and Sarratt could feel the burden of her position weighing down on her shoulders and everyone looked to her for the answer. The only option was for damage limitation in the immediate aftermath, as they couldn't shut down the Met, nor could they expect its ranks to be operating with a clear mind. The idea that some of their own had been murdered would play into every thought process of every police officer, either stoking thoughts and feelings of fear or revenge. There was also the snowball effect of social media, and one of the tech team had brought up a Twitter feed of the incident onto the big screen.

People were already talking about it.

It would only get worse.

It wasn't long before they were joined by Dipti Patel, the Mayor of London, who'd been woken by a panicked phone call from a member of her staff and now wanted to be fully involved in the response. Sarratt had a lot of respect for Patel, who, like herself, was a woman of colour in a position of power, and they were silently linked by the challenges that posed. Patel was also a firm ally of her predecessor, Bruce McEwen, and had written Sarratt a wonderful letter when she'd taken the top job to congratulate her and offer her support.

Patel cared about the city.

She cared about the people who resided within it, and those who protected it.

She was feeling just as mortified by the events as Sarratt was.

As the rain hammered against the glass windows of the meeting room, Sarratt looked out over the rain-soaked city she'd sworn to protect and knew that this was just the beginning. If someone was targeting police officers, then it was unlikely they would just stop at two. But there was no way to know when or where or even why. Many a grudge was held against the Met, whether for past or current reasons, and they came from all angles.

Known criminals.

Affected family members.

Disgruntled former officers.

Right now, Sarratt couldn't speculate on the reasons. Her role wasn't one of police work, but one of political practice, and she needed to grab the situation by the horns and guide the entire police service in the right direction. There were a number of highly skilled detectives who would get into the nitty gritty of each murder, and the process of assigning the work had already been passed on to Chief Inspector Mary Dummett, who'd leapt into action.

Now, Sarratt needed to keep the public calm, make the right assurances to the right people, and prepare herself for the busiest morning of her life. It was a little past one in the morning, and the city under her control should have been sound asleep. Instead, it was rocking with the very real horror of a murderous agenda against the system designed to protect it.

There would be calls for her head.

Someone had to take the fall for an outraged public who would see the deaths of two young officers a responsibility of those in charge. The government and their cost-cutting measures would sidestep their own responsibility, as they often did, and therefore the aim would be squarely on her.

But that didn't matter.

She'd face backlash with the respect it deserved, knowing she had allies in the likes of Dipti Patel.

All that mattered was that two of her officers had been murdered in the line of duty.

And the clock was ticking before it happened again.

CHAPTER FIVE

Everything hinged on split-second timing.

For over twenty years, Dominik Silva had plotted out every mission to the final second. It was a character trait that he knew had pissed off every politician, military leader or high paying client, but it was one he'd never waver from.

He couldn't.

Born and raised in Guadalajara, a vibrant and industrious city in western Mexico, Silva had spent the first eleven years of his life like any other child. He attended school, where he excelled in maths and any sporting activity, but by the time his twelfth birthday came around, his father was killed when the bank he managed was set upon by a gang of paid mercenaries. His father, Aurelio, was one of the most respected men in the capital state of Jalisco, and his high-end bank was rich with some of the wealthiest clients in the country. Beneath the bank was a tomb of safe-deposit boxes, which housed some of the most destructive secrets of the powerful men and women of the country, as well as access to unrivalled fortunes. The bank was heavily guarded, with gunmen at the doors, as well as a state-of-the-art security system that offered those who chose Aurelio's bank the comfort they required.

It meant his father worked long hours, dealt in secrecy, and was often absent.

It also meant the school that Silva attended was one of great renown, and the clothes he wore were the envy of all his friends.

But that fateful day, Aurelio put himself between a gun and the privacy of his clients and paid the ultimate price.

Silva paid the ultimate price.

His mother, Luisa, did her best to wrestle control of the bank from the lawyers who swarmed like vultures. But confidence in her wasn't shared by the rest of the board, and soon, Silva and his mother found themselves on the outside, with the money men ensuring they saw as little of his father's fortune as possible.

The impact was devastating.

Silva began faltering at school, where his temper began to flare and after too many physical altercations with other students, he was expelled. It helped the family out financially, as his transfer to a public school meant his mother wasn't burdened with the extortionate fees his father had agreed to. But the grief hit his mother hard, and while Silva's manifested in anger, his mother's festered in depression. Soon, she was drinking, and in a last-ditch attempt to get her back on track, Silva himself reached out to a friend's father who was a local doctor. It set off a chain reaction that saw his mother shipped off to rehab and Silva himself taken into care.

The perfect life, fractured by the murder of his father and the greed that drove it all.

His mother never recovered.

Over the years, his feelings towards her had softened, understanding that the grief and addiction had pulled her into a darkness she couldn't come back from. But as a child, it had only fuelled his rage.

How dare she not fight for him?

The anger spiralled.

His academic life crumbled.

At fourteen, he ran away from the foster home he'd been dumped in, made it across the border to America and found a job cleaning dishes in a Mexican restaurant in San Antonio and was taken in by the owner, who himself had lost his wife at an early age. Carlos Hernandez was a kind man, who'd devoted himself to the business he and his wife had made for themselves, and he became the first dependable adult figure in Silva's life in years. He pushed for Silva to return to school, but with his illegal status within the country, it was impossible.

For three years, Silva worked at the restaurant, becoming a decent cook and a strapping young man, with his physical gifts growing month on month. He began lifting weights and joined the local gym, where he grew fascinated with the Mixed Martial Art enthusiasts who rolled around on the mat and kicked the living hell out of each other.

One day he put on the gloves.

He was a natural.

Silva grasped the intricacies of fighting as quickly as he did the English language, albeit with a thick accent. As he grew into his imposing frame, his confidence grew and he soon caught the eye of one of the trainers, who trained at the gym. The man, known only as *Jefe*, was also a conditioning coach for the local army camp.

It took him less than three months to convince Silva to enlist, with the promise that he'd handle the finer details of his citizenship. With the right strings being pulled, Silva joined the army a few months shy of his eighteenth birthday, and he thrived in the environment. Physically fitter than all the other recruits, and a sharpness of mind that earmarked him for more.

He found it.

By the age of twenty, he was thrust into the Marine Corps, where he saw action across numerous continents. From search and rescue missions to all out assaults, Silva became one of the most lethal weapons the US Military possessed. But the pride and the reverence didn't match the pay, and when Carlos wrote to him to inform him that he'd lost the business that Silva had called home, his head was easily turned.

Farstone was a private security firm that masqueraded as a personal security detail, but was, in reality, a squadron of guns for hire that were always sniffing around the top recruits. Silva had been made aware of them by his colonel and had warned off a prospective scout on a boozy night in San Antonio.

They were relentless.

And they paid well.

Well enough for Silva to go AWOL from the marines. His record would be tainted, but he didn't care, and Farstone was more than happy to have him on the books. As guns for hire, he found himself carrying out multiple hits on both sides of the Mexican border, and as the years went by, he began to be requested by name. As his reputation as a *sicario* grew, it coincided with the rise of Jose Vasquez, a powerful drug lord who'd turned the barrios of Mexico City into his own personal playground. As his reach began to grow, Vasquez's right-hand man and cousin Raul would reach out to Silva and give him the names and the locations.

Silva would do the rest.

His reputation far outgrew Farstone's, and he struck out on his own, having to deal with the blowback from the jilted operation who now saw him as competition.

He saw them as a barrier.

After he put those he needed to in the ground, Silva became *the* gun for hire across the Mexican and American divide, and as Vasquez's influence grew, so did Silva's and his work soon began to be noticed by powerful people across the world.

He did a few jobs for a man name Ducard in France.

He'd helped deal with a few problems in South America for an Englishman named Wallace.

Silva didn't need to know those who were paying the extortionate fee he commanded. They just needed to know that if they didn't pay, or they tried to screw with him, he'd burn everything they knew to the ground.

Mercenaries were responsible for the fall and destruction of his entire family life. It was only right that down the same path; he was able to build a new one from the very same path.

Vasquez's reach extended further and further across the border. He soon came into conflict with the notorious Death Riders. Silva, who'd become a trusted confidant of the man, had expected to lead the removal of them and hand South Carolina over to Vasquez. At forty-three years of age, it would be one of his final jobs before he sat back on the riches Vasquez had promised him.

A seat at his table and more money and women than he'd know what to do with.

But Silva never received the call.

Vasquez was soon killed, and South Carolina stayed in the hands of the Motorcycle Gang. The DEA soon began to rip apart Vasquez's operation, and Silva went dark.

The names he'd relied upon for work soon began to tumble, and with the DEA on his tail, Silva burnt any remaining trace of himself and headed to Europe. With political tensions high and numerous countries on the brink of war, he'd be able to find work and re-establish himself.

He didn't need the money. Not really.

But the sense of purpose that it gave him and the pride he took in the mayhem he caused were reason enough for him to continue. There were always political figures that he could manipulate, always someone playing a dangerous game that needed a dangerous player.

After a few years of work, Silva once again had a list of clients willing to pay him to pull off jobs nobody else could.

He shifted people up the political ladder.

He removed others from the equation.

If the price was met, he could get it done.

But as he looked at his watch on a brisk, rainy night in London, he knew this one would have no margin for error. He'd spent an entire week in the capital city, unimpressed by the panicked nature of its civilians and the unappealing food. Some of the landmarks were impressive, but combined with the freezing weather, it only compounded Silva's dislike for England. But he followed the money, and a wealthy country where guns were illegal meant a man of his experience and means could charge extra.

Those who were signing the cheques, they didn't fully understand the nature of their request and when he laid it out to them, they were pretty easy to intimidate into adding an extra zero.

And if he pulled off this job, he'd never have to work again.

During his unenjoyable week in the city, with the only pleasures being the few women he'd taken to bed, he'd done all the required homework. He'd been able to bribe one of the security guards who worked at the Bank of England on Threadneedle Street. To be fair, he hadn't given the man a choice.

It was either take the money for the information or experience more pain than he could fathom until he spoke, anyway.

The guard soon relayed everything Silva needed to know, and it didn't take him too long to recruit the four men he'd need to pull it off. If you walk down the darkest, dirtiest streets of the city, you find exactly what you're looking for, and once he'd recruited his team he laid out the terms of their agreement.

They would all be paid handsomely.

They would listen to him at all times.

Any sudden moves, any ideas above their station or any disregard for a direct order would result in a bullet between their eyes and a warm stream of piss when he put out the fire that would eradicate their body from the earth. One of the men called his bluff, and Silva took the man's pinkie finger.

Everyone fell in line after that.

Everything had been planned to the finest detail. The necessary calls had been made and the assurances that people would be where he was told they'd be had been given.

The first call came in.

The deed had been done.

Silva checked his watch. The death of a police officer would have no effect on his conscience and karma wasn't an entity he put any stock in. If it existed, then he'd have paid for his sins a long time ago. The two men with him for the mission were already in the 4x4, one of them with a pinkie-less hand on the steering wheel.

The other in the passenger seat with the M16 assault rifle, locked and loaded in his lap.

From a discreet side street, a whole two blocks from the Bank of England, the armoured van turned out and onto the road. It looked nondescript, but Silva knew the value of what was locked away in the back.

The van would take one of six routes to Gatwick Airport, and Silva had memorised every single one of them. Based on the left-hand turn it took to disappear from sight, it narrowed it down to four.

'We ready to go?' the driver called from behind the wheel of the car. He'd lowered the tinted window to reveal his masked face.

Silva checked his watch again.

Less than an hour until the next call.

A minimum of sixty-four minutes based on the only routes available to the moving target.

The window was small.

But it was precise.

Silva nodded and then strode past the 4x4 to the jet-black Ducati Panigale V4 motorcycle behind them. Resting on the seat was a matching helmet and strapped to the side of the seat was his own M16. What was about to happen would shake the country to its core and nobody would know the reason why.

Silva took his seat on the motorcycle, and before he put the helmet over his head, he lifted the face mask that hung around his neck. As he fitted it over his nose and mouth, the terrifying imprint of a skeleton face became apparent.

He wrenched the hand grip a few times; the engine roaring a signal to the car in front, and they headed off on their mission.

And Silva *never* failed a mission.

Not once.

CHAPTER SIX

The November rain rattled the window of Sam's modest studio apartment, drawing him from his sleep. He'd come a long way from the recurring, haunting dreams of his dead son and now found that most nights passed in a dreamless slumber. It hadn't meant that he'd moved on from the agonising loss of Jamie, ripped from the world by a drunk driver over seven years ago.

Nor had he forgiven himself for failing to stop Miles Hillock from getting behind the wheel of the car that he'd drunkenly hit Jamie with.

It just meant that he'd accepted it.

It took a long time, and it had cost him everything, from his wife to what they once called a family home. The pain and torture caused by the gaping hole left in his son's absence had turned Sam into a machine, driven by vengeance against a justice system that just wasn't good enough.

That had failed too many people and that had rewarded those with the means to pay for it.

That was what drove him to keep fighting. Not to deal with the pain or the anger anymore, but to fight for those who couldn't fight back. That was the lasting legacy of his son's death.

Sam's one-man war on crime.

With a grunt of discomfort, Sam lifted himself from the bed and looked out of the rain-soaked window. The view was of nothing more than the back of another house, just one of many all crammed together on a nondescript street in North Greenwich. After returning home from Budapest with a new identity and little else, Sam had been thankful that Directive One had transferred everything over to his new name. It had been years since he'd even heard from Paul Etheridge, a former soldier turned tech millionaire, who'd eventually joined Sam's cause before going dark amidst a daring prison van rescue that had set Sam free. Etheridge was as near to a friend as Sam could have hoped for, and just another he'd lost along the way.

Some had seen the error of Sam's ways.

Others had laid down their lives for the cause.

Either way, he was eternally grateful for Etheridge's generous donation of money to keep Sam's war running. When Directive One had used the identity Etheridge had provided and turned it into one of the most wanted names across Europe, they provided him with a new start.

The passport and driver's license now said Ben Carter.

Hun, the tech whiz of the government outfit, even went as far as to create an entire financial history for the identity and ensured that every penny Etheridge had left for Jonathan Cooper now sat in the bank account of Ben Carter.

It meant all Sam had to do when he landed in Gatwick was pick up a laptop from one of the tech shops at the airport, and then check himself into the nearest hotel. Once connected to the wi-fi, Sam searched for a new base of operations, and with his ex-wife Lucy's fondness for

Greenwich market rushing to the forefront of his mind, he found a small apartment just a few miles away from it.

Good train links.

Busy enough to blend in.

He'd used one of the property websites that cut out the middleman, and when he offered to pay six months' rent up front, the landlord was more than happy to accept. Sam moved in the next day, and the owner had even left the flat furnished for him. His first order of business had been to head into town, where he purchased new bedding, towels and a kettle, as well as a stockpile of jeans and black T-shirts. With the biting cold of winter beginning to settle in, he even treated himself to a parka coat, along with a woollen hat and scarf. He picked up a SIM only mobile phone, along with a pre-paid internet dongle that would slot into the USB drive of his laptop. The last thing he wanted was to sign up for a broadband deal and leave a paper trail.

Then, he'd got down to the business of working through the names that Directive One had provided him, eventually focusing in on Simon Grant and the rest of his associates.

That morning, as he trudged to the open-plan kitchen to pop the kettle on, he turned on the television with the expectation that his name would once again be spread across the news like their new logo. As he joined the news-readers mid-conversation, he went about making his cup of tea until the next sentence snapped him to attention.

'As we've been discussing, two police constables were killed last night in what is being reported as a planned attack against the Metropolitan Police.'

Sam turned, pulled up the single chair from the small table affixed to the kitchen wall, and sat down, his eyes glued to the television. The entire story unfolded across a number of features, with various solemn-looking reporters talking to the camera in front of different locations. One of them was just outside the crime scene in Willesden, where PC Melanie Dyer, a thirty-one-year-old, eight-year veteran of the Met had been found in the alleyway behind. As the reporter relayed the seriousness of the crime, Sam focused on the movement behind them, as the public were held back by a police cordon as the departed's colleagues went to work. It then cut to another reporter, this time from an estate in Hackney, where a mid-twenties officer, PC James Harrington, had reportedly been lured to and murdered in the middle of the night. Although the reporters were doing their level best to report just the facts, Sam couldn't help but feel they were sensationalising the issue to spread panic.

Panic meant fear.

And fear meant more people would tune in.

After another bout of discussion in the studio with a crime psychologist, they cut to an interview from Commissioner Henrietta Sarratt, who looked like she hadn't slept a wink. Despite the apparent fatigue, the new commissioner carried herself with poise and authority, and Sam wondered how much she'd learnt from Bruce McEwen. The former commissioner had become an unlikely ally to Sam, having refused to back down to the threats of Dale Munroe after Sam targeted the billionaire's son on account of his sexual misconduct. The ensuing battle ended up costing Dale his life, his son Jasper his freedom and although McEwen had taken a bullet to the hip, it was Sam who'd saved his life and forged their trust.

If Sarratt had one-fifth of the integrity as her predecessor, then Sam knew she'd hunt those responsible to the ends of the earth.

As would he.

He lifted the remote control, switched off the television and marched into the cramped bathroom. He quickly brushed his teeth before he stripped off and stepped into the narrow shower cubicle that could barely contain him. At six feet one, Sam was a big man, and his impressive physique meant he had to draw in his round shoulders just to close the door. The pressure from the shower was good enough, and as he allowed the water to crash over him, he took a few breaths.

This wasn't his fight.

He'd walked through hell in Budapest, fighting some of the most dangerous criminals from the worst prisons across the globe. Each man had the promise of freedom dangled before them, which meant they were hell bent on killing him. But Sam had survived, and in doing so, had helped Directive One defeat a global terrorist organisation and a very imminent nuclear attack. Director Blake had embellished the sway he had with the British government with regard to Sam's actions, but he did provide him with the new identity and a list of powerful UK figures with ties to the organisation.

That was the fight.

To stop the potential backlash from the supporters of *Poslednyaya Nadezhda* in his own country from rising from the ashes.

But deep down, Sam wasn't just a fighter.

He was a soldier.

The nobility of justice had been embedded in him from the example set by his father, Major William Pope, one of the most respected men in the British armed forces. Sam understood, through his father's teachings and his own experiences, what it meant to serve.

What it meant to protect.

The young police officers who'd been murdered had signed up from that same belief that the cause was something they wanted to be a part of. Despite a salary that didn't match the responsibility, every police officer who strapped on a vest and took to the streets or responded to a call, did so knowing the danger they faced.

Their bravery may have been underplayed for years by the media, so much so that the public had turned against them, but Sam's opinion never wavered.

Anyone who was willing to protect the public was a hero, and although the police had been hunting Sam for years, he respected every single person behind the badge.

This wasn't his fight.

But then again, none of them had been.

But someone had to fight back, and Sam was a walking weapon who could ask the questions the law prevented others from asking and he could go places others weren't allowed to go.

As he switched off the shower and stepped out of the cubicle, the entire bathroom was clouded with steam. He reached out and wiped a hand across the glass, revealing the reflection of his soaking, naked torso. It was riddled with scars from a life of conflict.

A scar ran down his spine from his fight with Farukh at the top of the High Rise.

A bullet wound in his shoulder from where Mac, his friend and comrade who he'd assumed dead, had returned for vengeance for his perceived abandonment.

But it was always the two scars that dominated his pectoral muscles that Sam's eyes were drawn to. Two white eyes, staring back at him, from when he was shot twice and left for dead on a mission gone wrong.

He should have died that night.

That was the intention.

The betrayal of General Ervin Wallace during Project Hailstorm wasn't something Sam had discovered until many years later, but the two scars were a permanent reminder of what the most powerful people in the country were capable of. Wallace, respected and revered by the government as a hero, was a terrorist, and he'd tried to kill Sam to cover up that fact.

Sam had since had his revenge, with Wallace long since dead and his mercenary outfit, Blackridge, burnt to the ground.

But the scars always stared back at Sam, and he knew then and there, that his own fight would have to be put on hold.

The public was terrified.

The Metropolitan Police Service was shaken.

And the parents and loved ones of those two officers would be grieving for their senseless loss.

There was no doubt in his mind, from the words he'd heard during her interview, that Commissioner Sarratt would throw the full force of the Metropolitan Police behind it, but their resources only spread so far. The red tape and bureaucracy that they had to navigate meant things would take time. There would be hurdles to overcome and every hour wasted was another hour that justice got further and further away. An officer killed in the line of duty was one thing.

Two officers murdered within an hour of each other was something else entirely.

It was an act of war.

Or was it?

Sam quickly dried himself off and then flattened his short brown hair into something reasonably neat. The thickening stubble on his jaw could wait another day, and he quickly threw on his usual attire, wrapped himself inside the parka, and then opened the drawer beneath his wardrobe. The one thing Director Blake hadn't permitted was access to weapons, and Sam hadn't wanted to venture into the murky waters of gun trafficking to acquire one. He'd gone to war with Slaven Kovac to bring down his arms operation, so using the very same trade to buy a weapon would reek of hypocrisy.

As he slid back the drawer, he pulled up the Glock 17 he'd kept from his raid of Bakku two nights before, stood and stuffed it into the back of his jeans, before covering it with his jacket.

He might need it.

Then, with a purpose radiating from him, Sam headed for the door and off into the city.

Somebody killed PC James Harrington and PC Melanie Dyer for a reason.

And Sam was going to find out why.

CHAPTER SEVEN

A morbid atmosphere had flooded through the entire police station as news of the two deaths filtered through, with every member of the Met arriving to find out that two of their own had been killed in the line of duty. When DS Sutton had found out, she'd felt sick to her stomach. Both officers who'd been murdered were younger than she was, and she could only imagine the pain and devastation that their friends and families were going through.

Some of them were sitting in the very briefing room she'd been called into. Along with DS Vokes, the duo had found a space against the back wall of the room, which felt ten times smaller when it was packed to capacity. The rows of chairs that had been laid out were all filled with other police constables, all of them champing at the bit to get justice for their fallen colleagues.

Their friends.

That was the part of the job people failed to realise. Being a police officer was more a lifestyle than a career, and only those who truly understood were those who lived it. It forged friendships that would last the test of time, built on the trust of your colleague to follow you into any situation.

To always have your back.

That was why Sutton and Vokes had thrived as a partnership. The dated scenario of a male and female being unable to work together without a flicker of attraction was a work of fiction. Never once had a spark flown between the two of them, and Vokes had never been anything other than completely loyal to his loving wife.

But Sutton and Vokes trusted each other with their lives, and their friendship, like many of the officers in the room, had blossomed because of it.

And now that friendship meant the room was vibrating with an angry energy that Detective Chief Inspector Karim Hasan needed to get under control. In his early fifties, Hasan was three years away from retirement, leaving behind a well-respected if undistinguished career. He didn't ooze authority like many of the other senior figures did, but he was a reliable hand and at times, seen as a soft touch.

That morning, he had a face like thunder.

Standing at the front of the room, he looked out over the devastated team before him and offered them all his sincerest condolences.

'If anyone needs to take some time, or you need us to organise a meeting for you to talk, please let me know.'

Hasan knew what the response would be. Everyone would park their anger or their heartbreak, using it to fuel their efforts to catch those responsible. Beside him, Chief Inspector Mary Dummett stood with her arms folded. She was a stern woman, one who'd read both Sutton and Vokes the riot act a few times when she was in command of the Charing Cross Police Station. Now, she worked exclusively out of New Scotland Yard and was seen as one of Commissioner Sarratt's most trust assets.

'Thank you,' Dummett said, resting her hand on Hasan's shoulder before addressing the room. 'We know this is a hard time for you all. It's tough to even imagine what our fallen officers went through in their final moments, but it is our job to find out. I want everything gone through with a fine-tooth comb. If something needs pushing through, you find either one of us two. If something gives you even the hint of a lead, you chase that down to the end. We've had two good officers murdered in cold blood. This wasn't a coincidence. For those of you who know me, you know I don't subscribe to that notion. This was planned. This was premeditated, and this was executed without hesitation. I want the fuckers who did this. Right…get to it.'

With a firm clap of her hands, Dummett sent the vengeful team back to work, and then turned and struck up a conversation with Hasan. Sutton waited for the room to filter down before she and Vokes made their exit. As he made his way to the desk, she ventured down to the canteen, where the same sense of loss hung over the room like a dark cloud. Everyone, from the police constables to those serving food behind the counter, went solemnly about their business. As she joined the queue, she overheard a detective she didn't recognise discussing the night shift he'd just put in.

'Were you on the scene?' Sutton interjected, drawing the man's attention. He arched an eyebrow.

'Oh, no. Horrible business, that.' He shook his head sorrowfully. 'No, I was called out to that business near Gatwick.'

'Gatwick?'

'It's not being bandied about, so you didn't hear anything from me,' the man said, clearly keen to discuss it. 'But let's just say a fair amount of gold went missing last night.'

'Oh, really?' Sutton's eyebrow raised, although hers was considerably more shaped. The man sighed and nodded.

'I guess, you know…priorities.' He gestured to the open room. 'Pales in comparison to what happened, you know?'

Sutton nodded her agreement and then ordered her coffees. She allowed the man to veer off back to his day, paid the subsidised price before escaping the morose canteen and swapping it for a similarly morbid open-plan office. As the constables put their gear on to take to the streets, a few other detectives were either glued to their laptops or their phones.

Everyone was digging for answers.

Hunting for justice.

She placed Vokes's coffee down on his desk and he gave her a thumbs up, his mobile phone pressed to the side of his head. Sutton took her seat on the desk opposite, took a sip of the piping hot drink before logging into her laptop.

She opened the search bar and typed in Gatwick.

To her surprise, nothing from the night before had been logged into the system. She tried a few other searches, such as 'gold' or 'theft'. While the latter returned a number of reports that would unfortunately probably go no further, there was nothing to corroborate the story from the visiting detective. As she slumped back in her chair, Vokes peered over the top of the divider.

'You okay?'

'How long would you say it would take for a gold theft to appear in the system?'

Vokes sipped his coffee and then frowned.

'Not sure. Why?'

'It's nothing.' Sutton waved it off, and she began pulling up all the case reports that had been filed by PC Dyer over the past few months. The young constable had clearly been pro-active and every one of her write-ups carried the commitment and confidence of someone who lived being a police officer. A twinge of sadness flickered through Sutton's body as she read through them, realising that a promising light in the Met had gone out and a young woman had been thrown to her death from a fourth-floor window.

What the hell were you doing up there, Melanie?

Vokes offered a reason for needing to leave, but Sutton just waved it off and it wasn't until she needed a steer on something that she felt his absence. The part of detective work that they didn't truly highlight in books or on TV was the slow, methodical pace with which most things went. Trawling through page after page of paperwork was long and arduous work, and Sutton could have shrieked with delight when Vokes finally reappeared with another cup of coffee an hour or so later. As she sipped the necessary caffeine, she offered him a thankful smile.

'Where have you been?'

'I went down to Wembley nick to have a look in Melanie Dyer's locker. Nothing of any use, but it was worth a look. Can tick it off the list, anyway.' He nodded to her laptop. 'You?'

'I've been going through her call outs and reports for the past few months. Again, nothing of any real note. One thing I did notice was that she actually wasn't scheduled to work last night. Not officially.'

'Really?' Vokes stepped around the desk and peered over her shoulder at the screen. 'Overtime?'

'Probably. Fuck knows I did as much overtime as I could when I was her age.'

Vokes peered closer at her screen and then pointed to one of the open tabs across the top of her internet browser.

'What's that?'

'Oh, nothing.'

'Come on, Jess.' He insisted. 'You asked me something about gold earlier…'

She sighed.

The open browser was a search engine result for 'gold theft Gatwick' and she opened it up. There was nothing beyond a few posts on social media, but none of the papers or the news outlets had published anything to confirm what had happened. Vokes sipped his coffee and looked at her blankly.

'Dummett said to chase down anything, no matter how small, right?'

'She did. So, what you thinking?' He stared at her the way he had done a million times when he thought she was crazy. 'I just need to know what the thought process is when we inevitably get our arses kicked for wasting time.'

Vokes pulled a face at her, and she scrunched up a Post-it note and threw it at him. He marched back round to his desk, finished his coffee on route and then lifted his jacket from the back of his chair.

'Where are you off to?'

'Omar Kelmendi was released from hospital today, so I thought I'd go and pay him a little visit. You know, on account of the six men Sam Pope killed in his restaurant. Fancy it?'

Sutton looked around the room with concern, as if looking for DCI Hasan.

'All focus is on the two murders, Connor.'

'Don't give me that. You've been looking into bloody gold thefts.' Vokes countered. 'Besides, we still need to close that case down.'

'Which case is that, then?'

Right on cue, Hasan approached their desks, offering them both a warm smile behind his thick, grey beard.

Vokes took a respectful step to the side and smiled down at the superior officer he towered over.

'The Bakku incident from the other night.'

'I see.' Hasan rubbed his chin. 'Can it wait?'

'It can. But I figured we'd get to the owner of the place before he brought his lawyers in. He might talk a bit more…how should we say, honestly?'

'Make it quick.' Hasan sighed. 'I need you two focused on these two murders. The Yard is right up my arse on this and I want those responsible found yesterday.'

'Understood, guv.' Vokes nodded and then strode back across the office. Hasan turned to Sutton, who look troubled.

'Everything okay?' he asked. While Hasan didn't exude authority, he could read people better than most.

'All good, guv.' Sutton shook her head. 'Actually, no. Have you heard anything about the theft at Gatwick?'

'Gatwick?' Hasan frowned. 'I think we're a little busy here to be looking into any thefts. Where on earth has this come from?'

'There was a detective in the canteen earlier. I'd never seen him before, but I overheard him talking about it.' Sutton tried to recall the conversation. 'It was brief, but he said something about a gold theft last night.'

'A gold theft?' Hasan repeated, perplexed. 'It's not come across my desk today. And it shouldn't be taking priority.'

'I know, guv. Sorry.'

Hasan smiled kindly, as if to assure her that she wasn't in any trouble. As he turned to leave, he stopped himself.

'What was this detective's name?'

'I didn't catch it.' Sutton shrugged. 'He was bald. Forties. Pretty chatty.'

'I'll call around and see what's what. But head in the

58

game, Sutton. I need my best detectives to find out who killed our colleagues.'

The reminder of the severity of the situation was all Sutton needed to return to her screen, and she pulled up the recent reports submitted by PC James Harrington. The same monotonous process would be repeated, and Sutton knew it would be a slog. But she owed it to the two dead officers, as well as their families, to leave no stone unturned. If it meant reading through pages of poorly written paperwork, then so be it.

At least then she could tick it off the list.

'If something gives you even the hint of a lead, you chase that down to the end.'

Dummett's words were ringing in Sutton's ears for the next few hours, as she eliminated suspect after suspect through Harrington's recent work. All the while, that nagging feeling that she wasn't doing her job properly clung to the back of her mind.

Vokes returned and left to head home to his family, and Sutton promised herself she'd head off soon and get a good night's sleep.

That's what the investigation deserved.

It also deserved her to follow her gut, and she couldn't get the lack of evidence of a gold theft out of her head.

'Chase that down to the end.'

Sutton finished the final read-through of Harrington's reports, surmised that there was no information to go on, and then snapped her laptop shut. As she headed to her car, every part of her sensibility told her to head home.

To keep her head in the game.

As she dropped into the seat of her car in the under-ground garage beneath Charing Cross Station, she tapped Gatwick into the satnav, pulled out of the car park and knew she wasn't going to listen.

CHAPTER EIGHT

It hadn't felt right.

When Sam had arrived at Willesden, he was transported back to some of his prior visits to the area. Brent was a large borough of London, and one that unfortunately had the highest crime and poverty rates. Although it was home to the iconic Wembley Stadium, most of the area was a cramped collection of estates, all of them forgotten by the government and all of them a breeding ground for gang culture. It wasn't too far away in Neasden where he'd hung Sean Wiseman over the edge of a balcony to extract information. That was a long time ago, before Wiseman had pushed himself to become a better person and through the tutelage of Adrian Pearce, had trained as a social worker.

He'd grown up.

Found love in the form of the gutsy reporter Lyndsey Beckett.

He was also now recovering from the life-threatening injuries he'd sustained a year ago at the hands of Daniel Bowker, who'd since been put in the ground by Sam himself.

Sometimes, this war was personal.

As Sam had wandered into the estate, he quickly saw a few heads turn his way. The local neighbourhood was predominantly black, and a tall, muscular white man who clearly carried himself like a man used to a uniform was always going to draw suspicion. The authorities and the police had long since given up on the people who built their lives in the concrete high rises of Willesden, and Sam knew it wouldn't take long before someone questioned his motives.

They all looked out for each other.

Nobody else would.

If word spread around the estates that Sam Pope was in the area, he was expecting a backlash. A few years previously, a man named Leon Barnett ran rough-shod over the area, operating out of Wembley, which was a few miles down the road. The head of the 'Acid Gang', Leon would orchestrate acid attacks on innocent people as a way of initiation into his ranks. It was disgusting and cowardly, but it allowed him to discover how far someone was willing to go to serve under him.

Sam had given him a taste of his own medicine, and when Dana Kovalenko had put a bounty on his head, Leon had joined her ranks in a failed attempt at revenge.

He was dead now.

And there would certainly be loyal soldiers of his who would want Sam's head on a stick.

As he approached the building where PC Melanie Dyer had been found dead, he saw the limited police presence. A few young officers, no older than their colleague who'd just been killed, had been assigned to keep people off the crime scene. Sam also caught a glimpse of a Scene of Crime Officers, decked out in their overalls and masks, as the forensic analysis of the area was in full flow. Understaffed and underfunded, they would do their best to try to map out not only how PC Dyer took a four-storey drop to her death, but what she was doing in the building in the first place.

Something didn't feel right.

Sam cast his gaze down the street, where a few outlets were still fighting the good fight against the recession, and he pulled his parka jacket tight as he set off against the bitter chill of the wind. He stepped into the first one, an off-licence, where it quickly became apparent that the owner didn't speak very much English, nor was he willing to say anything even if he did. The next shop was a Caribbean barbershop, and as Sam pushed open the door, the ring of the bell drew three sets of sceptical eyes in his direction.

'You lost?' The large barber was sitting in one of the leather chairs and chuckled. 'You sure as hell don't have an appointment.'

'I dunno.' One of the other barbers stepped forward. 'I reckon I could give this man a fade. Maybe sort that beard out. What do you think?'

The third, more senior barber grunted before turning back to his newspaper. Sam held up both hands in a form of surrender.

'Sorry to intrude, guys. I'm not here for any trouble.'

The burly barber lifted himself from his chair, an act to show that he stood a few inches taller. Sam gave him a courtesy smile.

'That's what someone lookin' for trouble would say.' The large barber stepped right into Sam's personal space. 'You police?'

'He looks like police,' the other barber unhelpfully chipped in.

'Trust me. I'm the furthest thing from the police,' Sam said with a wry grin.

'Then what…you here to make us an offer? You one of

them rich mother fuckers trying to turn this place into somethin' it's not?' The hostility was rising, and the two barbers began to move strategically around Sam.

'Enough,' the older barber said. All eyes fell on the patriarch of what Sam assumed was a family business, and the man slammed his paper down and whipped off his glasses. With his white hair and neatly trimmed beard contrasting strikingly with his dark skin, the barber reminded Sam of Adrian Pearce. 'What the hell you want, white boy? You came in here for a reason and my boys want to know what it is.'

All eyes fell back on Sam again.

'The police officer who died across the road—'

'Wasn't us,' the burly barber cut in.

'I didn't say it was. Nor do I think it was. But I'm trying to figure out what happened. Wondered if any of you knew or heard anything.'

'You said you weren't police?' the younger barber spat.

'He isn't.' The older barber sat back in his chair. 'You're Sam Pope, aren't you?'

The two barbers spun back to look at Sam, and without realising, took a tentative step back. Sam smiled at the old man.

'Maybe. Depends on who's asking. I hear he isn't the most popular man around these streets?'

'Fuck these streets.' The barber chuckled. 'I made damn sure my boys had a business to run, so they didn't end up out there. Far as I'm concerned, you did this city a service when you took that acid prick out of the game.'

'Everything comes at a cost,' Sam said grimly. The older barber nodded. Sam liked him.

'If you're wondering if we saw any gangs of black kids beating up that officer and throwing her out the window, sorry, I ain't got that for ya.' The old gentleman eased himself up out of the chair with some difficulty and approached Sam. 'But nothin' happens on this street without my eyes seeing it. Yesterday, about two hours before that young girl got killed, there was a black SUV out the front of that building for some time. White guy, little older than you. I watched him go inside.'

'Anyone else?'

'All I saw.' The man shrugged. 'License plate ended in PMK. But that building's been empty for over two years now. Some rich prick ran out of money and left it to loom over my business like a reminder of how shitty this city is nowadays.'

'You boys see anything?' Sam turned to the two sons, whose aggression had lamented.

'Nope. Day off.' The burly one shrugged.

'Same as Dad.' The younger one motioned to his father with his thumb. 'The white guy had a black coat. But nah, we just thought he was a developer or summin'.'

Sam looked around the room, making sure he made eye contact with each man. Despite their initial scepticism, he appreciated their honesty. Just a close family doing their best to make an honest living. He nodded and then turned towards the door.

'Thank you, all. You should tell the police what you know. It might help them.'

Sam pulled open the door, the shrill bell echoing above his head once more. The two sons looked on in confusion as their dad stepped forward.

'What are you going to do, son?' he asked, and he offered Sam a knowing nod as he turned to face him.

He already knew.

So did Sam.

'I'm going to find out what really happened.'

It had been a relaxing few months of retirement for Bruce McEwen.

As he and his wife, Leanne, eagerly awaited the birth of their first grandchild, he'd found himself drawn to the idea of carpentry. Leanne had found his new hobby rather funny, especially as the first set of shelves he built from scratch collapsed as soon as he placed an object on them. Not one to back down from a challenge, McEwen had arrived back at the hardware superstore the following morning, restocked his supplies and went about converting the garage of their spacious home in the Farnham countryside into his own personal workshop.

It was time for himself, time he could dedicate to his family and most importantly, time to just live his life.

A world away from the stress and political pressures of being the Commissioner of the Metropolitan Police Service. With a stellar career of service behind him, McEwen adopted the top seat after it was vacated by Michael Stout, a man who'd since become a good friend and a wise sounding-board. He had helped McEwen steer the Met through some particularly muddy waters, especially when it ran afoul of the Munroe family, as well as the nasty business with Pierre Ducard. Despite the pressures from political allies of the Met, McEwen had never wavered from the integrity that had made him so suited for the role, and that was what ended up being his Achilles' heel. By putting the needs of the public above the money men, he was soon ushered towards the door and instead of trying to fight the system, he just assured that his successor, Henriette Sarrett, who'd served under him as his assistant commissioner, would be aware of what lay ahead.

He was an old man in a new world, and perhaps, a woman from her background and experiences could make a better inroad into the archaic regimes that still governed the country. He wished her well and made sure he was always at the end of the phone.

The only problem that McEwen had struggled to deal with was the return of Sam Pope, the vigilante who'd seemingly perished but returned to once again take down the wicked and corrupt. It was Pope who'd caused the issues with the elite and the French politician, and despite taking the law into his own hands, McEwen felt a kinship with the man.

After all, Sam did save his life.

But that was in the past, and since Sam had disappeared to France, McEwen had heard nothing from the man. He'd been kept up to date with the fall of the powerful oligarch, Vladimir Balikov, but there was no evidence that it was Sam.

It probably was, though.

McEwen chuckled at the idea of Sam now becoming an international pain in the arse.

As the winter rain clattered the roof of his garage, echoing loudly like a baby's rattle, he turned the volume up on his smart speaker as he began sanding down another recently-cut beam of wood. The orchestral strings of *Classic FM* echoed from the corner; he tried his best to smooth out the edges of the bookshelf he was building for the nursery that Leanne had insisted upon. Their son, Max, had made it clear that they didn't want them to go to any trouble, but they both knew it was moot.

Leanne had gone baby crazy, and as much as the idea of building things for his incoming grandchild filled McEwen with a sense of pride and purpose, it also meant he could shuffle away from the constant conversations around parenthood that he thought were long gone.

With his head down, and his hands delicately pressing the chipped wood against the belt, he heard the door to his garage open.

'Two seconds, love,' he called out over the noise. As he finished, he turned around and froze.

'Hello, Bruce.' Sam Pope stood in the doorway, casting his eyes around the workshop. Among the tools were some of the prototype creations he'd attempted, and McEwen foolishly felt a little twinge of embarrassment. 'I see you're keeping busy.'

'Aye. I could say the same to you.' McEwen chuckled. 'I take it that whole business at Bakku was you.'

'You know I can't confess anything to you.'

'I'm not in the police anymore, Sam.'

'No. But you're still a police officer. That doesn't leave you.'

McEwen shrugged and then reached across and turned the volume down on the speaker. He looked beyond Sam to the door, and Sam got the message and pulled it close. McEwen then reached into the cupboard beneath the workbench and pulled out a bottle of scotch and a glass.

'Oh, I don't drink anymore…' Sam said.

'It's not for you,' McEwen replied dryly and poured himself a generous measure. 'I have a feeling I'm going to need it.'

'That taxing, am I?'

'No. But you are the most wanted man in the country, and I'm a former police commissioner.' He took a sip and drew his lips back as he sighed. 'Bad optics and all. I take it this isn't a social visit?'

'Sadly not.'

'Shame. I was hoping to hear about Bulgaria.'

'These two officers who were killed. What are you thinking?' Sam said as he leant back against one of the workbenches and crossed his arms over his broad chest. The mention of them seemed to genuinely sicken McEwen.

'Awful business. But I take it you don't think this is a genuine attack on the Met?'

Sam shook his head as McEwen took another sip of his drink.

'It doesn't feel right. If this was a hate campaign against the Met, why did they stop at two? And why were they spread out?'

'Sarrett believes it was organised to show how thinly spread the Met are. Sort of like…proving to the public that we can't protect them anymore.'

Sam's eyebrow arched.

'Could be.'

'You just said that wasn't where your head was at?'

'No. But the idea that the Met are stretched across two of their own being killed means…'

'Means we're looking right while someone else is looking left.' McEwen and Sam nodded, both landing on the same train of thought. 'Tell you what, leave it with me. I'll do some digging. Sarrett is pretty busy, as you can imagine, but…'

'Tomorrow,' Sam said firmly. 'Sorry to be a pain in the arse, but whatever is going on, it's not going to wait. Trust me…the reason I'm a necessity is I can do this a lot quicker.'

It wasn't meant as a jab at the police, and McEwen wasn't even part of it anymore. But he still took it personally.

'I'll be in touch when I know something, Sam,' he said curtly. 'How do I contact you?'

Sam pushed himself forward and extended his hand to McEwen, who took it with a firm and well-practised handshake.

'I'll be in touch,' Sam said and then headed to the side door of the garage. As he pulled it open, the rain and wind howled through, dropping the temperature of the room instantly.

'Oh, and Sam,' McEwen called out and Sam turned. 'You may be sorry, but just so you know, you are *always* a pain in the arse.'

Sam smirked, nodded his thanks to McEwen and then disappeared out into the downpour, pulling the door closed behind him. McEwen stared at the door for a few moments and sighed.

He took a big sip of his drink and prepared himself for what was coming.

Sam Pope was going to war.

He just didn't know who with yet.

CHAPTER NINE

'Jesus Christ, Jess. I mean this is the nicest way possible, but you look like shit.'

DS Sutton looked up from her desk as DS Vokes walked across the office, his face still moist from the clean shave he'd had that morning. He was smiling, obviously to lighten the comment, and as he approached, she stood and knocked back the last of her umpteenth coffee.

He was right.

The funny thing about pulling an all-nighter was that those who'd experienced them could see it a mile off, and she made no excuse for her ragged appearance. The bags under her green eyes were heavy and her hair, pulled back into a messy ponytail, was screaming for a wash. As she stepped around her desk, she straightened out the creases in her jacket, and wrapped her hand around Vokes's arm and began to drag him away.

'Come with me.'

'What the hell?' Vokes uttered quietly, his brow furrowing with concern. The open-plan office of Charing Cross Police Station was sparse, with the day shift over a half hour away from taking over from the poor souls who were rostered for the night shift. Vokes looked at his partner with concern, as she twitchily looked up and down the corridor, before throwing open the door to one of the interview rooms and ushering him inside. He followed, then turned and sat on the edge of the table with his strong arms crossed over his chest.

'What the hell is going on, mate?'

His words were wrapped with concern, and Sutton offered a feeble smile to try to alleviate them.

'I think something fucking rotten is going on,' Sutton finally said, exhaling a large breath as if it was a relief to get it out in the open.

'Right.' Vokes shrugged. 'There's always something rotten going on.'

'No, I mean with the killings.' Sutton threw her hands up, flustered. 'I don't think these were attacks on the Met.'

'Mate, whoever did this killed two of our own. Even if it was a coincidence, that is still a fucking attack.' Vokes's body tightened. 'You want to tell all the uniform out there that this wasn't an attack? Seriously, go on. I'll grab a coffee and a front-row seat.'

'Listen to me, Connor.' Sutton was flagging. 'I followed up on that raid in Gatwick last night and...'

'Didn't guv tell you to drop that?'

'Yeah, he did. But you heard Dummett, she said to hunt down anything that felt off and something just didn't sit right with me.'

'Yeah, that will probably be guv's foot up your arse when he realises you didn't listen.'

Sutton closed her eyes and clenched her fist. She thought the world of her partner, but there was a steely arrogance that resided in Vokes at times that drove her mad. He was a stickler for the chain of command, and although he'd follow her into a burning building if he had to, he'd do everything in his power to avoid it if he could.

To keep things on track and to have them follow orders.

'I know you're just looking out for me, Connor, and I appreciate that.'

Vokes stood and rested a caring hand on her shoulder. She looked up at him with envy. Despite the pressures of the job and two young kids, he looked well rested.

'I am, mate. Also, I hate to piss on your parade, but we have more important things to do than look for some stolen gold. Now, I know you're upset that the elite may have lost some of their fortune…'

'Fuck you.' She playfully thumped him on the bicep.

'…but we need to focus on Dyer and Harrington. They gave their lives for this job, and we aren't doing them any good in this room talking about some robbery that took place miles away.' Vokes reached for the door handle. 'So, let's get to work, shall we?'

Sutton fixed him with a cold stare, hating the fact that he was right. Hasan would only reprimand her if she took it to him anyway, especially after his strict orders to drop it. After a few more tense moments, Sutton placed her hands on her hips.

'What if I told you I think those murders were an inside job?'

Vokes stepped back and his eyes widened. He relinquished the door handle and turned to her.

'I'd say that's a fucking big leap.' He spoke in a hushed tone. 'And a very serious allegation.'

'Look, I'm only telling you this because I've been pulling my hair out all night trying to make this not make sense. But while we're all charging out into the streets, knocking on doors and telling the world we'll find who hurt our own, where are we not looking?' It was a rhetorical question and Vokes treated it as such. 'I checked the rosters, and both Harrington and Dyer were shifted on with a day's notice.'

'Overtime,' Vokes said, playing devil's advocate.

'No one else was clocking overtime that day. They didn't request it, they were moved onto it. So, were they selected?'

'Rosters change like that.' Vokes snapped his fingers. 'It's a hell of a stretch...'

'Neither call out that they attended was of a serious nature. One was for vandalism and the other was for a potential trespass. Nothing that would indicate violence.' Sutton knew she was losing him. 'So, both of them were handpicked for those shifts and *both* of them received calls in their areas for non-serious crimes?'

'I mean, yeah, it's a coincidence but...'

Sutton cut him off, hitting her stride.

'So, Harrington gets his throat cut and this whole place goes into an understandable meltdown. An hour or so later, Dyer takes a four-storey drop to her death and the entire country is focused on what the hell we do next.' Sutton had begun to pace, working her theory through in her head. 'Then, at that immediate point in time, someone just so happens to roll over an armoured truck that's stacked with gold bars? Hell of a coincidence, right?'

She could tell she had him. While Vokes would do everything in his power to stay on order, at his heart, he was a good detective. His duty to the police and the public was never in doubt, and as he ran through the scenario she'd just laid out for him. She could almost hear the cogs in his brain turning.

He frowned a few times.

He rubbed his strong, hairless jawline.

Eventually, he sighed.

'Fine. You have something,' he admitted. 'But if you take this to Hasan, he'll shut you down.'

'That's why I need you…' Sutton playfully tapped his arm with her fist. 'Old buddy, old pal.'

'Gee, thanks.' Vokes huffed as he opened the door. 'I'm honoured.'

The two detectives left the interview room, and the corridor was now filled by a slow-moving group of officers and other workers who were filing towards the incident room at the far end of the corridor. One of them told Vokes that there was a briefing, so he and Sutton followed, weaving into the stream of people who filtered into the room. All the chairs were already taken, so the duo crammed into a space in the corner, with Vokes moving Sutton ahead of him so she could see. Lined across the back of the room were a number of senior figures within the Met, some of whom Sutton recognised. At the front of the room was Detective Chief Inspector Hasan, along with Chief Inspector Dummett. It was apparent that until the murderers were brought to justice, these meetings would be daily and as Hasan ran through the information they had up to that point, Sutton could feel her knuckles whitening as she clenched her fist. Even if she wanted to interrupt and offer her theory, she knew that her run-down appearance would be used as evidence of her delusion.

Dummett wrapped up the meeting with another rallying cry, channelling the anger and pain of the other constables to push them to seek justice for their fallen comrades.

It was admirable stuff, but Sutton couldn't help but feel that it was a show for the higher-ups who nodded with appreciation at what they witnessed.

Even the deaths of police officers could be used to gain political points.

Before Dummett sent everyone out to fight the good fight, Hasan opened the floor up to questions.

Sutton's body stiffened as she bit her tongue.

As ever, Vokes could read her mind.

'Yeah, just one from me, guv.' Vokes lifted his hand up, and his deep voice held a certain gravitas that he knew drew people's attention. 'Just a theory I think we should look at.'

For the next five minutes, as Vokes relayed out the work Sutton had done and then the chastising he received in front of the station, Sutton wanted the ground to open up and swallow them both.

Dummett doubled down on Hasan's calls for them to focus on the task at hand, and when Vokes apologised and stepped back, Sutton glanced over at the row of senior figures, who all shook their heads with disappointment.

It was time to give up the enquiry.

But when she glanced back to Vokes, the spark of anger that emanated from his dark eyes told her otherwise.

There was something there.

And now Vokes was on board, too.

There was something liberating about a no-name policy that made Dominik Silva's work more enjoyable. His time working closely with Jose Vasquez had led to a friendship that inevitably led to sloppiness. When the man's operation was taken down, Silva had made a promise to himself then and there that he'd only do jobs with those willing to be ghosts.

No names.

No niceties.

They presented their proposal, and he either took it or not. If they failed to meet his demands, he'd burn them to the ground. His reputation was bulletproof, and whenever he raised his price mid-mission, it was never questioned.

You paid for quality, but in Silva's case, you paid to stay alive.

The robbery of the armoured truck had gone swimmingly. They had tracked the truck across its route to Gatwick, and Silva had sped ahead, cutting it off at an underpass as it turned on a side road that would have taken them through a private passage through to a secret and heavily guarded entrance to Gatwick Airport, where no doubt, the contents would have been loaded directly onto a similarly guarded plane.

One thousand gold bars.

Valued at just under fifty-one million pounds.

Silva had arrived at the underpass with enough time to enjoy a ritualistic cigarette before the bright lights of the truck exploded into view. As it hurtled towards the overpass, Silva kept to the shadows, and then rolled out the puncture tringles that obliterated the front tyres of the truck, causing it to swerve, slam into the side of the tunnel and spin wildly out of control. To his credit, the driver kept the truck steady and brought it to a safe stop, just in time for the 4x4 to pull up on the bridge above. As his two henchmen hopped out and trained their M16 assault rifles at the truck, the passenger foolishly stepped out, his fingers already wrapped around his handgun.

Silva nonchalantly sent two bullets through the man's shins and then trained his gun on the driver who held his hands up in fear. The passenger howled in agony, and as he stepped over the fallen man, Silva shut him up with a brutal boot to the temple. With a beckoning finger, Silva drew the driver out of the vehicle and then pointed up the bridge above, where the man stared up at the two rifles and turned a deathly shade of pale.

'If you're going to shit your pants, do it quietly,' Silva warned the driver, and then took a quick look at the truck and then signalled up to his men with two fingers. One of the men disappeared, and moments later, two tyres appeared over the brick wall, with a rope looped through the centre and tied in a sturdy knot. As they were lowered in stages, Silva let his rifle swing to his side, and he pulled a Glock 17 from the back of his jeans and held it under the driver's quivering jaw.

The man squealed, and while he hadn't shat himself, Silva could smell the distinct aroma of urine.

'You have five minutes to change both tyres,' Silva said coldly.

'That's n-n-not enough time,' the driver pleaded.

Behind them, the fallen passenger began to stir, groaning in pain as the blood loss from his legs was beginning to kick in. Silva stepped over to him and pointed the gun at him.

'Shall I put a bullet in his head and then tell you that you have four minutes?' Silva pulled the gun back and then clicked his fingers. 'Come on. *Ándale. Ándale.*'

Fear was a hell of a motivator, and four minutes later, Silva took the driver's keys and phone and drilled him with an uppercut to the stomach for good measure. Then he sped away, where five miles out in Sidlow, he'd pull into a warehouse where the transfer of gold bars would be made across four smaller vans, all marked with different trade companies. The warehouse owner would be happy with one of the bars, which was a small price to pay, considering the haul.

Now, Silva sat in the warehouse on one of the tatty sofas in the staff room, ignoring the no smoking signs as he enjoyed a cigarette and watched his hired help play a game of cards. They'd get three gold bars each, as would the two who'd killed the officers.

Then he'd discuss the new arrangements with those who'd hired him in the first place. The initial fee of ten million felt a little generous in retrospect.

As he smiled to himself at his sudden increase in value, his mobile phone buzzed and blew out a plume of smoke and lifted it to his ear.

'Yeah?'

'Am I talking to Silva?'

Silva sighed.

'We do not use names, *vato*,' Silva said dryly.

'Oh, sorry. This is Chief…'

'No names. What are you an idiot?' Silva ashed his cigarette in frustration. 'Shipment is in place. Fly out in two days once my people have secured the airspace. In that time, we can discuss payment.'

'Oh, I don't think I'm at liberty to…'

'Then hang up the phone call and tell the person who is to call me. Otherwise, I leave with everything.'

Silva pulled the phone away from his ear but before he hung up, the voice echoed through.

'We have a problem.'

'I do not have problems, *vato*. You do. I can handle the problem for a fee,' Silva said with a grin.

'We've done our best to cover it, but there are two detectives looking into…'

'I do not need reasons.' Silva took another drag on his cigarette. His two cronies had stopped playing and were listening intently. 'Just give me the names and it will be done.'

The voice on the other end of the phone hesitated, and Silva stubbed out his cigarette and sat up. It angered him to deal with amateurs.

He'd take the whole damn score.

Eventually, the voice spoke under serious duress.

'DS Jess Sutton and DS Connor Vokes. I'll send you the addresses.'

'No need,' Silva said confidently. 'I'll find them.'

He hung up the call and shot a look to his henchmen,

who smirked at the likely increase to their payday. With a chuckle, they returned to their card game as Silva stood and marched across to the window of the staff room. The warehouse was in the middle of nowhere and the view was of a nondescript town, under siege by the torrential rain from above.

He reached into his pocket, drew another cigarette, and lit it.

As he drew the smoky goodness into his lungs, he exhaled, wondering if he should be concerned that murdering two detectives meant nothing to him.

CHAPTER TEN

With a reluctant sigh, Bruce McEwen shoved open the door of his pristine BMW iX M60, the winter sunshine shimmering off the dark paint work that was streaked with the morning dew. The vehicle had been a present to himself upon retirement, and the heated leather seats had been a godsend that morning. There were only three other cars in the car park, which was peppered with the rays of the sunlight that managed to break through the surrounding woodlands.

Why on earth had he agreed to take up golf?

Leanne had told him he needed a hobby when he'd retired from his duties as the commissioner, and foolishly, he'd signed up for the local golf club. Numerous former colleagues had sworn their lives by the game, but after a few rounds, McEwen had deduced it was because they didn't want to spend time with their families. He wasn't a natural, and while he still kept his weekly round in the diary, he found himself yearning for the warmth of his garage and the challenge of another woodwork project. He stepped out onto the gravel that coated the car park, retrieved his clubs from the back of the car and hoisted them over his shoulder. He was welcomed, as always, by a friendly and polite receptionist behind the counter along with a complimentary coffee. The decadent reception was in keeping with the extortionate annual membership fee, and as he waited for his latte to be made, he heard the clap of hands and excited footsteps approaching.

'Bruce. Ready to lose some more money?'

McEwen turned and felt a smile spread across his face as Michael Stout approached him, his hands clasped together and his golf clothing neatly pressed. The man who held the commissioner's seat before him had become a good friend during his retirement, but unlike McEwen, seemed to derive all his post-career enjoyment from the eighteen holes that lay ahead. McEwen greeted his predecessor with a firm handshake.

'Nice to see you, Michael.' McEwen turned and thankfully took his coffee. 'How are things?'

'Oh, you know.' Stout shrugged. Despite their friendship, Stout didn't talk much about his life. McEwen knew the man had three adult sons and four grandkids. But beyond that, their chat was strictly sports or, as Stout put it, *'the good old days'*. 'How's Leanne?'

'She's fine. Baby crazy right now, but hey-ho.'

'Not long now, eh?' Stout smiled as he collected his own golf clubs. 'Trust me, they'll keep you young. More so than your golf swing, anyway.'

'What was that famous quote? "*Golf is a good walk, spoilt*".' McEwen joked, and the two men made their way to the first hole. As always, Stout ran through the usual rigmarole of a few practice swings while McEwen finished his coffee. The briskness of the morning was refreshing enough, and with the delicious coffee now pumping through his veins and the good company he had with him, McEwen looked out over the immaculately kept grounds and decided there were worse places to be.

He could have been in Henrietta Sarrett's shoes.

As they made their way through the first few holes, they noticed a larger group gathering around the first tee. There was no chance they'd catch them up, and as the only other players that early in the morning, the conversation between the two men flowed effortlessly. Their respective times as commissioner meant they shared a unique bond, and it didn't take long for Stout to bring up the heart-breaking murders of PCs Harrington and Dyer.

'Truly disgusting.' Stout shook his head as he mourned them.

McEwen had contemplated mentioning the visit from Sam Pope the night before, but it was hard to gauge Stout's reaction. The man was as by-the-book as McEwen had known, but there was a shade of grey when it came to Sam. Stout was in seat when the deranged Matthew McLaughlin had stormed UCLH in Euston and held an entire floor hostage. Sam had willingly walked into the firing line, and it was Stout who'd given Sam the choice of another chance or prison.

Sam had chosen the latter, and while his subsequent escape from the police escort hadn't been on the cards, Stout had seemed okay with Sam having another taste of freedom. By the time Sam had returned from the dead, Stout was already comfortably living off his pension.

'You're up,' Stout said with a firm nod, as he slid his own driver back into his bag, which stood firm on its two legs. Somewhere down the course, Stout's ball was resting neatly on the fairway.

'I'm already down one fifty,' McEwen grumbled. Their decision to play for fifty pounds a hole was akin to burning money at this point. With a grunt, McEwen slid out his driver, placed the ball down on the tee and then lined up his shot. The sun cut through the clouds and bathed the course in a glorious glow, and McEwen hoisted the club up and swung through. The connection was satisfyingly strong, but as the ball soared up into the winter's sky, it began to veer worryingly to the right. Stout hissed through his teeth, and McEwen felt his shoulder droop as it disappeared into the surrounding trees.

'I thought all coppers played golf?'

The voice caught both men by surprise, and they spun and froze in shock as Sam Pope walked up the grass verge to the tee. With his hands stuffed into his parka coat, he nodded his greetings to both men.

For the first time all morning, Stout was speechless.

'Sam?' McEwen stammered. 'What the hell?'

'Morning, Commissioners.' Sam shook his head. 'That seemed weird.'

'Well, this is a surprise.' Stout snapped back to the situation and stepped forward to Sam. The few seconds of tension eased as he extended his hand. 'They really do let anyone in here, don't they?'

Sam took the man's firm handshake. It had been over three years since he'd sat opposite the former commissioner and shared a few drinks before accepting his fate behind bars.

A lot had happened since then.

'Judging by the surprise, I take it Bruce here didn't tell you?'

Stout raised an eyebrow in McEwen's direction.

'No. He didn't.'

'Sam's looking into the murders...' McEwen began, but Stout lifted a hand to cut him off.

'That checks out,' Stout said with a sigh. 'I take it telling you to leave it to the police won't change your mind?'

'With all due respect, sir. There are some places the police can't and won't look.' Sam looked out over the course. 'Something doesn't feel right about it.'

Stout looked at McEwen accusingly, but then smiled.

'Neither of us has the same pull we used to, Sam. In fact, once we get the handshake and the generous pension, we kind of get put on the shelf.' Stout ran a hand through his hair, that was thinner than the last time they'd spoken. 'But an attack on the Met still boils my piss, and if you can do whatever it is you do and find the bastards responsible, then I'll look the other way.'

Sam glanced to McEwen who nodded.

'That's as good as we can promise,' McEwen agreed.

'I didn't come here for permission.'

'No. I assumed as such,' Stout said firmly and then sighed. 'I haven't heard too much. A few gangs in London have been sending encrypted messages among themselves about taking a run at the Met. Threats of violence, etc.'

Sam drew his lips into a line and frustratingly shook his head. McEwen cleared this through.

'There was one theory that got passed around.' He began. 'I made some calls after you visited me last night, and there were two detectives who were trying to link the attacks with the robbery of an armoured truck heading to Gatwick Airport. Apparently, the hit was within a few minutes of the second murder.'

Sam's focus snapped to McEwen.

'You got any names?'

'Err…Sutton. DS Sutton.' McEwen pulled his mobile phone out of the pocket of his gilet. 'I assumed you'd want to speak to her, so I got her address. Gave them some lies about wanting to discuss a memoir I was writing…'

As McEwen handed the phone over to Sam, he glanced at Stout, who seemed impressed.

'Never had you as a spy, Bruce,' Stout joked.

Sam glanced over the screen and committed the address to memory. There was no way he'd send it across to his own phone.

He didn't leave a trail, no matter how small.

'Thanks, gentlemen.' Sam handed the phone back. 'At least give me five minutes before you call this in.'

Stout stepped past Sam and hoisted his golf bag up onto his shoulder.

'Now now…we have a game to finish.'

The warm smile told Sam he was in the clear, and he nodded to both men, turned on his heel and headed back down the verge to the vast woodlands surrounding them. It was a mile walk back through the trees to the wall he'd scaled to trespass on the golf club, and beyond that was his car. As his boots crunched over the crisp, frost-kissed grass, McEwen called after him.

'Don't make too much of a mess.'

Sam couldn't promise anything.

Within a few minutes of turning up to the office, Sutton could feel the shift.

Although the mood of the station had been morbid since the deaths of Harrington and Dyer, there had been a sense of togetherness from everyone working within its walls.

An attack on one was an attack on all.

But the few times she'd left her desk, either to venture to the cafeteria or the bathroom, Sutton could feel the cold shoulder that seemed to be thrust in her direction. Vokes had commented on it, too, sensing that ever since he'd posed the theory that the deaths had been a distraction, the entire station had decided to cut them out. Usual greetings had been reduced to the odd grunt of acknowledgement. Friendly small talk had evaporated and when Sutton tried to call in a few favours with one of the uniform teams, she was met with excuses.

Whatever it was, pointing out that the deaths of two police officers may have been for nothing more than money had alienated them both.

To his credit, Vokes didn't blame her. In the twenty-four hours since she'd dumped her wild theory on his lap, he seemed to have become transfixed with the idea that it was all a double bluff. The senseless killings were indeed a distraction, and Vokes had been hammering down the door of the Bank of England only to be told it was already being handled by the police.

Someone wasn't talking.

When he pushed for answers from other parts of CID, he was shut down. When they went to Hasan, he chastised them loudly for the rest of the office to hear. Every search into the system for anything to do with the supposed hijacking of the truck was either missing or behind a password.

Something didn't add up, and the more the duo dug, the harder the pushback. It was infuriating, and when Hasan scolded Sutton over the lack of progress on the Bakku incident from a few nights before, he questioned whether her head was truly in the game.

It was a personal dig and one that Sutton took to heart. Vokes decided to call it a day after a final pushback, and with the clock ticking past six that evening, Sutton decided to join him. The two of them ventured nearer to London Bridge Station, where Vokes would usually hop on a train to Epsom where he lived with his young family. Sutton lived in a small flat in Finsbury Park, which while not offering her much in way of space, was a hell of a nest egg with the skyrocketing price of London real estate.

Before they went their separate ways, they'd stopped for a drink in one of the numerous pubs that surrounded the enormous station. Despite the cold and the dark, the bustling London life was still in full swing, and the two of them managed to perch on a small side table in a pub that was alive with drunken banter and after work frustration.

They didn't say much.

A few gloomy resignations that their cards were marked and Vokes even posed the idea of just letting it go. Fall in line and help find the person who pushed Dyer, or the one who ran a knife across Harrington's throat.

What annoyed Sutton most was that, as always, Vokes was right. It was the sensible move for them, especially if they wanted the opportunities they both knew they'd worked for. But there was a feeling in the pit of her stomach that it would go against her oath as a member of the police service.

To protect the public and uphold the law.

They couldn't look the other way.

A glum goodbye followed, and Sutton felt a twinge of jealousy as Vokes disappeared into the chaos of London Bridge Station knowing he was going home to a loving family that would distract him from the failure they'd felt.

Sutton was heading home with her thoughts, and the idea of wrestling with her conscience all night took her into the local off-licence to pick up a bottle of wine and regrettably, another packet of cigarettes.

As she puffed her way through the first one, she promised herself that unlike the previous times, this would be for one night only.

Her third-floor flat sat in a trendy apartment block a few streets away from the aforementioned park, and she stepped through the thick, black gate that surrounded the well-kept grounds. Lost in her own self-deprecation and cloud of cigarette smoke, she completely bypassed the black 4x4 and the three men who were watching her enter the building. Thankfully, she didn't run into any of her neighbours as she ascended the staircase, and the idea of small talk turned her stomach. So did the idea of dinner, and as she pushed open her front door, she knew it would be a bottle of wine and then bed.

The room was pitch-black; the only light was that of the street light peeping in through the bay window that overlooked the street below. She flipped on the switch and stepped into the open-plan kitchen, oblivious to the usually neglected dishes that now sat washed on the drainer beside the sink and the man sitting on the sofa behind her. She uncorked the wine, poured herself a large glass, and then placed the bottle on the side. After a large gulp, she turned around and stumbled back into the fridge.

'Jesus fucking Christ!'

Sam Pope pushed himself off the sofa and held his hands up. After a few moments to let her catch her breath, he fixed her with a hard stare.

She knew who he was.

But not why he was there.

'We need to talk.'

CHAPTER ELEVEN

Over his career, Silva had killed dozens of police officers across numerous countries. To him, the fact somebody had dedicated their lives to a badge held zero weight, and any institution that tried to govern the world was living a lie. He believed in hierarchy, which was why he never sought to overthrow the wealthy and powerful people who paid well for his services, but he was also against the idea that it could push down on him.

It was why he'd burnt Farstone to the ground and why he held no remorse for killing people who fought to protect the law.

The law was a construct to keep the weak and afraid intact, offering them a warm, comfortable blanket to shield them from the real world.

Anything he desired could be taken, and Silva knew his talents and mentality meant that there was nothing out of his reach. He could have killed the two men in the truck had he so wished, but it would have just sensationalised the robbery when it had been agreed to be swept under the rug. Putting two bullets in the passenger's legs had earnt him some push back, but a swift threat of his own soon put that to bed.

In two days, he'd be long gone, but now, two unfortunate detectives had done some actual police work and were now firmly in his crosshairs. The encrypted file that was sent through a number of backdoor email addresses soon ended up in his inbox, and as he cast his eyes over them, he found himself in a moral quandary.

DS Connor Vokes had a wife and kids.

DS Jessica Sutton was attractive.

Although he had a penchant for pretty women and no qualms about widowing a wife and orphaning children, the smart move was to kill one and scare the other off. Unfortunately for Sutton, she had less collateral damage and would most likely be lumped in with the other killings that Silva had orchestrated. Vokes would be too messy, and Silva had taken his two men with him in case the operation threw up any surprises.

Perhaps she wouldn't be alone?

There was nothing in her file to suggest a partner, but there were always curveballs to be thrown. Perhaps she'd got lucky that evening? As he'd sat in the backseat of the 4x4, he looked out of the window at the city of London as they slammed headfirst into the London gridlock. Impatience spread through every road like a tidal wave, but Silva was content to bide his time. The detective would still be at work, and besides, growing up in the heart of Jalisco had more than readied him for a bout of traffic. He drew down the window and lit a cigarette, not even asking if the two men in the front of the vehicle had any objection.

They weren't allowed to. They were being paid handsomely.

As he blew the smoke out of the window, he placed the cigarettes on the seat beside him, and then rested his hand on the loaded Glock 17. The plan was to make it look like a robbery gone wrong, but if all else failed, he'd be more than happy to put a bullet through her pretty little skull.

Slowly, they progressed, and Silva felt no affection for the city of London as they were swallowed by the towering skyscrapers. He'd been numerous times before, and while he understood the pull of the iconic buildings to tourists, to him it was nothing more than a concrete jungle filled with arrogance.

They arrived in Finsbury Park a little after four and the sun was already beginning its descent. A chilling wind had picked up and Silva sent the thug in the passenger seat to check if Sutton was home.

She wasn't, and so his next order was for the man to return with the best coffee he could find.

Then they waited.

And waited.

A little before eight, the forlorn figure of DS Sutton emerged around the corner, a white plastic bag swinging a wine bottle in her hand and Silva watched as she meandered through the unlocked gate and then through the front door of the apartment complex. Despite all the reasons for its existence, the residence had done away with the auto-lock function on the door, which meant his hired gun would be able to walk right up to her third-floor apartment and end her life.

After a few moments, the light in her apartment went on, and the adrenaline of the henchman caused him to spin in his seat.

'Shall I go?' he asked, his excitement a little unnerving.

Silva smiled to himself and lifted his cigarettes and tapped one out of the box.

'Give her five minutes, *Ese*,' Silva said calmly as he lit the cigarette, refusing to open the window due to the cold. As the smoke swirled around them, he looked up at the window once more. 'Let's allow her one final drink before she dies.'

It took DS Sutton a few moments to collect herself, and Sam caught her off guard by offering to get her some water. As he did, she kept her eyes locked on the man she'd been hunting for weeks. As he lifted the glass to the tap, she noticed the full draining board beside him.

'Did you do my dishes?'

Sam looked at them, smiled up at her, and shrugged.

'I was bored.' He stepped back around the breakfast bar that overlooked the living room and handed it to her. 'Force of habit, I guess.'

'How the hell did you get in here?'

Sam lowered himself onto the arm of her sofa, a few feet from the bar stool where she sat. He was an impressive sight, Sutton admitted to herself, with his muscular frame filling out the black jumper that clung to his body. His strong jaw was coated in a thick stubble, and the eyebrows that sat above his dark eyes were intersected with scars.

Mementos from his previous misdeeds.

'I can take apart and reassemble an L96A1 Sniper Rifle with my eyes closed.' He boasted jokingly. 'Your piddly little lock was a walk in the park.'

'You picked the lock?' Sutton snapped.

'I wasn't going to kick your door down, was I? Then I wouldn't have the opportunity to scare the hell out of you.'

He offered her his disarming smile, and she took a slow sip of the water. The tales that were spread about Sam often verged on the ridiculous, especially among the young recruits who seemed almost in awe of the path of destruction he'd left over the years. Sutton had always been quick to remind them that the man wasn't just a wanted criminal, he was a stone-cold killer. Yet, through those rumours, the notion that Sam himself was a decent man had often filtered through.

Dangerous? Yes.

Troubled? Certainly.

But in his heart, he was a soldier and the fact that those who ended up in his crosshairs were some of the most deplorable men and women in the world was evidence of a heart in the right place.

But Sutton shook that notion away, slammed down her glass and stood powerfully.

'Sam Pope, you are under arrest for the murders of countless people. You do not have to…'

Sam lifted his hand and shook his head.

'Please, save it. You're not arresting me.'

'Excuse me?'

'You're not arresting me. Now sit down so we can talk.'

'Are you resisting arrest?' Sutton goaded. 'If I get my cuffs, will you physically stop me?'

Sam sighed and then held his arms out, his wrists together and his hands balled into fists.

'Go on then. Arrest me. But I'm more use to you out of prison than in it.'

'Oh, really?' Sutton said sarcastically as she leant across the kitchen counter for her bag. 'How do you reckon?'

'Because I think someone killed those police officers so they could hijack an armoured truck.' He let the statement hang in the air as Sutton stopped in her tracks. She dropped her bag down and spun back in her chair to face him. 'Can I lower these?'

'How did you know about that?'

Sam lowered them anyway and rested his hands on his thighs.

'Probably best you don't know. But I know that you and your partner are the only ones pulling at that thread, and somebody doesn't want it to unravel.' Sam stood. 'That's where I come in. I can pull on threads very fucking hard if I need to.'

Sutton raised her hands to her head and massaged her temples. Sam knew he was putting a tough decision on the detective, but he hoped his intuition was correct.

Sutton wanted justice.

Whatever the cost.

A few moments of silence felt like hours to her, and she finally looked up at Sam and shook her head.

'I can't let you. I'm sorry. You're a wanted man and I would be neglecting my duty if I didn't bring you in.'

Sam heard a car door slam shut and then walked across the room and carefully poked his head around the curtain, just in time to see a burly man pull open the door to the apartment block and disappear below.

'What about those officers?' Sam said, snapping his attention back to her. 'What if they died for nothing? And the police did nothing?'

'Why do you care?'

'Because someone has to do something,' Sam said firmly.

'Leave it to the police, then. You can't just do whatever you want, Sam. There are laws. Chains of command.'

'Not to me, there's not.'

Knock! Knock!

Sutton startled and turned to the door, and Sam took a step towards it. As he did, he held a finger up to Sutton for her to stay silent, and then he moved carefully to the door.

Knock! Knock! Knock!

'Delivery for a Miss Sutton.'

The gruff voice echoed from behind the wood, and Sam turned to the detective.

'You order anything?'

She shook her head.

The banging grew louder and more aggressive, and Sam took a few steps to the side of the door and then pulled the handle down. Within milliseconds, the thug barged through, his beady eyes glaring from the bald head that was speckled with rain. They latched onto Sutton in an instant, and the murderous intent in his every muscle exploded. Sutton stumbled back off her stool, but as the man cleared the doorway, Sam booted the door and it snapped backward, the hard edge colliding with the man's eyebrow. As the intruder fell back into the wall and held a gloved hand to the gushing wound, Sam slammed the door shut and turned right into a solid right hook. The blow sent Sam back into the kitchen and the man charged at him, his bloodstained face distorted in a crazed scowl. He had a few inches on Sam, along with a good twenty to thirty pounds, and as he drove his shoulder into Sam's midsection, he sent the air shooting out of his lungs. Sam drove his elbows down into the man's neck before he reached for a metal pan and slammed it into the man's skull. The man stumbled slightly, and Sam kicked him back a few steps, creating a little space between the two of them. The man shook the wooziness from his brain and then pulled a knife from his pocket. With only a few feet between them, he wildly lunged at Sam who weaved to the side, but the man swiped it back and the blade sliced across Sam's shoulder. It ripped through the fabric of his jumper and drew blood, but Sam threw up his arm as the blade came lunging back towards his throat. Expertly, he drove his elbow into the joint of his attacker's arm, and it loosened his grip on the blade. With his other hand, Sam clasped at the attacker's wrist and found the pressure point.

The fingers lapsed, and the blade dropped.

Sam caught it before it hit the ground and drove it down into the flesh above the man's kneecap.

The man collapsed to his other knee and howled in

pain, and Sam shut the noise off by drilling his boot into the side of the man's jaw, crushing his head against the glass oven. The man dropped to the kitchen floor motionless, leaving a bloody smear across the cracked glass. Sam stretched out his shoulder, grunting with pain before turning to a shell-shocked Sutton.

'I think we need to go,' Sam said calmly and although Sutton nodded, she was frozen to her spot. 'NOW!'

The rise in Sam's voice snapped Sutton out of it and she quickly gathered her bag and threw on her coat. All her training came flooding back to her and the fearful statue from a minute before was replaced by a figure of authority.

'We need to call this in...'

'Who the hell do you think sent them?'

The penny dropped, and Sutton looked down at the motionless body in her kitchen and then at the pool of blood beginning to spread across the tiles.

'Shit,' she said to herself.

'Shit, indeed,' Sam said calmly, easing himself uncomfortably into his jacket. He could feel the warm blood beginning to slide down his arm. 'Is there a back way out of here?'

Sutton looked up at him.

'Yeah. Why?'

Sam pulled open the front door and ushered her out.

'Because he didn't come alone.'

CHAPTER TWELVE

Silva ashed the cigarette onto the footwell of the car and then casually looked at his watch. He took another puff and then stomped it out under his foot, glanced up at the apartment across the road, and then tapped the driver's seat in front of him.

'Your boy always take this long?' Silva said, doing little to mask his annoyance. The driver turned.

'Do you want me to go and check?'

'You're very clever. *Vámonos*.' Silva sat back and shook his head as he watched the driver amble across the street and made the decision to deduct their pay. The driver yanked open the door to the building and disappeared inside, and Silva anxiously straightened the cuffs of his jacket. When he glanced back up to the building, the driver was leaning out of the window, waving to him. Silva frowned and stepped out of the car, his fingers wrapped around his handgun.

'She's fucking gone,' the man yelled through the rainfall.

An engine roared to life down the other end of the street, and Silva watched as a car sped past and instinctively, he smoothly lifted the Glock and unloaded a few roads that shattered the back window. The gunfire elicited a scream of terror from a passerby, and Silva threw open the driver's door and hopped in.

Seconds later, he was in hot pursuit.

As the back window blew out, Sam reached across from behind the steering wheel and put his hand on the back of Sutton's head, pushing her down into the seat.

Another gunshot echoed from behind them, the bullet embedding in the back of the car as Sam hit the corner at full speed.

'Stay down,' he warned, wrestling control of the wheel again and straightening the car.

Sutton looked panicked, and she glanced back through the gaping hole as the wind and rain ripped into the back of the car. The headlights appeared swiftly behind them, and she looked back at Sam.

'They're following us.'

'I know.' Sam's eyes were locked on the rear-view mirror. 'Hold on to something.'

As the car shot down Seven Sisters Road, he lifted the handbrake and spun the wheel, the tyres screeching like a banshee into the night as he cut through a red light. A flurry of car horns erupted as he cut off the traffic, spinning the car around the Manor House Train Station before slamming down the handbrake and roaring forward up Green Lanes.

The 4x4 slammed between two other cars and continued its pursuit, drawing a foul-mouthed utterance under Sam's breath. As he weaved through the thankfully light traffic, he turned to Sutton with a frown.

'What the hell are you doing?'

'I'm calling it in,' Sutton said firmly, unlocking her phone. Before she could lift it to her ear, Sam knocked it into her lap.

'Are you crazy?'

'No. I'm a fucking police officer.'

'Have a think, Jess,' Sam said, spinning the wheel again to avoid a bus and then turning sharply down a side street towards Wood Green. 'How the hell do you think these people found you in the first place?'

The question hit Sutton like a freight train, and she lowered the phone. For all her pre-conceived ideas about Sam Pope and the dangerous road he walked, he'd just saved her life. Whoever was at her door, they'd intended to kill her and now they were being pursued through the London rain by a man who'd already unloaded a gun at them.

But who?

Sam was right. Only a few people knew that she was snooping around the Gatwick robbery and the information surrounding it had been washed away by the blood of innocent police officers. Quietly, she tapped out a message and hit send, just as Sam turned down another side street and cut past Wood Green station. Somewhere in the distance, the wailing of sirens could be heard, no doubt responding to the gunfire outside her building.

Wherever Sutton and Sam were heading, they were on their own.

Sam's eyes were fixed on the road, and as they approached another traffic light, it turned to red.

'Hold on.'

Sam slammed his foot down and hammered through the red light, drawing a few irate car horns as a few cars skidded to a stop. Behind them, the pursuing 4x4 slammed on the brakes to avoid the collision. Sam flashed a look to the mirror before speeding down a road and rounding

Wood Green Common, which was shrouded in darkness. Beyond that were rows of railway tracks, separating them from Alexandra Park, home of the London Football Academy. The New River ran parallel to the train tracks, and it was clear from Sam's scanning of the local area that there wasn't a plan, but then as they approached an old, run-down industrial park, Sam shut off the lights of the car and pulled into an old, abandoned warehouse. It had once been a storage facility for a low budget retail company that had long since collapsed, and Sam weaved the car between two tall pallets and killed the engine.

'Who did you message?' He turned to Sutton and gestured for her phone.

'Excuse me?'

'Back there. You sent a message.' Sam shook his head. 'You can't trust anyone, Sutton.'

'It was to my partner, DS Vokes.' Sutton held onto her phone tightly. 'We can trust him.'

'Phone. Now.'

Reluctantly, she handed it to Sam, who held down the power button and shut it down. Sutton looked a little concerned, and Sam shrugged.

'They can trace your sim.'

'Fine.'

Sam smiled, but before he could hand it back, the glare of two headlights illuminated the entrance to industrial park and Sam snapped his head back. As he peered through the jagged remnants of the back window, he felt his muscles tighten as the 4x4 came into view.

'Out of the car. Now.'

Sutton understood and as quickly and as quietly as possible, they left Sam's rental where it was, and he led her further into the warehouse. It was filled with large wooden pallets, all wrapped in plastic sheets that were thick with dust. The only light was that of the moon above, which burst through the gaps in the roof in long, powerful streams. The rain clattered against the rusty, corrugated iron roof and the howl of the wind caused some of the sheets to rustle. Across the far side of the warehouse were rows of tall metal shelves, all of them now stacked with old store equipment. Relics of an old business model that couldn't change with the times. As Sam ushered Sutton forward, he shot frequent glances over his shoulder. The sound of a car door slamming shut echoed through the old building, followed by the sound of high-quality shoes on concrete.

The man was walking confidently into the warehouse, seemingly undeterred by whoever had saved his target.

When he spoke, his voice was laced with a thick accent and the undeniable arrogance of a man with no fear.

'Let's make this quick, shall we?'

Sam and Sutton rounded another pallet, and Sam motioned for her to hide behind one of the desks that had been stacked lazily in the corner. As she did, she turned back and Sam raised a finger to his lips, lifted his gun, and then stepped away.

The smell of cigarette smoke began to filter through the damp air.

'Hey, Mr Hero. You looking for a job?' The follower joked, the voice getting louder as he ventured deeper into the warehouse. Sam pressed against one of the crates, his ears tuned into the sounds of his environment.

The patter of rain against the roof, and the plastic sheets as it invaded the warehouse.

The relentless drip of a broken pipe.

The plastic sheets writhing in the wind.

And the footsteps.

Closer.

On the other side of the pallet.

With his gun at the ready, Sam took a deep breath, just

as the man came into his eyeline and instinctively, Sam drew the gun up and held it against the side of the man's skull. There was no panic, and the hitman held both hands up, allowing the handgun to flop and swing by the trigger that hung around his finger. In his other hand, clasped between his index and middle finger, was a half-smoked cigarette.

'Oh, you're good, *ese.*'

'Who are you?' Sam barked from the shadows, his finger a mere twitch from ending the man's life. The man turned to face him, realigning the gun with his forehead, and he took a confident pull on his cigarette as he peered into the shadows.

'Can I at least look into the eyes of the man who wants to kill me?' Silva stepped back, his hands still up in surrender, inviting Sam to step forward. As he did, Silva's eyes squinted in the moonlight. 'I seen you before? You look familiar.'

'Doubt it. I'm not in the business of killing police officers.'

The man took the insult and nodded, drawing again on the cigarette that was nearly done.

'Well, let's make an introduction. My name is Dominik Silva.' He then gestured to Sam who stayed stoic. 'This is the part where you tell me your name.'

'How about I just put a bullet through your skull?' Sam spat back, his muscular arm at full stretch as he pressed the barrel of the gun against Silva's skull. 'Or you tell me who you're working for and I'll go straight to the top of this food chain.'

Excitedly, the man slapped his thigh and his rugged face broke into a smile.

'You're him, aren't you? The great Sam Pope.' Silva chuckled as he looked at Sam. 'You know, *vato*, you cost me a lot of money when you killed Vasquez back in the day.'

'I didn't kill him.'

'So you say.' Silva took the final drag on his cigarette and let the smoke filter from his lips. 'Say, is that bounty still on your head? What was it…three million dead?'

Sam adjusted slightly, getting ready to pull the trigger.

'I'm afraid Dana Kovalenko can't fulfil that contract on account of my putting a bullet through her skull.'

'That's a shame, *vato*,' Silva said as he looked beyond the barrel of the gun directed straight at his skull and into the eyes of the man who intended to fire it. 'Because I'm now going to have to kill you for free.'

Without warning, Silva flicked the cigarette butt forward and the hot remnants of it blinded Sam as they crashed against his face. As Sam pulled the trigger, Silva shunted Sam's arm upward and the wayward round clattered onto the roof. Sam tried to blink through the pain, just in time to see Silva spin the gun round his finger and clasp it in his palm, but before he could turn it on Sam, Sam drove his elbow into the man's jaw, sending him backwards. Silva dropped his gun, and as Sam went to raise his again, Silva wrenched Sam's arm to the side and drove his fist into Sam's wrists, sending the weapon sliding off into the dark. With his grip strong, Silva spun Sam around and slammed him into a pallet before drilling a knee into Sam's midsection. Sam absorbed the blow with a grunt of pain and then wrenched his arm free. Silva responded with a hard right that sent Sam stumbling to the side and Silva smirked and cockily rolled his shoulders and stretched his back.

'You really want to do this?' Silva asked. 'Just hand me the woman and I'll be on my way.'

'Who sent you?' Sam asked again, spitting a dribble of blood onto the floor.

'Again with the questions. Let me tell you something:

the less you know, the less you care. It's a lot easier that way.'

Sam launched forward and threw a left jab that Silva dodged, but then caught him with the following right hook that sent him spiralling into one of the wooden pallets.

'Hard way it is then,' Sam said, shrugging as Silva wiped the blood from his own lip, smirked and then threw his fists up. Sam threw a few more punches, but Silva weaved expertly, picking his spots and snapping Sam's head back with a hard jab. Slightly shaken, Sam went for a similar response, but Silva spun out of the way, spun around Sam's back and drilled him in the back of the head with an elbow that sent Sam stumbling onto all fours. As Sam's brain ricocheted inside his skull, Silva casually strolled across to the Glock that Sam had knocked from his hand and picked it up.

'I'm a little disappointed, *homes*,' Silva said as he drew the gun up. 'I expected more.'

As Sam pushed himself up onto his knees and tried to shake the grogginess, Silva lifted the gun. As he did, a swarm of footsteps filtered into the warehouse behind them.

'Drop the fucking weapon, now!'

It was DS Vokes, and beside him, filtering out through the warehouse, was an armed response unit. Silva looked back at Sam and arched an eyebrow.

'To be continued.'

Silva then turned and raced towards the sanctity of the shadows, unloading his gun in the direction of the oncoming tactical unit, who all took cover behind the multiple pallets and equipment. Silva raced between the shelving units and without stopping, he leapt shoulder first into the old fire exit door, which was drawn together by a rusty chain that swung from a decrepit padlock. The velocity combined with his impressive frame obliterated the lock as he slammed through the doors, sprawling onto the wet concrete and then straight up into a sprint. Behind him, he could hear the orders being thrown out by the police unit, and he leapt up and cleared the chain-link fence in a matter of seconds. As the first armed officer appeared in the doorway, screaming at him to stop moving, Silva pushed himself off the top of the fence and he crashed into the river below. Under the camouflage of the downpour, along with the cloud shrouding the light of the moon, it didn't take him long to disappear into the night.

CHAPTER THIRTEEN

Sutton knew explaining it to Hasan or Dummett would be impossible, but she'd thought Vokes would have been more understanding. After the armed response had chased Silva through the warehouse and seemingly lost him in the darkness beyond, she'd emerged from her hiding place just in time to see Vokes pin a woozy Sam Pope to the ground and slap some cuffs on him. Despite her protests, Vokes, quite rightly, pointed out that Sam was the most wanted man in the country, and they *had* to bring him in. Sergeant Brian Hayes, the leader of the armed response unit swept the building with the rest of the team, before demanding Sutton and Vokes return to Charing Cross Station for a debrief. It was all standard procedure, but through it all, Sutton could only think back to what Sam had asked her in the car.

'How the hell do you think these people found you in the first place?'

As Sam began to shake the cobwebs, he showed little resistance to being lifted to his feet by Vokes, who then guided Sam back through the warehouse to the car. As he dipped Sam's head and shoved him into the backseat, he closed the door and turned to Sutton with a warm smile.

'I'm glad you're okay.'

'I'm not fucking okay, Connor.' She spat. 'Those men came to my house to kill me. Thank God Sam was there.'

Vokes shook his head.

'Are you listening to yourself? That's Sam Pope. You know, the guy you've been obsessed with catching for the past however long. And besides, why the hell was he there as well?'

'He was waiting for me when I got home.'

'Jesus.' Vokes put his hands on his hips. 'Do you know how that's going to look? There're already rumours that Pope has connections in the police. You really want to be lumped in with those? Because I can tell you what happened to their careers if you like?'

'Save it.' Sutton held up her hand. 'He wanted to talk about Gatwick and the killings and—'

'How does he know about Gatwick?' It was a fair question. 'There's fuck all in the press, and barely anymore in our systems.'

'Is it too lame to say he seems to find a way?'

'Unless he's in on it? You ever think about that?' He looked at Sutton who chuckled. 'I'm serious.'

'If he was, wouldn't he have been there to put a bullet in my head? He's the only reason I don't have one.'

Sutton stomped around the car to the passenger seat of the squad car that Vokes had arrived in. As she went to pull open the door, she hesitated.

'How did you get here so fast?' Her question ramped up the tension.

'Excuse me?' Vokes seemed genuinely offended.

'You went and got on your train hours ago. It's not like you live round the fucking corner.'

'Oh, thanks, Connor, for answering my call for help.

And for saving Sam Pope's life, too. Fucking hell, Jess.' Vokes yanked up the car door with frustration. 'My train was cancelled by the way. You can check on the fucking app.'

Vokes dropped into the driver's side of the car and slammed the door, and Sutton cursed herself for mistrusting him. For years, they'd been thick as thieves and the last thing she wanted to do in that moment, when it felt like the institution she'd given her life to wanted to snatch it from her, was alienate the one man she could always rely on. As the armed response unit filtered out of the warehouse, Jess tentatively opened the door and got into the car. The duo sat in silence for a few moments, refusing to look at each other. Sam watched them with interest.

'Look, I'm sorry,' Sutton finally offered. 'It's just been a hell of a night.'

'Apology accepted.' Vokes shunted a thumb towards Sam. 'I know he thinks the Met is crawling with corrupt cops, but there are reasons for everything.'

'Vokes, is it?' Sam piped up. 'As nice as it would be to be as oblivious as you are, it's hard to be subjective when you've had the actual British government turn on you.'

'Yeah, well, maybe you shouldn't kill people then.' Vokes said coldly and started the car, before reversing in a semi-circle and heading back towards the road.

'You don't have to like me. I get it. But you have to let me go otherwise you're both in *very* real danger.'

'You're not the first criminal to threaten me, pal.' Vokes's East London swagger had returned.

'No, but I bet I'm the only one who's saved your partner's life.'

Vokes grimaced slightly and then glanced at Sutton who was staring at him hopefully.

'Don't look at me like that.'

'Connor, you need to listen to him. And that's coming

from me. Someone who thinks he's a dangerous piece of shit.' She turned to Sam. 'No offence.'

'Trust me, I've been called worse.'

Vokes chuckled and then caught himself, replacing it with a frown.

'Look, I appreciate you saving Jess. I really do.' Vokes glanced into the mirror to make eye contact with his prisoner. 'But the sensible thing to do is to bring you in, take everything up the flagpole and get us put in protective custody if need be.'

'Protection from who?' Sam asked, his stare burning through the reflection. 'Ask yourself this, Vokes, how many people knew you two were looking into Gatwick?'

'Quite a few. I pitched it in a meeting earlier yesterday.'

'And before you did that, how many times had a hit team turned up at either one of your houses?' The silence was chilling. 'Be thankful it wasn't your house. Because if you weren't there, what do you think they would have done to your family?'

'You keep my family out of your fucking mouth.' Vokes's anger was abrupt. 'You understand me?'

'Jesus, Connor. He's not goading you.' Sutton cut in as they turned past Wood Green station and back to civilisation. 'But we're detectives. We know when something is wrong and you're telling me you feel comfortable going back to the only people who knew what we were up to? What we were looking at?'

Vokes shuffled uncomfortably in his seat. He tightened his grip on the steering wheel and kept his eyes on the road ahead.

'It's the sensible thing to do.'

'And what if he's right?' Sutton asked, arching her neck towards Sam. 'Two officers were killed so a lot of gold could be stolen. Killed, Connor. They tried to kill me because I'm looking in the right place. And so are you.'

They sat in silence for a few moments as the detective tried to gather his thoughts. Sutton flashed a smile back at Sam, a silent thank you for saving her life, and he returned in kind. His lip was split open, and dried blood had crusted down the stubble that clung to his chin. The turn off that would take them back towards Charing Cross was fast approaching and, as he approached, Vokes sighed.

'Fuck it.'

He turned the wheel in the other direction.

There was a strong chance the armed response unit, which was somewhere further back on the road, had seen them veer from the route, but Vokes slammed his foot down and sped down several winding roads until he was comfortable they'd put enough distance between themselves and discovery. A large McDonald's burst into view, with the large, yellow M still as offensively bright despite the inclement weather. Vokes pulled into the car park and then guided the car to a vacant spot behind the drive-thru. He killed the engine and then turned in his seat.

'So, what are we doing here?'

He looked to Sutton and then to Sam, who rolled his shoulders, stretching out the pain from his brawl with Silva. His head was thumping from the sharp blow to the back of the skull. What hurt more was the fact that Silva had him beaten and he'd have been killed if Vokes hadn't shown up.

'You okay, Sam?' Sutton asked, clearly seeing his distress.

'First off. Vokes. Thank you. You saved my life,' Sam said. 'Second, can we take these cuffs off?'

Vokes unclipped his seatbelt, and quickly hopped out of the car. He gave a cautionary glance around the car park, and then quickly opened Sam's door and removed the shackles that had bound his wrists to his spine. He pulled out his vape stick and took a puff as he stood by Sam's open door.

'So, what's the play?' Vokes asked.

'Run it back,' Sam said. 'Who *really* knew what you were up to and who tried to shut it down?'

'Card on the table.' Sutton countered. 'Who put you on to me?'

'I can't say.' Sam shook his head. Vokes and Sutton shared a look of annoyance.

'You have to do better than that, Sam,' Sutton said firmly. 'Gatwick is big, but trust me, you are bigger.'

'I can't tell you that. But I can give you something else.'

'This isn't a fucking market, mate.' Vokes chimed in. Sam ignored him and looked straight at Sutton.

'Bakku. I was there, I killed those guards, and I targeted Bloom, Grant and Wilson.'

'We know,' Sutton said with a shrug. 'We're pretty good detectives.'

Sam smiled. Sutton had a determination that was as attractive as her sharp features. Despite the situation, she smiled back. Vokes noticed it and rolled his eyes.

'Shall I go?' He joked.

'Bakku will be shut down, maybe? The owner has a lot of money. And those three men, they'll walk. We know that.' Sam leant forward. 'But I targeted them because they were connected to Vladimir Balikov. I have the evidence that proves they were funding a global terrorist unit. Now, we already met the guy who pulled off the heist tonight. Silva. The name rings a bell but a man that good costs a lot of money. Which means someone hired him to hit Gatwick and organised for those officers to be killed. Arranged for them to kill you, Jess and most likely, Vokes... they'd come for you next.'

As Sam bluntly laid out the situation, the two detectives swapped a fearful look. They weren't trained for combat.

Their jobs were to hunt for evidence and shift through the details to nail suspects to crimes.

Not go to war with mercenaries and murderous senior figures. After a few nervous puffs, Vokes turned back to Sam.

'So, what do you want to do?'

'First. I'd quite like to go in there and get something to eat.' He pointed to the McDonalds. 'Then, you're going to tell me all the people who knew what you were doing and have the power to cover it up.'

Sam turned on the seat and swung his legs out. The bitter cold hit him like a slap to the face, and the chill sliced into his split lip and caused him to wince. As he stepped past Vokes and headed towards the fast-food restaurant, Sutton stepped out of the car and called across the roof to him.

'And if we do? Then what?'

Sam turned his head back but kept on walking.

'I'm going to get some fucking answers.'

By the time Silva had emerged from the river, his shoulders were aching. He'd swum for over a mile, keeping as low to the dark waters of the river as possible and ignoring the freezing cold that had eaten at his body. Once he'd stepped onto the banks, he knew it wouldn't be long until the combination of the freezing wind and the sodden clothes became a problem. He ventured down the nearest high street until he found a charity shop, and he expertly drove his elbow into the corner of the window that sat above the door handle to the store. The glass shattered and triggered the alarm, but Silva entered anyway.

Considering the police radios would be awash with rumours of gunfire and Sam Pope, he hedged his bets that a potential break in at a charity shop would be the least of their concerns. The Met was too thinly spread as it was, and with the shockingly low response rate to burglaries only plummeting, he took his time to find a change of clothes that would at least fit his impressive physique. He was a man of fine clothing, but needs must.

He left his sodden, designer clothes on the counter as a form of reimbursement for the damages, and sauntered out in a black puffer jacket, a jumper, jeans and some black boots.

It would do until he got back to the hideout, where his suitcase was waiting.

He travelled light, but there were a few outfits neatly folded, along with four more Glock17s, his M16 assault rifle, two Bowie knifes and a set of grenades.

When he had over fifty million pounds' worth of gold to protect, he was damn sure ready to go to war.

He stopped in the next off-licence that he passed to purchase some cigarettes and a lighter and then took cover in a phone box to light one. The cubicle smelt of piss and was lined with crude images of scantily clad women offering a vulgar phone call at a premium price. Silva lifted the receiver, called the operator, and requested a reverse charge call. As he waited for the receiver to confirm the charge, he peered out into the downpour and puffed his cigarette.

'*What the hell happened?*'

'Your detective. She had a friend, eh?' Silva took a jovial puff. 'The name Sam Pope ring any bells?'

'*Sam Pope?*' The shock was obvious.

'Interesting. I would have put a bullet through his fucking skull if your men hadn't shown up.' Silva's tone swiftly changed. 'If you try to fuck me, I'll set your fucking family on fire in front of you, and then use you to put out the flames. Is that understood?'

The silence was as good as a confirmation.

'*Where are you?*'

'You do not need to know.' Silva dropped his cigarette and crunched it underfoot. 'I need an hour or two to realign and then I'll take care of this problem for you. We can discuss the cost afterwards.'

'*Look, we can't renegotiate the price. You know he is a powerful man who…*'

'Who will do what every powerful man does when I put the barrel of a gun in his mouth,' Silva said calmly. 'They do as I say.'

A deep sigh on the other end of the phone.

'*What do you need?*'

'I need you to send me the phone location of either one of the detectives. They'll be running scared by now, and if they have any brains, they know they can't come to you.'

'*Fuck you.*'

Silva chuckled.

'Just send me the location and give me some room to work. Oh, and if you ever curse at me again, I will take your teeth out with a pair of pliers. Understood?'

Silva slammed the phone down and hung up the call. He kicked open the door of the phone box and watched as the torrential downpour danced across the ferocious wind. He tapped out another cigarette, lit it and then pulled the hood of the recently stolen jacket up over his thick, dark hair.

Then Silva headed off into the darkness of the city.

Ready to kill whoever he had to.

CHAPTER FOURTEEN

'A myriad of shit.'

That was what Bruce McEwen had laughingly told Sarrett he was handing over to her, the same way his predecessor had to him. At the time, she'd laughed. The man had just come through a life-threatening bullet wound, as well as being caught up in the chaos of the Olivier Chavet incident. She'd seen it as just a down-beaten man, ready to retire.

It turned out he was prepping her for what was to come.

The meeting room was already full, and as her assistant knocked on her door to once again tell her she was late, Sarrett felt bad at snapping back.

She knew she was late.

She was stalling.

As she blew out her cheeks and gazed out at the window, she wondered if Jordan had to deal with such pressure. As always, his restaurant was fully booked, and she'd heard enough stories from him, and seen enough cooking shows, to understand how a kitchen operates. A constant stream of commands, with everyone working at breakneck speed.

Only it wasn't life or death.

And Jordan loved what he did. Sarrett was concerned that she wasn't sure if she felt the same anymore.

With a sigh, she left her office and strode powerfully down the corridor, nodding to the officers who stood respectfully to attention before she pushed open the door and greeted the eager eyes with a smile.

'I take it we're all briefed?'

'Yes, ma'am,' Dummett said with purpose. Sarrett took the seat next to her and smiled.

'So, what do we think?' Sarrett opened it up to the room. Along with Dummett, she saw the familiar faces of DCI Hasan, as well as Graham Henshaw, who looked his usual grumpy self. There were a few senior people from the PR team in the room, along with a representative from the Office of Professional Standards. Sarrett had been certain Henshaw would be the most despised face in the room, but even the Minister of State wasn't frowned upon as much as someone who hunted criminals *within* the Met.

As the silence threatened to continue, Hasan tentatively put up a hand.

'I think we need to focus all our energy on finding Sam Pope.'

'You think?' Henshaw barked sarcastically. 'You think maybe we should find out where the two missing detectives are, along with Sam Pope?'

'I'm just saying…'

'I think we can agree that it's a priority.' Sarrett cut through the bickering. 'Have we tried to establish contact?'

'We have. But nothing so far.' Dummett offered. 'He's either got them captive or…'

'You've got more snakes in your house,' Henshaw said unapologetically. 'I'm sorry, but this isn't the first time Sam

Pope has had…how should I put this? Assistance from this organisation, is it?'

'That's a very strong accusation,' Dummett said, scowling over her glasses.

'But not one without merit,' Sarrett said with a sigh. 'It's why I invited OPS here. Look, no one ever wants to look inwards, but we owe it not just to the public, but to the families of PCs Harrington and Dyer to find out what really is going on here. And *if* someone from within this organisation had a hand in their deaths or is aiding and abetting Sam Pope, then they'll feel the full force of my size six boot where the sun doesn't shine.'

The threat lingered in the room for a while. A few glances were shifted towards Detective Inspector Thomas Gayle, who was scribbling scrupulous notes. OPS operated within the Metropolitan Police to snuff out corruption and collusion, but their reputation had taken a hit ever since then-Assistant Commissioner Ruth Ashton had run Adrian Pearce out of the organisation. Gayle was a fair man but lacked anything even resembling a personality.

'So, what's our move?' Dummett asked.

Sarrett pressed her fingers together and rested her chin on the tips.

'Armed Response said there was another man at the warehouse. Uniform is still searching, but if he managed to leave Sam Pope in a bloodied heap on the ground, we can probably safely assume he's in the wind.'

'We're still running with that angle, are we?' Henshaw scoffed.

'What, the facts?'

'Depends what way we look at them,' Henshaw said. 'We're spinning this story of Sam Pope fighting off some mysterious man. Yet from my side, the one that's been tasked with ensuring the safety of our nation and that our systems do their jobs, it seems that Sam Pope has now gone missing, along with the two detectives who were looking into his latest killing spree.'

'What about the gunshots at DS Sutton's apartment?' Dummett offered. 'It was called in not long before the armed response was called in by Vokes.'

'A warning shot?' Henshaw shrugged. 'There was a lot of blood found at the apartment and signs of a clear struggle. I mean, why are we looking at alternatives here?'

'Because we need to look at *everything*,' Sarrett said, maintaining her calm. 'Right now, the priority is to find our two missing detectives and then, after that, we can piece together this mess. Until we have Sutton and Vokes safely back in our protection, this is red alert. I've already lost two officers this week. I will *not* lose two more.'

'Yes, ma'am'. The chorus went up from the room as Sarrett stood, adjusting her crisp, white shirt.

'Now, Graham, you and I need to discuss how we will brief the PM. Join me in my office, won't you?'

Henshaw sighed and then stood, making no effort to hide how laborious he found it all. The man had made it clear through numerous speeches and interviews that he found the Met to be a broken institution and Sarrett knew he was using every possibility to turn the knife. She needed him onside, especially if they were going to keep things from spiralling out of control. As she held the door open for him, she looked back to Dummett, who was in conversation with Hasan.

'Mary, keep me posted. The second we hear…'

'You've got it, ma'am.'

Sarrett closed the door behind her, leaving the rest of the meeting to filter out. As she headed towards her office, and another inevitable clash with one of the most unlikable men she'd ever met, her thoughts went out to Sutton and Vokes.

What the hell was going on?

She wouldn't have to wait too long to find out.

DCI Karim Hasan yawned as he sat down behind the desk of his office. It was nearly midnight by the time he'd got back to Charing Cross Police Station, and once again, he'd have to make it up to his wife and kids for another evening of absence. They understood the job he did, but that still never stopped them from milking his guilt when it suited them.

A new games console.

Expensive jewellery.

The cost of his absence wasn't just the time he missed with his family. His bank balance was starting to feel the pain, too.

It was why he'd agreed to go along with it.

Hasan gave a quick, cautionary look through the blinds that draped the windows of his tiny office and then pulled open his bottom drawer. The bottle of Jack Daniels had originally been bought for emergency or celebratory purposes, but he was finding it was becoming more of a regular occurrence. He placed one of the glass tumblers on the desk and poured out a generous measure, before screwing the cap back on tight. Was it worth putting the bottle back just yet?

Hasan took a long swig of his drink and then a deep breath.

Twenty-five thousand pounds.

That was what the offer was, simply to rearrange two shifts. Nobody would bat an eyelid, and it would all be swept up as 'wrong place, wrong time'. Hasan had been hesitant at first, especially as he'd been squeaky clean for the entirety of his career within the Met. Three years away from a respectable pension and the time to actually be a part of his family again.

But twenty-five grand for ten seconds' worth of work was too good to turn down, and when the offer was put to him, he'd found it hysterical.

Not just the amount, but where it came from.

It had taken a few hours for the original trepidation to disappear once he'd made the required roster changes, but after that, he'd simply forgotten about it. If it meant one of the young officers would be accused of something, or be the patsy for a bust gone wrong, then so be it. They'd get rapped on the knuckles, have it chalked down to inexperience and probably face twelve to eighteen months of reputational damage.

They'd be fine.

He never thought that assigning those shifts was signing their death warrants.

As the guilt flooded back through him, he knocked back the rest of his drink and got busy pouring another when the curt rumble of his mobile phone startled him. Nearly spilling the whisky, he screwed the cap on and lifted the phone as it vibrated again.

DS Vokes.

Panicked, he slammed the bottle back in the drawer and answered the call.

'Connor. Jesus. Are you okay?'

'I'm fine, sir.'

'And DS Sutton?'

'Pain in the arse. But what's new?'

Hasan smiled and then felt that guilt twinge again.

He knew what was really going on. Whoever had put together the entire operation was tying up loose ends. Hasan had been given strict orders to push any attention away from Gatwick, and he'd tried his best to steer Sutton clear of it. When Vokes had cast the theory out to the wider team, Hasan had felt his heart break.

The two of them had now become part of the problem, and Hasan regrettably knew what was to come next. He'd pass on the location, and both Vokes and Sutton would be just two more unfortunate victims of a calculated attack on the Metropolitan Police.

The public would go into panic.

The media machine would go into overdrive.

The Met itself would throw the barriers up, looking to protect its officers as well as its reputation.

And fifty million pounds' worth of gold would simply disappear, and Hasan would have another twenty-five thousand pounds in his retirement pot.

'Where are you?' he asked, sipping his whisky.

'I can't say, sir.' Vokes paused, and Hasan could hear a faint, muffled voice before Vokes returned. *'Things are complicated.'*

'I understand.'

'It's just…we have Sam Pope, sir.'

'Excuse me?' Hasan stood, struggling to contain his excitement.

'We have Pope, sir. Unconscious,' Vokes said firmly. *'But after what's been going on tonight, we weren't sure if bringing him in was the best idea.'*

'Are you somewhere secure?'

'For now,' Vokes replied. More muffled speaking. *'But we need to keep moving.'*

'Tell me where you are, and I'll come to you.'

'I can't do that, sir.' Vokes sounded shaken. *'We'll come to you. Can you meet us by London Tap?'*

'Yes. When?'

'Just head there now. We'll be there as soon as possible.'

'Good work, Vokes. I'm heading out now.'

The call disconnected, and Hasan straightened his tie

and helped himself to the rest of his drink. He was a little over the limit, but not enough to worry about, and he ripped his coat from the hook and headed to the exit. As he walked down the stairs towards the station exit, he tapped out a message into his phone.

London Tap. Outside London Bridge Station. They have Sam.

Hasan sent the message on and let out a deep breath.

Three more death warrants signed.

He'd need to be there, otherwise Vokes wouldn't show. It meant he'd be involved more than he'd ever asked to be, but there was every chance he'd be able to negotiate a bigger pay day.

After all, all of it was Blood Money.

Every last penny had cost every last drop.

———

'Did he buy it?'

Sam asked with his arms folded as Vokes hung up the call. He was leaning against the backdoor of the car. In the open driver's seat, Sutton looked up at Vokes, too.

'I think so.'

'If he's in on it—' Sutton began.

'Then he won't come alone,' Sam said with a nod. 'But I doubt it will be the boys in blue again. If he's involved, then we can make a logical guess that they'll send Silva.'

'Who is this Silva?' Vokes said with a shrug.

'No idea,' Sam replied. 'But I can tell you this, he hits like a fucking freight train.'

Sutton slapped her thighs and stood.

'So, best-case scenario, Hasan isn't involved, and maybe he can help us.'

'Worst case, he brings a team of hitmen with him, and we all die.' Vokes shrugged. 'What a shit fucking day, eh?'

Sam looked at Vokes and smiled and patted him on the shoulder.

'Could be worse. You could be Hasan.'

'Why'd you say that?'

'Because if he is in on it, then he's going to regret ever stepping foot out of that station.' Sam walked around the vehicle and dropped back into the backseat of the car. Vokes and Sutton exchanged a few concerned exchanges, and Vokes leant forward and whispered under his breath.

It was barely audible through the downpour.

'What do you think he's going to do?'

Sutton looked back over her shoulder at Sam, who was sitting calmly in the backseat, peering out of the window in the opposite direction. Everything she'd trained herself to believe about the man was slowly unravelling.

He was still a dangerous man, with a long list of dead bodies to back that up.

But he wasn't a criminal.

He had saved her life. And now he was fighting for the truth, just like they were.

Fighting for the justice of two dead police officers.

As the rain clattered on the roof of the car, and exploded into wet fountains, she turned back to Vokes and reassuringly clutched his arm.

'What's necessary?' she finally said, and the two of them exchanged one more hopeful look and got into the car. Vokes brought it to life. The headlights illuminated the raindrops, and they headed back towards London Bridge, ready to fight for the truth.

CHAPTER FIFTEEN

As the four men were led through the secure warehouse, Silva didn't even look up from the table. Having changed out of his clothes when he'd returned to the safehouse, he'd dumped his wet clothes in the corner and swiftly changed. Black jeans and a white shirt, which clung tightly to his impressive frame. The sleeves were rolled up to the elbows, contrasting nicely with his tanned forearms, which were hard at work.

He was prepping his arsenal.

Fully aware that the group had their eyes on him, Silva expertly ejected the magazine from the Glock 17 and turned to them.

'This them?' He waggled the magazine at the henchman who'd acted as his driver. After Silva had given chase to Sutton and Sam, the driver had acted on instinct and hauled his bleeding colleague out of Sutton's house and after stealing a car, dumped the man at the nearest hospital. The police would likely make the link between the man and the blood in Sutton's apartment, but it didn't matter.

It was one less payout and Silva would be long gone

before they even started cleaning up the mess he'd leave behind.

'Yup.' The driver nodded confidently. 'Been rolling with these boys for years now. This is…'

'No names.' Silva stated as he stood, assessing each man with his cold, calculating stare. All of them tried their best to appear unphased and Silva smiled. 'You brief them?'

'Yep.'

'They know who we are dealing with?'

'Sam Pope.' One of them spat angrily.

'Hey, *pendejo*, was I talking to you?' Silva stepped forward; his eyes locked on the young man. He was barely in his twenties, with a tacky neck tattoo that curved up towards his jaw line. Silva's anger dropped and he smiled, reaching out and brushing imaginary dust from the man's shoulder. 'I'm sorry. It has a been a long night, *vato*. Thank you for volunteering.'

The young man frowned in confusion as Silva stepped away from him.

'Volunteering for what?'

Silva slammed the magazine back into the gun, lifted it, and shot the man squarely between the eyes. As the gunshot echoed, followed by the gasps of shock by the rest of the crew, the young man's head snapped back and he collapsed to the ground. His eyes were still wide open, as if shocked that the contents of his skull had been emptied on the ground beside him.

'Now, thanks to that young man's brave sacrifice, I take it I don't have to give a speech about what happens if you let me down?'

The rest of the group stood stoic, shaking their heads. Silva nodded to the driver, who looked on in shock, and then he casually returned to the table and began prepping the rest of the weapons. After a few moments of tense silence, the driver stepped forward.

'Was that necessary?'

'Necessary? No. Efficient. Very much so.' Silva reached up and patted the man on the side of his bearded face. 'I hope you two were not close.'

'No, he was a prick.'

'Then I did you a favour, no?' Silva flashed his charming grin as he tucked the two Glocks into the back of his waistband and then pulled his leather jacket over his shirt. 'They bring their weapons?'

'Yeah, all of them are packing.' The driver took a step closer, and Silva sighed. 'I told them ten each?'

'Thousand?' Silva raised an eyebrow. 'That's a big number.'

'Well, you did just save twenty-five per cent.'

Silva looked down at the man he'd just killed and chuckled.

'I like how you do business, *vato*.' Silva lifted the M16 Carbine off the desk and turned to face the other three men. 'Whoever kills the detectives gets that man's share of the money.'

The group shared a greedy glance between them, accepting the friendly yet murderous competition.

'What about Sam?' the driver asked.

Silva grinned.

'Sam is mine. We have some unfinished business.' Silva's phone buzzed and he turned the screen. 'They will be meeting another policeman in London Bridge. Once they settle on a location, we move in. Kill whoever you have to.'

With Silva's curt orders rattling in their minds, the gang made their way to either of the two vehicles and took their seats. Silva lit a cigarette and stood, turning his gaze to the trucks that housed the fortune that he'd spilt blood on.

He'd want nothing more than to disappear with it all, but the avenue out of the country wasn't possible without the others.

Powerful people, who were behind their façade of protection for the public, were just as greedy and as dirty as he was.

The between himself and them, and it was something he prided himself on, was Silva knew who he was.

Not only that, he embraced it.

He was a merchant of death. And in a few hours, he'd have Sam Pope in his sights once more.

As he blinked his vision back into focus, DCI Karim Hasan could feel a throbbing in the back of his head. The last thing he remembered was standing under one of the shop awnings to shield himself from the rain. Scattered across the entire side street were black bags of charity donations or rubbish, blending in with the alarming number of people who called the street their home. Those were people who had nothing, yet here Hasan was, standing in the downpour, ready to sanction the probable deaths of more good people just so he could have more than his fair share. The longer he stood, the further he fell into self-loathing, and Hasan had breathed a sigh of relief when the car slowed outside of the now closed London Tap pub. Hasan scurried out from under the awning, yanked open the door, and dropped into the passenger seat. As he turned to face DS Vokes, he was met with a regretful look from the young man.

'Sorry, guv.'

That was all Hasan could remember, as before he

realised that Sam Pope had sprung up from behind his chair with a chloroform drenched rag, the world had gone black.

But now, as the edges of his vision began to sharpen, he looked around a desolate room in a clearly abandoned building. A few pieces of furniture were covered with sheets, coated with dust. The walls were stripped bare of any paper or decoration, and the floor beneath his feet was strips of thick wood. A real estate development abandoned, most likely due to a lack of funding, and a place where nobody would look.

'Hello?'

Hasan called out. There was the faintest glint of light through the doorway, and as Hasan stood to follow it, he found himself pulled back against the chair. The chains clanged loudly, and only then did he notice the thick metal links that bound him to the chair. Two sets of handcuffs had been used to lock his wrists to each respective armrest, and his feet were bound to the legs of the chair with another chain.

'What the fuck do you think you're doing?' Hasan yelled again, trying his best to impose his authority over the hopeless situation. He arched his neck as hard as he could, trying to decipher the muffled voices that emanated somewhere outside of the small room that had become his cell. Down the hallway from the room, the two detectives were pacing another lifeless room, trying to decide what the next move was. Behind them, Sam was rifling through the rotten cardboard boxes that had been stuffed under a sheet to be forgotten.

'So, how do we want to play this?' Vokes asked.

'We need answers,' Sutton said firmly. 'Guv was the one who kept trying to steer me away from the Gatwick job. So, I say we just flat out ask him.'

'And what? He says he did it and then everything has

128

been forgotten?' Vokes posed with a frown. 'We've essentially kidnapped a senior officer and made a deal with a violent vigilante. No offence.'

Sam held up his hand and continued his search, as the two officers stopped and anxiously looked down the hallway.

'We don't have a choice, Connor. Even if he isn't involved, we can't trust anyone at the moment. They sent people to kill me. What if they'd sent them to you?'

The notion had already been broached before and Vokes felt his stomach flip at the thought of someone knocking on the door to his home, and his wife and children being at the mercy of a hitman. From what Sam and Sutton had told him, Silva was a dangerous man.

A man they needed to stop.

'Okay, fine. Do you want to ask him?' Vokes offered, gesturing towards the hallway. Before Sutton could answer, Sam stood, lifted something in his hands, and walked past them.

'I'll ask him.'

Sutton glanced down at the rusty claw hammer in his grasp and darted in front of him.

'Sam, he is a *senior* police officer.'

'We don't have time for this,' Sam replied calmly.

'What if he's innocent?' Sutton begged.

'Then I'll find out pretty quick.' Sam looked at them both and offered them an understanding nod. 'Look, this place you're in right now. It's a world away from what you're used to. This is the dark, dirty reality of this city. To survive in it, your hands get a little dirty.'

'But we have laws we have to abide by,' Sutton said feebly, clinging to the life she had before.

'Not tonight.' Sam readjusted his grip on the hammer. 'Tonight, you have me.'

Neither of the detectives made a move to stop him as

he turned back towards the hallway, and Sam marched through the abandoned apartment that still belonged to his good friend Paul Etheridge. Somewhere in the world, his good friend was probably living the good life. The fortune he'd amassed in his lifetime had ensured a comfortable new beginning wherever he'd laid his hat, and Sam always found himself filled with warmth when he mused on where he'd ended up. As he stepped through the cold, barren apartment, he thought back to the week the two of them had spent within its walls, lying low after Etheridge had bust him out of a police convoy. They'd shared stories of their lives, reconnecting after years apart after serving together in the army, and it was only Sam's relentless hunt for a teenage girl that had brought them back together.

Sam stepped past the main living room of the apartment, glancing towards the broken windowsill where Olivier Chavet had discovered the locker key a few hours before he'd been killed.

This flat, despite its anonymity and its listless charm, held memories that would echo through Sam's mind for the rest of his life.

It was time to make another.

Sam stepped through the doorway and he stopped. Hasan's eyes widened with terror at the sight of the most wanted man in UK and the very clear reality of his situation.

'Look, Sam…we can discuss things. I can help you.'

'Why were PCs Harrington and Dyer killed?' Sam responded, ignoring the man's offer. He took another step closer.

'Never mind that. I have a seat at the commissioner's table. We can work something out, you know? The things you've done…'

Sam took a few more steps until he was only a foot

away from the trapped, squirming Detective Chief Inspector.

'Last chance.'

With his bargaining card clearly failing, Hasan turned to rage, and he struggled against the chains that locked him in place as his face twisted into a vicious snarl.

'I'm a chief inspector, Sam. Do you have any idea how much fucking trouble you would be...'

The man's sentence shifted abruptly into a sickening howl of pain as Sam slammed the hammer down as hard as he could. The crack underneath told Sam he'd shattered Hasan's pisiform, breaking the man's wrist instantly.

He felt nothing.

'Breath through it,' Sam said calmly. 'And then I'm going to ask you again.'

Hasan was weeping. The agony of the shattered wrist, combined with the clusterfuck that his life had fallen into had reduced him to nothing.

'I don't know.' He whimpered. 'I don't know.'

CRACK!

The hammer turned the man's left index finger to dust as Sam drove it downwards, extracting another scream of torture and the immediate sound of onrushing footsteps. Sutton appeared in the doorway, her face fraught with worry, and she froze at the sight of her boss.

'Sam. I think we need to stop.'

'Sutton. Jesus, help me.'

'Sam,' Sutton said again, but Sam stepped forward, flipped the hammer round so the claw side was facing up and he pressed it against the man's wobbling Adam's apple.

The whole room fell silent, and Hasan gasped with fear.

Outside, the streets of Richmond were deathly quiet, and nothing but the rain accompanied them.

'I'm going to ask you one last time. If you don't tell me what the fuck is going on and what you did, I'm going to rip your throat out with this. Do you understand me?'

Hasan's wide, tear-filled eyes leapt to Sutton for help.

She relented.

'One.'

'Sutton. For god's sake, I'm your boss.'

'Two.'

'You know me, Jess. For fuck's sake…stop him.'

'Three.'

'Okay…okay.' Hasan finally broke, and as the tears fell down his cheeks, Sam slowly removed the hammer from his throat. 'I was given the two names. I don't know why. Maybe they were just unlucky.'

'Given the names?' Sutton stepped forward, her face making no effort to hide her disgust. 'You mean Dyer and Harrington?'

'Yes.' Hassan wept. 'I was given the names and told to make the arrangements, so they'd be on the shifts at those times.'

'Who?' Sam barked. 'Who gave you those names?'

'I can't…'

'Sir.' Sutton lowered herself down onto one knee as she approached him. 'The only way out of this is to tell the truth.'

Hasan took a few deep breaths to compose himself and he then turned to Sutton, his eyes vacant.

'You don't understand, detective. There's no way out of this. For any of us.'

The interrogation came to an abrupt end as the sound of the front door being forced open snapped Sam and Sutton's attention to the doorway.

They heard Vokes yell in shock.

Then the harrowing explosion of a gunshot.

CHAPTER SIXTEEN

'Connor!'

Sutton turned on her heels in a panic and sped towards the door. The thundering of footsteps across the floorboards filled the hallway beyond the doorway and just as Sutton was about to burst through and into a barrel of a gun, Sam dived and wrapped his arms around her, spinning her to the wall and pinning her against it.

Before she could react, he lifted a finger to his lips, his eyes wide with intent.

'They're in here.'

Hasan called out to the corridor, before shooting an apologetic look to Sutton who shook her head in disgust.

The footsteps grew louder, and Sam pressed himself to the wall, the hammer hanging by his side, just as the black-clad figure stepped over the threshold, the gun held tightly by his side.

Hasan tried to call out to him, but it was too late.

Sam swung the hammer with all his might, the two rusty, metal claws ripping into the side of the gunman's throat and then with a powerful wrench, he pulled the man's throat open. A mixture of horrified shrieks from

Hasan and Sutton, combined with the man stumbling forward as he tried to close the wound with his hand, drew another set of footsteps towards them, and this time, Sam stepped out and drilled the hammer towards the attacker's skull.

The second gunman swerved, and Sam connected with the man's shoulder. He grunted in pain, but his leather jacket absorbed most of the impact and he charged into Sam, sending both of them sprawling over the flimsy, covered furniture which collapsed under their weight.

The gun and the hammer spilt to the floor, and the man tried to wrestle the advantage and mount Sam, drilling his elbow down ferociously as Sam lifted his forearms up to protect his face. As the man arched back to generate more power, Sam shot a right hand up, connecting with the man's jaw and sent his head snapping backwards. The man woozily rocked backwards, and Sam rolled to the side, sending the man across the floorboards, and then they both scrambled to their feet. The man stood, holding his jaw, and then he swashed the saliva in his mouth and spat it out across the floor.

A broken tooth slathered in blood.

The two men locked eyes, raised their fists, and without removing his focus from his opponent, Sam spoke.

'Get to Vokes.'

Sutton didn't need a second invitation, and she pushed herself from the wall and raced through the doorway, just as the man swung a few rights at Sam, which he evaded, before drilling the man with a knee to the ribs. The man buckled a little, then charged once more, slamming his shoulder into Sam's stomach and driving both of them into the wall. Sam drove his elbows down into the man's spine, but the man frantically reached up and wrapped his hand around Sam's chin and slammed his head back against the brick.

The impact rocked Sam's skull, and as his brain shook within it, he walked right into a hard right hook that sent him tumbling to the ground.

'Up you get, sweetheart.'

The cocky London twang of the man's voice echoed above him, and Sam turned, just in time to see the boot headed towards his face. He got his hands up just in time and caught the steel capped boot a few inches from his face and then wrenched it to the left, toppling his attacked to the floor once more. As the man tried to kick himself free, Sam hooked the man's foot under his arm, locked on his grip, and then rolled in the opposite direction.

The man's ankle snapped like a twig.

As he howled in agony, Sam rolled to his feet, and then drilled him in the side of the head with a vicious kick.

The man went limp.

Sam lifted his hand to the back of his head and winced. His fingers returned with blood across them but then he swiftly stepped over the blood that was pooling around the first attacker and lifted the Glock from beside his dead body. As he turned to head out of the room, a shocked Hasan called after him.

'Please. Don't leave me here. I can help you.'

Sam looked back at the treacherous Detective Chief Inspector and then headed out of the door, ignoring him completely. As he headed towards the living room, he could hear the laboured steps and Sutton emerged, holding up Vokes who had his hand pressed to his stomach.

His shirt was soaked with blood.

He was dying.

'We need to get him to a hospital,' Sutton stated, her worry plastered across her face.

'Connor.' Sam leant in to look the man in the eyes. 'Breathe slowly, okay? We're going to get you out of here.'

'Just get her out,' Vokes said with laboured breaths, and

as they went to take another step, he stumbled onto one knee.

'Get up.' Sutton shrieked. 'Don't be a fucking hero.'

Sam tucked the gun into his jeans and then hooked Connor's arm over his shoulders, hoisting him up.

'Keep pressure on that wound,' he ordered, and Sutton clasped both of her hands over Vokes's feeble attempts, the warmth of the blood filtering through her fingers. They turned and headed out into the corridor of the building, but Sam turned away from the stairwell and further down the corridor.

'Where are we going?' Sutton asked, clearly panicked.

'Fire exit.'

Before Sutton could respond, Sam turned around the corner, and then booted the metal latch bar of the fire exit, flinging the door open. The bitter wind and the relentless rain rushed through, just as another black-clad attacker made his way onto the top step.

His eyes widened in shock, and he reached for his gun.

Sam had already dropped Vokes's weight onto Sutton and charged forward, slamming his shoulder into the man's chest and sending him backwards into the railing.

The small of the man's back hit the metal, his weight toppled backwards, and gravity did the rest.

As he plummeted down the two-storey building, his head clipped the edge of the first-floor fire escape, splitting his skull open and he was dead before his body shattered against the wet concrete below.

Sutton looked on in shock.

Not at the second brutal killing she'd witnessed in five minutes, but by the worrying efficiency with which Sam carried it out.

Without mercy.

Sam glanced over the railing at his handiwork, scouted the rest of the escape and alleyway, and turned back to the two detectives. He shifted the weight of Vokes back onto himself, and then turned to Sutton with a clear and forceful order.

'Go.'

Silva heard the first gunshot from the lobby of the abandoned apartment block and smiled. The driver, who'd finally introduced himself as Jay, looked to Silva for his orders and Silva told him to hang back. To him, all the men were expendable, but Jay had shown at least a sliver of competence. He'd used his initiative to get his fallen friend out of Sutton's apartment and had a seemingly long list of undesirable men willing to break the law for a quick buck.

They'd sent two armed men up to an apartment with the element of surprise. No matter how good Sam Pope may have been, there was no way out of it.

The only request he'd made was that once they have Sam Pope cornered, they call down to him and he be the one to send Pope to the grave.

As he puffed on his cigarette, he even offered one to Jay, who gratefully accepted.

There was no small talk, but that gesture was enough for Silva to know he had Jay's loyalty for the rest of his stay in the country.

He might even let him live.

As the time ticked by and the cigarette burnt to ash, Silva felt a small twinge of unease. He flicked the dead cigarette into one of the dusty, shadowy corners and then ordered the last of Jay's friends to go round the back of the building and block off the fire escape. Then he turned to Jay, who seemed to have read the situation and stubbed his smoke out underfoot.

'They're taking too long,' Silva said as he made his way to the stairs, passing the elevators that had long given up the ghost.

'My guys can be pricks.' Jay shrugged as he followed. 'Maybe they're just taking their time?'

'With Sam Pope?' Silva arched an eyebrow. The two men pulled their handguns and began climbing the stairs, with Silva taking the lead. As he approached the landing to the second floor, he could feel the bitterness of the outside world infiltrating the corridor and he sighed.

'They're gone,' Silva said glumly. Then, he slammed his foot into the nearest door in a rage. *'Estúpidos hijos de puta.'*

Jay stepped past his irate boss and jogged down the corridor to the open fire exit, which was swinging wildly on its creaking hinges. The rain splashed against his face as he peered over the railing, and he grimaced at the crumpled heap that had once been his friend. Blood had pooled around his broken body and somewhere in the distance, the dim hum of an engine could be heard under the torrential downpour. As he stepped back inside, he followed Silva through the broken door to the apartment. There was blood on the floor but no body, but from somewhere within they could hear panicked cries for help. Silva nonchalantly walked through the hallway and then stepped into the room, which was slick with blood. The corpse of one of his men lay strewn across the floor, with the side of his neck brutally torn clean from the bone.

On the other side of the room, another man laid motionless but breathing, with his ankle hanging by a thread.

As Silva's footsteps squelched in the blood, he approached the chair where DCI Karim Hasan lifted his head. His eyes were red with tears, and his left wrist and index finger were bruised.

Broken, most likely.

A smile spread across Hasan's face.

'Oh, thank god. Please, get me out of here. We need to speak with D—'

Silva put a bullet in his head.

Jay jumped at the gunshot, and Silva casually looked around the room as if ending a man's life was no different from swatting a fly. He tucked his gun back into his jeans, readjusted his jacket, and then pulled his phone out of his pocket.

'Leave them for the police,' he told Jay and motioned to the door. Obedient as ever, his driver exited the room and Silva lifted the phone to his ear and tapped out another cigarette. As he lit it and blew smoke over the carnage of the room, the call connected.

'Is it done?'

'No,' Silva replied calmly. 'I think one of them might be hurt, but they've gone.'

'You said you would handle this problem.'

Silva smiled to calm his anger.

'This problem should not have been allowed to happen. You said you would pull these detectives away, but then you sent me to clean up the mess. For that, my cut has increased.'

'That isn't possible.'

'Are you going to stop me? Tell me, are you going to send more detectives after me? I'll just leave them like I've left this one here.'

'What are you talking about?'

'Hold on.' Silva pulled the phone away, flicked through to the camera, and took a picture of Hasan. The body was rigid in the chair, his head tilted backwards and blood pouring down his face. Silva sent the picture to the caller. 'Is it still not possible?'

He heard the audible gasp on the other end of the phone and chuckled.

'This is not what we agreed.'

'I didn't agree anything with you. I dealt with my client, who told me you would make this job easy. In that case, I'm afraid you've failed.'

'You're the one who didn't get there in time.'

Silva took a long, concentrated pull on his cigarette and then flicked it at the dead body of Detective Chief Inspector Hasan. The man was a disgrace to the badge. As was the voice on the other end of the phone.

People who'd sworn to protect the public and uphold the law, who were just as driven by greed as the rest of the world. At least he saw it clearly enough to know who he truly was.

'Let me make something very clear. I do not take accusations lightly. I'm calling with the courtesy to say one of them might be injured. Check the hospitals or something and shut it down.'

Silva could hear a little commotion at the other end of the line. Fingers desperately tapping across keys.

'Stay contactable. When I have their location, I'll send it through.'

'You don't understand. This is your problem now.'

'Until this problem is taken care of, I will advise your client that shutting down the airspace for your swift departure might be...tricky.'

Silva felt his fists clench and his knuckles turn white.

He took a breath and calmed himself.

'I like you. You're a piece of shit.'

'Charming.'

'I am a piece of shit, too.' Silva chuckled. 'Fine. Send me the location and I will end this. Hopefully, for your sake, I might have made up my mind whether to find you and kill you by then.'

Silva hung up the call, hoping his final threat would

resonate like an echo in their mind for the rest of the evening. Then, he turned and marched back out of the apartment and back down the stairs, finally admitting to himself that Sam Pope had become a problem.

One that needed to be solved quickly.

CHAPTER SEVENTEEN

Watching someone who was closer than family cling to their life was a harrowing experience.

Sutton tried to take comfort from the fact that the blood loss, combined with the shock, meant that Vokes didn't really feel much pain, but it did little to appease her.

The worry for her friend.

The terror of the whole situation.

The guilt that she'd dragged him into it.

As Sam had sped through the streets of Richmond, leaving two dead bodies in his wake, and a beaten and surely guilty DCI Karim Hasan, Sutton had sat in the backseat of the car with her hands pressed to Vokes's bleeding abdomen. Sam cut through the minimal traffic, weaving between the few cars and showing little concern for any speed cameras.

They needed to get to a hospital.

Sam raced down Twickenham Road, cutting through a portion of the famous Richmond Park and over the River Thames, before taking St Margaret's Road towards Isleworth. West Middlesex University Hospital was the closest one with an A&E Department, and without urgent and immediate care, Vokes would die. The torrential downpour had finally worked to their advantage, as the horrendous weather had clearly discouraged most people from being out beyond midnight. When they'd pulled through the gates of the hospital entrance, Sam veered away from the car park and slammed his foot down, launching the car towards the doors of the hospital and drawing the attention of a number of paramedics who were heading towards one of the ambulances. One of them had angrily stomped across to confront Sam, but when Sam told them they had a man with a gunshot wound, the paramedics snapped into gear with impressive efficiency and calm. Sutton stood to the side as they tended to Vokes, and as a few nurses had run out to help, Sutton was in awe at their expertise.

She was banking on it.

As quick as they'd arrived, Vokes had been loaded onto a gurney and rushed through the hospital doors, with his chances of surviving diminishing by the second. Sutton took a deep breath and followed, as Sam headed back to the car and dumped it into one of the car parks. When he'd caught up with her, she was sitting in the emergency waiting room, surrounded by an eclectic mix of the public.

A drunk who'd taken a nasty fall.

Two young men, one of them holding a clearly broken arm, who were laughing and joking.

An elderly man who looked like his world was about to end.

It was a depressing place, and despite its high ceilings and long walls, Sutton felt the claustrophobic crush of the situation permeating from its walls. She thought about his wife, Laura, and their two boys.

She should call them.

Sutton patted down her pockets, looking for her phone, but was then distracted as the doors to the emergency theatre flew open and a serious-looking surgeon stepped out. He marched to the reception desk, conveyed a message, and then disappeared.

For what felt like an eternity, they sat in silence, and one nurse even asked Sam if he wanted her to treat the battle scars across his face. He politely declined and suggested to help someone who was in more need than him.

Another confusing aspect to the man that just twenty-four hours before, Sutton had pegged as the most dangerous man in the country. In some respects, he was. But what she was struggling with was the fact that she and Vokes, if he pulled through, owed their lives to the man.

None of it was anything to do with him.

The deaths of the police officers.

The robbery at Gatwick.

The attempts on their lives or the betrayal by their boss, DCI Hasan.

But here he was. Sitting beside her, waiting to see if Vokes pulled through. When she'd walked into the hospital, she wondered if she'd ever see him again but sure enough; he'd emerged through the door and even brought her a cup of water. As the background noise of the hospital began to grate, and her worry rose, she turned to Sam.

'Why are you here?'

'Excuse me?' Sam turned to her. The cut on his lip had scabbed, and a small bruising had appeared under his left eye. Sutton looked at him, wondering if the sudden fondness she had for him was born out of her worry for her friend.

'Why are you here? Like…why haven't you left already?'

Sam smiled and leant forward, resting his forearms on his knees.

'About a year ago, I had to make a decision on whether to do this again.' He looked at Sutton who lifted her eyebrows. 'It's true. When I "died", I actually came back and lived in London for eighteen months. Nobody batted an eyelid. Nobody knew who I was. It was nice, actually?'

'Well, if that's the case, why did you start again?'

'Because a good friend of mine was beaten to the brink of death because he knew someone who'd pissed off a powerful person.' Sam's jaw tightened as he thought back to the horrific injuries Sean Wiseman had received at the hands of Daniel Bowker and his crew. 'Trust me, I did everything to convince myself that I wasn't a necessity. But since then, I've seen powerful men try to kill young, abused women. I've seen politicians bend over backwards to break the law and keep it quiet and I have lists of influential people who were funding a terrorist network. You want to know why I'm still here, well there you go. Someone has to do something.'

Sutton sat forward, finally understanding the man she'd been hunting for months. She rested her hand on his shoulder, and he forced a smile.

'But why does it have to be you?'

Sam turned to her, looked her dead in the eyes, and spoke with more conviction than she'd ever heard in her life.

'Because I can.' The moment lingered between the two of them, and then Sam slapped his knees and stood. 'Coffee?'

Sutton smiled for what felt like the first time in ages.

'You read my mind.'

Sam turned and headed towards the door, venturing out into the hospital for any machine that would produce a semi-decent coffee. Sutton slumped back in her chair, and found herself staring at the door, hoping a surgeon would burst through with good news.

She shuffled a little, cursed herself for losing her phone, and then folded her arms, ready to wait as long as it took.

The smart thing to do would be to walk away.

It was a sobering thought, and one that would often swim through Sam's mind for a brief moment whenever he knew he was about to cross the point of no return. Humans were inbuilt to analyse risks and turn around and walk away from them. As a species, the idea of conflict was usually one that pushed people away. It was usually the ones who understood that who got ahead by bullishly pushing ahead with conflict until the others backed down.

Most people, when push came to shove, were more flight than fight.

And that was the problem.

Sam blew out his cheeks as he ventured down one of the sterile, beige corridors of the hospital, smiling politely at an old patient who shuffled by with his wrinkled fingers clasping the IV drip that rolled beside him on squeaky wheels. The police were no doubt on their way, responding to a nurse's report that a man had been brought in with a gunshot wound. Sam and Sutton had deliberately held back the fact that Vokes was a detective to bide more time, but the final grains of sand were tumbling through the hourglass.

When the police arrived, Sam would need to be gone, which is why he'd parked the car in the furthest corner of the furthest car park. Somewhere to lie low before the next step.

Whatever that was.

He could just turn and walk away.

The thought tap danced across his mind once more as

he approached one of the exits of the maze-like hospital. Although the rain wasn't exactly a welcoming sight, the freedom beyond would mean he'd have done enough.

He'd kept Sutton safe and given Vokes a fighting chance of survival.

Wasn't that enough?

Sam eventually found a coffee machine, and after shuffling through his pockets, he found his bank card and tapped the machine to activate it. As the coffee dribbled out of the machine, he wondered if he needed to make another.

Would he return to Sutton?

The police would be there soon and maybe she could find the right set of ears to ensure their safety. Maybe he could call in another favour from McEwen, just to ensure that whoever the rat was, they were hunted down and smoked out.

Sam knew what the answer was.

The idea that he was even contemplating walking away made him chuckle, as if the briefest opportunity of freedom had been waved in front of him like a cruel taunt.

He had to stay.

He had to fight.

The Met and most media outlets had made him out to be a menace, but the reality of it was that he was a balance. Money and power had become so skewed that those who had it were beyond reproach.

It was why people like Andrei Kovalenko or Harry Chapman had been allowed to build criminal empires. Why people like Slaven Kovac were able to infiltrate the country and spread weapons and drugs throughout the poverty-stricken cities that were kept under the oppressive regimes and constructs put in place by those with the means to build them?

It was why wealthy men like Jasper and Dale Munroe

had lived their lives with little regard for the have-nots, or how a CEO like Nicola Weaver could have an innocent beaten nearly to death.

Why bother with the law when you have everything and the financial power and political sway to ensure it doesn't apply to you?

But the real reason Sam was the balance was because of the corruption by those who were behind the wheel of the institutions that had allowed it to happen.

Inspector Michael Howell.

Detective Sergeant Colin Mayer.

General Ervin Wallace.

People who'd worked their way into positions of authority and who abused them for their own gain.

That was why Sam couldn't walk away. Because it was happening again.

Someone beyond DCI Hasan had set Dominik Silva onto DS Sutton and DS Vokes and pressured Hasan to move Dyer and Harrington into position to be murdered.

The Metropolitan Police, the institution that held the public's safety in its hands, were killing their own.

Someone was pulling the hangman's switch.

All for money. Blood money.

As Sam pressed his card against the machine once more, confirming his decision to fight it out until the bitter end, he glanced out of the window to the car park. Through the rain, he could see across the vast parking lot, which depressingly, was almost filled. A damning inditement on the government that half of the cars probably belonged to the brave staff of the NHS, who had to pay for the right to park their cars to perform their life saving jobs.

In the distance, he could see the ambulances that he'd nearly hit when he'd swerved to a stop what felt like hours before. It shocked him how far he'd walked on his quest for coffee, and how long he'd been lost in his thoughts.

Sam's eyes widened, and without retrieving either of the coffees, he turned on the spot and began sprinting as fast as he could back through the hospital. He didn't care if he attracted any attention.

Not when, despite the rain, the distance and the feeble lighting, he'd seen the unmistakable figure of Dominik Silva marching towards the doors of the hospital with a clear purpose and a few loose ends to tie up.

Sam's feet pounded the tiles of the hospital corridors, hoping against hope that he got back to the emergency room before Silva could do just that.

CHAPTER EIGHTEEN

Sutton looked down at her bloodstained hands and shuddered. Her friend was clinging to his life in another room, yet she was struggling with the idea of calling Laura and letting her know what had happened to her husband. After Sam had left to get coffee, she'd fished through her pockets and retrieved Vokes's phone, which she'd taken from him when they'd arrived at the hospital. Without her own phone to make the call, she quickly tapped in the birthdate of Vokes's eldest son and felt her heart break at the image of Laura and their two boys.

What would their life be without him?

As she navigated the menu to his contacts, she pulled up Laura's number. Her thumb was centimetres away from the screen when the commotion from the corridor grew louder and a palpable panic grew within the A&E. Sutton stood, pulling out her warrant card to try to ensure some calm when the door to the A&E burst open by the thrusting boot of Dominik Silva.

Sutton froze.

Those nearest the door clambered away from the soaking wet man, dressed in black, and he was shortly joined by another man, his head shaved to the scalp to counteract the thick, bushy beard that hung from his jaw. Silva didn't say a word as he slowly scanned the waiting room, his handsome face dripping with rainwater.

His eyes were burning through everyone until they stopped on Sutton.

They flickered with excitement and cries of terror rang out as he lifted his hand and Sutton's life flashed before her eyes.

The gun was drawn up to his eye level, and without hesitation, he pulled the trigger.

With all the focus on his target, Silva hadn't reacted to the oncoming pounding footsteps, and as his finger touched the trigger, Sam wrenched his arm upwards, sending the gunshot into the roof tile that instantly shattered and collapsed upon them in an avalanche of debris. The entire waiting room erupted into a panic, with terrified parents shoving their children towards the corner, and those waiting for care screaming as they tried to move away.

Sam tried to wrench the gun from Silva's grip, and the two men swayed together as Silva refused to relinquish his hold. As Sam began to overpower his enemy, Jay wrapped his arm around Sam's neck and hoisted him backwards, wrenching onto his hold as he dragged Sam away from Silva. Instinctively, Sam dropped to his knees, using the momentum to flip Jay over his shoulder and the man crashed spine first onto the hard floor. As Sam stood, Silva drew his gun up again, but Sutton tackled Silva by the waist, dragging him down to the ground with her.

The gun sprawled out of his grasp, but Silva swiftly rolled over and drilled Sutton with a hard elbow strike. The impact sent her head slamming back against the tiles and the world went woozy, but before he could deliver another blow, Sam caught him with a knee to the side of the head that sent him crashing into the nearby chair. Security had formed at the doorway, hesitantly looking for their moment to intervene, but as one of them found his bravery, Jay stood up and stuck the gun in his face.

'Feeling fucking brave, son?' Jay spat, and the man held up his hands, went white as a sheet and stepped back.

Jay turned and Sam's fist collided with his jaw, rattling it loose, before Sam wrenched his wrist and released the weapon. Sam yanked the arm, and as Jay moved with it, Sam spun and caught him clean on the nose with an elbow. The impact shattered the man's nose, and as it exploded down his lips and chest, Sam stepped back and rocked him with a brutal uppercut that took him off the ground and tumbling over the plastic chairs.

He hit the ground motionless.

Sam turned back, and amid the panic, he could see Sutton beginning to stir, just as Silva stood, stretching the ache from his neck as he slid his arms from his sodden jacket.

'Round two, then?' Silva said with a cocky grin, tossing his jacket and limbering up his muscular arms. Both men threw their fists up and as they narrowed the distance between themselves, sirens could be heard howling in the distance.

They didn't have much time.

Silva exploded forward with a barrage of body blows, and then he snuck a jab through Sam's guard and sent him back a couple of steps. Silva frowned, as if expecting more, but as he went to throw another punch, Sam stepped into it, deflected it with his forearm and then carried his momentum forward and drove his elbow into Silva's jaw. More audible gasps echoed from the terrified civilians who clung to the edges of the room and Silva took a few steps back, rolling his shoulders as he sized Sam up. As they squared up once more, the card activated door to the actual hospital area opened up as a few doctors walked through, and Silva barrelled into Sam, sending both of them through into the medical facility. Panic spread among the doctors and nurses as the two men slammed into the nurses' station. As the doors closed behind them, Silva pressed Sam back over the counter, his hands wrapped around his throat and the few nurses shot backwards from their seats and screamed for security. Sam reached back across the desk, his hand scrambling for anything until his fingers clasped onto a hole punch, which he then lifted and swung into Silva's skull. The stationery equipment struck Silva above the eye, splitting his eyebrow and relaxing his grip, and as he took a step back, Sam lifted up his foot and drove it into Silva's chest. The impact sent Silva stumbling backwards through a curtain until he hit an unused gurney, and as a few doctors screamed at them to stop, Silva emptied out a drawer of medical equipment in the curtained off section of the A&E until his eyes locked onto the scalpel. Sam charged at Silva, who whipped up the blade, spun out of the way and then sliced Sam across the back of the arm. Beyond the walls of the hospital, the ringing of police sirens hung heavy in the night sky, signalling the arrival of the police, and Silva smirked.

'They're not here for me, *vato*,' he said with a smirk, before he flipped the scalpel over in his hands, pinched the blade between his index and thumb and then launched it at Sam. The blade spun through the air, slicing its way to Sam who managed to duck out of the way just in time. As the blade embedded in the cheap, plywood wall, Sam turned and Silva drilled him in the face with his knee, sending him backwards into the medical equipment that lined the walls. Sam grunted, spat out some blood, and Silva squatted down in front of him.

'This has been fun.' Silva yanked the scalpel out of the wall and smiled. 'Disappointing, but still fun.'

Silva drove the scalpel towards Sam's eye, and the blade stopped a mere inch away from his pupil. Despite the blood dripping from the fresh slice across his tricep, Sam held onto Silva's wrists, his muscles shaking as he tried to hold off the pressure as Silva tried to force the blade into his eyeball. Slowly, Sam lowered back onto the ground, and Silva arched over him, leaning his entire bodyweight onto his arm as it began to slowly take its toll on Sam.

His muscles began to buckle.

The blade began to lower.

Ironically, the two police officers who swarmed in through the locked doors saved his life as they hauled Silva off Sam and dragged him back a few steps. As they barked at Silva not to move and began going through the formalities of his arrest, the door burst open again, only this time, it was Jay, his face smeared with blood, and he limped towards the first officer, lifted his handgun and pressed it to the man's shoulder.

The bullet blew through the man's collarbone and as he spun to the ground in a pool of blood and a scream of agony, the other officer stood, his hands held up as he tried to calm the gunman down.

Jay put a bullet through his kneecap.

With both officers writhing in a pool of blood, Jay helped Silva to his feet and Silva reached out and patted Jay on the shoulder.

'Thank you,' he said sincerely. 'Perhaps, when this is done, I have some more work for you. Now…gun.'

Silva held out his hand, ignoring the nurses who'd bravely dashed to the aid of the fallen officers, and he turned back to the curtained off area.

But Sam was gone.

'Boss. We need to go!' Jay yelled from the doorway as he watched more police cars arrive. Despite the auto-lock's best efforts to close off the exit, Jay held it open with his foot, and with a grunt of dissatisfaction, Silva turned and headed through. The two men went bounding off towards the other side of A&E, heading into the labyrinth of the hospital to find another exit, and leaving behind a trail of carnage and panic that would keep their pursuing officers busy enough to allow them to escape.

Although every instinct in his body had begged for Sam to stay and help the officers, he knew he had to move. With Silva pinned to the ground and the police beginning to swarm the building, the only hope of getting to bottom of everything was for him to get out of there. It meant abandoning Sutton and Vokes and he hated himself as he pulled himself up via the gurney, stepped around it and then, cloaked by the curtain that surrounded the area, he slid behind it and the wall into the next closed-off area. A young man was lying on the next bed, his eyes closed, and his arm linked to a drip via a thick, plastic tube. Carefully, Sam stepped around the bed, just as two gunshots echoed behind him, and the two police officers hit the deck in more pain than they'd ever known.

Sam understood it.

He'd been shot more times than he cared to remember, but another bullet would surely put him down for good.

He had to get moving.

He had to keep fighting.

As he heard Jay helping Silva to his feet, Sam ducked out of the curtain and further into the closed off area of the hospital. All the rooms were locked, with staff and patients all in hiding at the terrifying sound of gunshots, giving Sam a clear path through. He quickened his pace, ignoring the thumping in his skull and the burning pain of his tricep and eventually, he came to an emergency exit.

With little care for the alarm it could trigger, he slammed into the security bar, pushed open the door, and stumbled out into the cold, bitter night. The sky was alive with flashing blue lights, and as more police cars arrived on the scene, Sam faded into the shadows of the buildings, creeping around the outskirts of the hospital until he came to the row of trees and bushes that lined the overpriced car parks. The mud was slick beneath his feet, and he had to catch himself a few times before he hit the ground. With no streetlights to guide him, he was swallowed by the darkness caused by the greenery, and he looked back across the car parks as a swarm of officers descended on the hospital.

There would be widespread panic.

Three more officers shot in one faithful night.

Too many witnesses to not put Sam at the scene of it all, and there would be no denying that a full-blown attack on the Met was underway.

Whoever was pulling the strings for Silva would likely point the finger in Sam's direction. It wasn't anything new, and another round of police press conferences that painted him as the villain were par for the course at this point.

But it meant that without Sutton or Vokes, he had no finger on the pulse.

No feed into what the police were doing or where they were looking.

He also had no way of tracking Silva or the missing gold.

All he had was a faint hope that both Sutton and Vokes would still be alive by the time the sun rose. As Sam edged his way around the parking lot, he eventually exited the trees in the far corner where his hire car was. He unlocked it, dropped into the driver's seat, and started the engine. Carefully, he pulled out of the car park, heading out of the exit the police had yet to cover, and drove off into the London night.

There was nowhere for him to go.

No leads for him to chase.

But he had to keep fighting.

Otherwise, all this blood would have been shed for nothing.

CHAPTER NINETEEN

The aftermath of Sam and Silva's brawl through the hospital was unlike anything Sutton had ever seen.

Within moments after she heard the terrifying gunshots on the other side of the doors, more police officers began flooding into the emergency reception, all of them quickly doing their best to establish calm and a sense of order. Patients who'd scattered to the edges of the room began flocking towards them, each telling their version of events in varying stages of terror, and none of them coherent. One of the officers was guided to Sutton by another patient, and as he helped her to her feet, she showed her police warrant card and immediately drew his attention.

'What happened?' the officer asked, scanning the room at the panic and the chaos. The security guards, who'd proved next to useless, had collected the weapon that had been sent sprawling from Silva's grasp. They were in the process of handing it over to another officer, who was being directed to the obliterated ceiling panel and the debris beneath it. Doctors had opened up the security doors, and were tending to the two fallen police officers, neither one having suffered any life-threatening injuries.

But they'd both been shot in the line of duty.

All of this had been in the line of duty.

The officer blew out his cheeks and then looked back at Sutton once more.

'Well?' He shrugged.

Where could she begin?

The fact that she was investigating the deaths of two of his comrades over the past few days, but her gut was telling her it was a distraction. That they'd been killed to allow corrupt police officers to rob an armoured truck filled with gold. Or that she'd somehow aligned herself with the most wanted man in the country to investigate further, which had seen them kidnap her commanding officer and wilfully watch as Sam Pope interrogated the man with a hammer? Or that by kicking the hornet's nest, her partner, a well-respected detective, was lying on an operating table under-going lifesaving surgery?

None of the optics looked good, and as Sutton took a seat and the throbbing in her skull threatened to overpower her, the officer told her to wait where she was until someone more senior got there. A nurse soon scurried over to her, applying a cold compress to the cut that had been opened above her eye before checking her for any signs of a concussion.

Sutton wasn't sure if she had one or not.

She didn't care.

She just wanted to get up, get back out there and find the corrupt bastards who'd sanctioned her murder. The people who were responsible for the needless deaths of police officers.

All so they could get rich.

Or richer.

The severity of the situation hit her when she reached for her phone, wanting to call Vokes, as he was the only person she could trust. A cold dose of reality washed over her as she thought about her friend somewhere beyond the doors, fighting to hold on to his life and to return home to his kids. She felt her stomach turn. The guilt of dragging him into her investigation and putting him in the firing line was almost too hard to bear. She needed to call Laura, and tell her what had happened, and as she fished Vokes's phone from her jacket pocket, she grunted at having misplaced her own.

Vokes's phone was locked, but it wasn't hard to crack it with one of his children's dates of birth, and she thumbed through the contact list to find Laura's number. Sutton and Laura had a great friendship, and she knew if anyone needed to be the one to break the news to the devoted wife, it should be her.

Plus, she felt a sense of responsibility. She'd tell Laura this was her mess, and that Vokes had saved her life in the process.

It would be scant consolation, but in the horrible yet very real scenario that he didn't pull through, she didn't want Laura to think she'd lost her husband for nothing.

It had to mean something.

It just had to.

'DS Sutton?'

Her concentration was broken by a voice she sort of recognised above her, and she arched her neck up, feeling the heaviness of her head almost topple her to the side. It took a few moments, but she soon recalled speaking with the detective in the canteen the day before. As she placed him, he seemed to do the same.

'You're…' Sutton began, gesturing to imply she didn't know.

'DS Finch,' he said with a smile, and extended his hand. 'Or Paul, if you prefer.'

Sutton took it and shook firmly.

'You were at Gatwick weren't you?' Sutton said,

wincing slightly, and he took the uncomfortable plastic stool beside her. Before he could respond, another wave of panic washed over the room as the armed response unit filtered through, their automatic weapons held in their proficient arms, as they swarmed through the now open secure doors and past the pool of blood left behind by the fallen officers. As they began to sweep the A&E, Sutton turned back to Finch, who sighed.

'I got taken off that.' He shrugged. 'I guess I started asking a few questions about it and they shifted my focus onto the double homicide. I hear you and your partner raised it in a meeting?'

'We did,' Sutton said through gritted teeth as she looked beyond the armed response. 'He's back there somewhere, on a fucking operating table because of it.'

'Jesus,' Finch said solemnly. 'What the fuck is going on?'

'Trust me. The less you know the better.'

'Well, I do know I have orders to get you back to the station safely. Have the nurses checked you over?'

'Yeah.'

'You good to go?'

'I'm pretty fucking far from good,' Sutton said and then softened. 'Sorry. It's been a long night.'

'I can imagine.' Finch held a hand up to an officer who seemed to gesture that they needed to move. 'Look, I know this has been a rough night, but we need to get you out of here. According to the witnesses, you were the intended target and considering your partner has already taken a bullet, Dummett can't risk you out here.'

'Dummett?' Sutton frowned.

'Nobody can get hold of DCI Hasan, so Dummett has stepped in. She wants you back at the station, in our protection, and wants to know what the hell is *actually* going on.'

The idea that a senior officer was ready to listen had caught Sutton by surprise, and as she contemplated the idea that she might just get the support they needed, a surgeon marched through the chaos, looking around at the waiting room in confusion. The man had been in the theatre for a few hours, and having missed the show, had walked out into an absolute circus.

Armed police.

Terrified patients.

A partially destroyed emergency centre that was now stained with blood. As he surveyed the scene, Sutton moved away from DS Finch and approached him.

'Doctor.' Sutton got his attention. 'How is he?'

'He's a fighter,' the surgeon said with a warm smile. 'The surgery has gone well, although there was significant damage done to his kidneys and a partial tear to the stomach wall. We've done everything we can, and he's now being put into recovery. He should pull through. The man's as strong as an ox, but it's a long road to recovery.'

Sutton didn't even try to fight the tear of relief that slipped over her eyelid and slid down her check. She thanked the surgeon who obviously had more pressing things to take care of then turned back to Finch.

'Give me a minute.'

Finch nodded and then stood to the side as Sutton marched through the doors of the A&E and headed out into the freezing downpour. A few uniformed officers looked her way, but she held up her police warrant card to satisfy them. The police had now fully swarmed across the hospital, and she could see the armed response unit sweeping through the car parks, tactfully covering each other as they cleared every gap and every potential hiding place.

It was no use.

Silva and his friend would be long gone.

So would Sam.

With her concerns for Vokes now slightly lowered, her mind now turned to Sam. There had been every chance that the police would have hauled him out in cuffs, or even worse, a body bag. All she'd heard was gunshots, but the fact that Sam's name hadn't been mentioned once made her confident he'd somehow got through it.

That he was in the wind.

Which meant they still had a fighting chance.

Sutton glanced over her shoulder and saw Finch speaking with one of the officers, and it was clear he was under strict orders to not let her out of his sight. In Chief Inspector Dummett, Sutton would have a very powerful ally, and as long as she could steer her away from what happened with DCI Hasan, there was a chance that she could convince the chief inspector to really look into things beyond the narrative of a 'an attack on the Met'. The deaths of those officers had been a tragedy, but they were being used to cover up what was really happening, which meant they would have died for nothing.

Sutton couldn't let that happen.

As she lit a cigarette and welcomed the rain that crashed against her, she chuckled at herself for sounding like Sam Pope. This was the man who she'd been hell bent on catching.

Now, she was relying on him to put things right.

There had been rumours swirling around the Met for a few months that Amara Singh's obsession with Sam Pope soon evolved into love, and while Sutton didn't believe it was that extreme, she could understand how someone's view on Sam could change. Strip away the good looks and the wry delivery of a quip, it was then the magnetic pull of his nobility that drew people in.

The dedication to the do the right thing.

Even in the worst of times.

Channelling that thought, Sutton lifted Vokes's phone and made the call. Laura answered after the second ring, clearly fraught with worry.

'Connor. Where the hell are you? It's four in the morning—'

'Laura. It's me.'

'Jess?' The horror quickly set in. 'Oh no…'

'Laura, Connor is okay.' Sutton quickly stated with authority. 'It's a long story and we'll have time go over it. But earlier tonight Connor was shot in the stomach.'

Laura gasped, but Sutton continued.

'We got him to the hospital in time and he's just come out of surgery. It went well, all things considered, and he's in recovery.'

'Where is he?' Laura began scrambling on the other side of the call.

'West Middlesex Hospital.' Sutton took a drag on her cigarette and looked back at the hospital. Finch noticed her on the phone and began to march towards her. 'The place is crawling with police. But I've got to go.'

'You're not staying with him?' Laura sounded furious.

'I can't.' Sutton looked up just as Finch approached her. 'I'll be in touch.'

She disconnected the call and turned to Finch, who looked at her with interest.

'Making a call?' He stated the obvious.

'Yeah. To the wife of my partner who nearly fucking died to let her know what's happening.' Sutton dropped the cigarette and crushed it under her boot. 'That okay?'

Finch held his hands up apologetically, and Sutton felt a small twinge of guilt. The man didn't deserve her frustration, but considering the night she'd had, she wasn't going to apologise. Finch gestured for her to follow, and she did so, falling in line a few steps behind as he marched through the chaos of the car park, weaving through the police cars that painted the sky and the rain blue in intermittent flashes. As they approached the Black BMW, Finch opened the passenger door for her and gestured for her to get in. Sutton pulled her drenched hair from her eyes and shot one more cautionary look back at the hospital.

Vokes would be okay.

He'd pull through.

She dropped down into the seat and Finch slammed the door shut. Swiftly, he got in, started the engine and switched on the heaters for her before he backed out carefully between the scattered police cars and headed for the exit.

Sutton looked out of the window as the hospital disappeared and the rough streets of London rolled by. Dummett would hear her out, see the damage and the truth, and they would go about putting this right.

But something in the pit of her stomach told her that it wasn't over.

Not yet.

And as they headed back towards the haven of the Metropolitan Police, she hoped Sam Pope was ready to fight again.

CHAPTER TWENTY

The myriad of shit she'd been promised had turned into a relentless shitstorm, and as Sarrett sipped at her third coffee of the morning, she thanked God that her office door was closed. There had been no respite since her meeting about the incident at Sutton's apartment, with DCI Hasan going missing followed swiftly by the fallout that happened at West Middlesex University Hospital.

As she'd tried to make order out of the chaos, information kept coming through in dribs and drabs.

DS Connor Vokes had been shot.

Sam Pope was spotted at the hospital.

A gunman laid siege to the hospital and two more officers had been shot.

As the Met went into overdrive to get a handle on the situation, she'd pulled her Brains Trust back into another emergency meeting, batting back the criticisms that were being sent her way by Graham Henshaw, who saw the wheels falling off the wagon. While this sort of thing had happened under the leadership of McEwen or Stout, there had never been such a price paid by her officers. Chief Inspector Dummett had been a strong ally in the meeting room, deflecting the blame from the Met itself and onto the facts of the situation.

Sam Pope was a wanted vigilante with a long list of deaths attributed to his name. A man who'd made many powerful enemies and who'd likely put himself in this gunman's crosshairs. If Sam's motive for action was injustice, what better way to serve it up than murder innocent police officers? DI Gayle was still in attendance, and he posed some excellent and worrying points about someone needing to feed the information for this chain of events to happen.

To him, *everyone* was a suspect.

It was when the call came in from Richmond that the heat in the room rose exponentially.

DCI Hasan was dead.

He'd been found strapped to a chair with a bullet in his skull, with his wrist and fingers clearly broken in some horrific method of torture. Two other men were in the room with him, too.

One was barely alive.

The other had been killed ruthlessly.

Another body had been found at the bottom of the emergency stairwell; his skeleton shattered from the plunge he'd obviously taken. They were working to identify the men in question, but it didn't help with the serious issue.

Who was the gunman?

Swiftly enough, the CCTV footage from the hospital was sent across, and Sarrett had her IT support hook it up to the main screen in the meeting room. The first footage was from the car that raced to the entrance of the hospital, where the unmistakable image of Sam Pope alerted the nearby paramedics. The room collectively squirmed in discomfort as the footage of Vokes being lifted from the car to a gurney followed, his shirt thick with blood as he was then raced in through the doors with his life hanging in the balance. Sarrett gave the order for that footage to be sent to the cyber team to get a number off the plate and to track down the car.

Sam Pope was clever. He'd likely dump it, but they had to follow it up.

As they watched on, Henshaw made some unhelpful remarks about the way Sutton and Sam were interacting, and when the wanted man took a seat beside the clearly worried detective, the speculation only grew.

Why wasn't she arresting him?

Dummett did make the point that Sutton had been working the Bakku incident from a few nights before and had been quite bullish in her want to stop Sam's war on crime. DI Gayle seemed interested, making a few notes and asking a few probing questions as he connected some dots.

Dots that couldn't be explained. Yet.

Why was Sam Pope at Sutton's apartment last night?

How exactly did Sam, who'd been handcuffed, over-power both Sutton and Vokes that led to them disappearing?

Sarrett rubbed her temples as the theories flew around the room, and when Henshaw suggested that Sutton was responsible for Hasan's death, she snapped at him to keep quiet. Speculation wasn't what was needed.

They needed to follow the facts and find their officers.

The room unanimously agreed that Sutton had been the target of the gunman, who'd stormed bullishly into the waiting area and without hesitation, had drawn the gun at Sutton. Sarrett had her tech operator take the clearest still of the footage and pass down to cybercrime to run a trace to see if they could identify him. They needed to know who he was.

Then, they might be able to trace back to what he wanted.

The one thing they could prove was that Sam had saved Sutton's life.

As the man drew up the gun, Sam barrelled into the room and diverted the shot upwards, drawing praise from Dummett for not allowing the stray bullet to head into the crowd of innocent and terrified civilians. The ensuing brawl was an uncomfortable watch, especially when Sutton was driven into the ground with a hard elbow.

'She's tough,' Gayle said, seemingly impressed.

As the fight spilt into the actual emergency room, the footage shifted, offering a partial oversight of Sam and the gunman as they brawled into a curtained cubicle.

The police officers arrived, hauled the gunman back into view, only for the other man to enter, and put a bullet through both officers.

Sarrett felt her heart break on both pulls of the trigger. As the footage ended, Sarrett asked for a few bits to be replayed, especially when it came to Sutton trying to help Sam in the waiting room, and the direction the two attackers had fled the hospital. There was further CCTV footage to arrive, most likely showing Sam Pope making his own exit from the hospital, but it was moot by now.

They didn't have him in custody, which meant he was long gone.

He was still out there in the city somewhere, as were the two gunmen.

Sarrett thanked the tech operator, who quickly scurried from the room, and then she opened the meeting up to an avalanche of angry opinions, wild theories and snide remarks about their ability to operate.

A myriad of shit seemed like heaven in comparison.

The whole city was going to hell in a handbasket, and Sarrett called for a ten-minute break for everyone to regroup and calm down. Now, as she stood at the window of her plush office at New Scotland Yard, she gazed out over the city she'd been sworn to protect and felt nothing but failure.

Three brave members of the Metropolitan Police were dead.

Two more were in hospital.

Something was going on, and despite having several pieces to the puzzle, none of the edges fit.

Her thoughts were interrupted by a gentle knock on her door, and Dummett entered. Sarrett finished her coffee and turned to her ally.

'Well, this is a fun night, isn't it?' Sarrett said dryly as she stomped back to her desk to retrieve her phone.

'It's a rough one.' Dummett agreed. 'But I just had contact with DS Finch. He's got Sutton safe and secured. He said that the armed response is sweeping the hospital, but it looks like our shooters are long gone.'

'And Pope?' Sarrett looked up.

'No sign of him.'

'Okay. Right now, Sutton is a target. First and foremost, we need to bring her in and keep her safe. They went to her home, and they went to the hospital. We saw that they came in looking for her, not Sam.' Sarrett shook her head. 'I need to know what the hell she's got herself into.'

'She was talking about the robbery at Gatwick,' Dummett offered. 'I've spoken with the team who are looking into that, but none of it feels connected.'

'Get me a meeting with the lead detective of that case. As soon as possible.' Sarrett leant against her desk and puffed her cheeks. 'As soon as Sutton gets here, I want you to put her in the safest place possible.'

'Yes, ma'am.' Dummett nodded and then looked at the commissioner with concern. 'You okay, ma'am?'

Sarrett shook her head. With her arms folded across her chest, she looked out once again through the rain-soaked window at the city beneath her.

'Not really. When I was working with McEwen, I always told myself that when the time came, I'd be able to step up into the role. He said the same thing, but it was never meant to be this soon.' She shook her head, trying to send away the doubt. 'I just…I just feel like we're failing.'

'With all due respect, ma'am, this did come to you quickly. Whatever happened with McEwen, it's between him and those who made the decision.' Dummett reached out and put a friendly hand on Sarrett's shoulder. 'For what it's worth, I think you're handling this as well as you can.'

'Thank you.' But it's not enough is it? We've got Sam Pope treating this city like the Wild fucking West, and two gun men killing police officers. Something is happening out there that we are not seeing. We can't lose any more people.' Sarrett suddenly had a jolt of realisation and turned to Dummett. 'How are you? I know you and DCI Hasan were friends.'

Dummett forced a smile and looked at her feet.

'Not great. But we don't have time to grieve right now, do we?'

'He had a family didn't he?' Sarrett asked and Dummett nodded. 'Well, let's make sure they know their father didn't die for nothing.'

'Yes, ma'am. Shall we head back?'

Sarrett stepped from her desk and returned the friendly hand to the shoulder.

'I will. You take five, process what you need to and then get on the phone to DS Finch, was it? Right now, I don't trust Sutton being left alone with anyone else. So I want you to take her to the safe house, let me know the location and then I'll be there as soon as possible.'

'Will do.' Dummett nodded purposefully. 'I'll need protection.'

'Whatever you need.'

'Thank you, ma'am.'

'We'll get through this,' Sarrett stated. 'If it costs me my job, I don't care. Right now, we need to get this city back under our control and I need to get this whole police force swimming in the same direction.'

With a firm nod, Sarrett pulled open the door and ushered Dummett through and then followed. The two women went their separate ways, and as Sarrett disappeared back down to the meeting, Dummett headed back down the building towards the hot desk she'd been using in the open-plan office on the floor below. It was empty, with the night shift out and about, working their way through the carnage that Sam Pope had left in his wake.

Dummett lifted her phone and called in a favour, and within a few minutes, two plain clothed officers walked through the door. She took them down to the basement, through an array of key card activated access points, to the armoury, where, under her authority, they both signed out their firearms. With her armed protection in tow, Dummett led both men to the car park that resided underneath the building, and one of them took charge of the situation and led them to his car. The bitter chill of the turbulent night had filtered into the underground facility, and Dummett took a seat in the back of the car as the officer kindly put the heater on for her.

They waited.

Ten minutes later, the ramp way to the car park erupted with the bright lights of DS Finch's BMW, and as he rounded the corner into the dimly lit, sparse parking garage, one of the officers flagged him down. Obediently, Finch pulled the car in beside them. He waited until they held their badges to the window before he stepped out, and then felt foolish as he was greeted by Dummett, who also emerged from her car.

'DS Finch,' she said as she reached forward and firmly shook his hand. 'Excellent work.'

'Thanks, Ma'am.'

The passenger door opened, and Sutton stepped out. Dummett smiled at the woman, but she could sense the shift in her. This wasn't the same woman who'd meekly stood to the side as her partner got shouted down in the meeting room yesterday. There was a hardened look to her sharp, beautiful face that was only enhanced by the fresh cut that sliced through her eyebrow and the gentle bruising under her eye. The cuffs of her white shirt were stained with her partner's blood, and the woman looked like she needed a good meal and a hot drink.

'DS Sutton. Thank goodness,' Dummett said, ushering her to the car. 'Let's get you somewhere safe.'

'We're moving?' Sutton raised her split eyebrow, looking at the three men surrounding her.

'Commissioner Sarrett wants to speak to you, but she's currently in a meeting.' Dummett smiled. 'With everything that's been going on and the danger you've been placed in, we think it's best we head to an undisclosed location until we can guarantee your safety here.'

'Can you guarantee it there?' Sutton asked bluntly.

'These men here are armed,' Dummett offered. 'Now come on, dear. Let's get you out of this mess.'

There was a warmth to Dummett that hadn't always been there, and after the night Sutton had been through, it was welcome. Tentatively, she nodded her thanks to Finch and then accepted Dummett's offer of the backseat. The chief inspector shut the door, said something to the two armed officers and then walked around and joined her in the back of the car.

The two armed officers made themselves comfortable in the front seat, pulled out of their parking spot and headed towards the exit. Sutton looked back to Finch, who watched them go, and she then dropped her head back against the headrest and shut her eyes.

At least she was safe now.

CHAPTER TWENTY-ONE

After the adrenaline finally wore off and he'd managed to get accustomed to the uncomfortable chair, Jay had managed to doze off for what felt like only a few minutes before Silva slammed his hand down on the table on which Jay was resting his head. The impact and the noise combined caused him to sit bolt upright, and he almost wobbled from the chair.

'Sorry, did I wake you?' Silva grinned. Having cleaned up in the barely functioning bathroom of the warehouse, Silva looked unfathomably refreshed.

'Sorry, boss,' Jay mumbled, and yawned. 'What's the play?'

'The play? Check you out, *vato*,' Silva chuckled. 'You spend a few days with me and you're acting like a true criminal.'

Jay couldn't hide his smile. For years, he'd been nothing more than a petty thief or a heavy for some of the more meagre gangsters in London. This was an opportunity to work with, and become trusted by, one of the most dangerous men in the world, and he didn't want to waste the opportunity to sit under his learning tree.

Also, he had the chance to become very rich.

Although it hadn't been said out loud, Jay was sure that Silva had no intention of paying the men who'd helped him, despite his promises. The two associates of Jay's who'd died would be forgotten about, and the one now sitting in a prison cell would never hear from them. By proving his worth and his loyalty to Silva, Jay wasn't just hoping for a job working with the man.

He was hoping Silva wouldn't kill him.

Silva clicked his fingers and beckoned Jay to follow, and they climbed down the metal stairs to the main floor of the warehouse where the four vans were parked. Each one was emblazoned with a fake trade company, and each one had enough space in the back to transport a quarter of the gold. The plan was for them to arrive at the airspace in ten-minute intervals, but with their ranks depleted thanks to Sam, Silva looked to Jay to solve the problem.

'I can make some calls.' Jay shrugged. 'But I can't promise anything.'

'I don't like the word can't.' Silva frowned. 'Get it done and if this gold is ready to go by five o'clock this evening, then maybe there is a space for you on that plane with me, eh?'

Jay's eyes lit up, and Silva smirked as he pulled his cigarettes from his pocket and lit one up. He was still debating whether Jay would survive the rest of the day, but the more the man came through for him, the more he saw the benefit of keeping him around. Although Jay had none of the training that Silva had, he'd proven himself willing to get his hands dirty and, had he not put two bullets in those police officers at the hospital things could have been playing out a little differently. Silva's contacts would have seen him walk free, but it would have thrown a real spanner in their plans.

For that, he owed Jay.

Perhaps he could make an asset out of him yet.

'Do you know if they took Pope in?' Jay asked as he began flicking through his phone.

'Do I look like the policia?' Silva replied. 'But I think a man like that, he's a survivor.'

'You think he's coming for us?'

Silva's eyes narrowed as he gazed out towards the door of the warehouse, where the rain was still falling, and their remote location felt even more secluded.

'I think if there is any way that he can find us, he will.' Silva flicked the cigarette. 'Tell your boys they'll be on security, too. I'll strap them up.'

'Yes, boss.'

Silva slapped Jay firmly on the back, a show of appreciation, before he turned and stomped back through the warehouse. He climbed up the steel steps once more and then moved to the table where his armoury was laid out. After losing his weapon at the hospital, he had enough Glock 17s to arm Jay and the potential three-man crew, but it would mean he'd had to sacrifice his back-up weapon. He doubted he needed it, and if any problems were to arise, his M16 would be more than capable of wiping them from existence. Silva checked all the magazines to ensure they were full, expertly releasing each one from the handgun before snapping it shut once more.

He lifted his phone, thumbed to his recent calls and tapped the screen. The call connected and his contact was in transit.

'I can't talk right now.'

'Then just listen,' Silva said firmly. 'We are still on track for delivery this evening. Five o'clock as agreed. That means from four o'clock, I need that airspace cleared and any resistance from airport security pulled back.'

'I'll see what I can do.'

Silva felt his fist clench and his biceps bulge and he gritted his teeth.

'I had assurances. Your boss said he could make this happen for me, so if I arrive there at four, and anyone tries to stop me, I'll make a widow of their wives and an orphan of their kids. Do you understand me?'

There was a shuffle on the other end of the phone, and the sound of a car door slamming shut. The voice then spoke at full volume.

'They have you on CCTV. I can protect you a little, but they'll be looking for you at every airport, dock or tunnel out of this country.' The voice sighed. *'You said you could handle the problem.'*

'It was your officers who stopped me,' Silva barked. 'So this is *your* mess!'

'We are doing what we can to clear up it up this end. But…'

'But what?' Silva huffed impatiently.

'There are things we can't do.'

The pause told Silva enough, and he began to chuckle. He could hear the irritated tut on the other end of the line and he lit another cigarette to bask in his enjoyment.

'If you want me to do it for you, then you tell your boss my price has changed.' Silva luxuriated in the fact that she couldn't talk. 'I want half.'

'Half?' the voice snapped, and then quickly quietened down.

'I'll leave you to discuss it. But if you turn up here with the girl, and I don't have that price confirmed, I'll be putting a bullet through two police officers. *Entender?*'

Silva disconnected the call and tossed the phone onto the table among his array of weapons. The threat was clear, and although it was inevitable that they would bring DS Sutton to him for him to pull the trigger, there was no way those involved wanted another senior figure of the Metropolitan Police to be killed along with her.

He didn't know much about Chief Inspector Mary Dummett, only that she was a cold and calculating woman.

She'd do the right thing.

Otherwise, he'd kill her as well.

It had been a long time since Sam had been shunted awake by his dreams. In the years following Jamie's death, he'd tried everything not to fall asleep, knowing that the haunting images of his son's dead body would flood his subconscious and threaten to drown him.

Night after night.

Image after image.

It had all stemmed from the guilt of knowing he could have stopped it, knowing that he should have thrown Miles Hillock against the car he'd drunkenly tried to get in and throw him in the back of a cab.

But Sam hadn't acted.

He and Theo, his best friend, had been finishing their last drink, toasting to a future outside of the armed forces when Hillock had stumbled past and while they turned a blind eye to the man's clearly inebriated state, the consequences would be earth shattering. The man drunkenly swerved round a corner and killed Sam's son, who along with his ex-wife, Lucy, had come to meet him.

The whole world ending in a second.

Ever since Sam had finally confronted his guilt and shame, the two burning factors in his quest for justice, he'd been able to sleep dreamlessly every night. It wasn't perfect, but knowing he was now fighting the good fight in honour of his son's memory, as opposed to the guilt, meant his conscience was clean enough to allow him to rest.

But not that night.

After dumping the hire car a few miles from the hospital, Sam had walked the three miles back to Greenwich in the pouring rain. Once he'd entered his small flat, he'd stripped his wet clothing off and collapsed into the shower, hoping the hot water would wash away the pain that was ricocheting through his body. Silva had come close to killing him, and as the water beneath his feet had turned red, he inspected the slash across the back of his tricep.

It probably needed stitches, but there was no way he'd be able to walk into a hospital with the whole city in turmoil.

His face would be everywhere.

Once dried, he pulled a roll of bandages from the cupboard and wrapped his arm as tightly as possible, enough to stem the bleeding, and then he collapsed on the bed for some rest.

His eyes were shut before he hit the pillow.

It was Theo who'd greeted him in his dream, his dearest friend offering his million-dollar smile and a few charming quips, the way Sam remembered him. He beckoned for Sam to follow him and even in a dream state, Sam knew he didn't want to.

But he did.

As they walked, Theo's skin began to char, burns from the grenade that had killed him, and by the time they emerged into a park and Theo sat down at the bench, his body was an obliterated mess.

He told Sam he didn't blame him.

Then Sam was confronted by Frank Jackson, his shirt blood red and his body riddled with bullets, who questioned what made him and Sam so different considering the blood that was on Sam's hands. Before he could form a response, Jackson collapsed onto the ground, beside Sergeant Carl Marsden, gasping for breath as he clutched the bullet hole in his chest.

He told Sam to keep fighting before he also died,

drawing a tear from Sam who tried to reach down to him but couldn't find the strength to do so.

Then he heard the blood-curdling scream of his wife, and as he turned, the park had evaporated and he was on the humid streets of a London evening; the buildings bathed in the blue lights of police cars. Lucy was on her knees, her agony roaring from her throat, but she didn't move when Sam placed a hand on her shoulder.

All the details of the city and the surrounding street began to melt to black as he stepped forward, where the motionless, broken body of Jamie lay. Blood pooled around his fragile skull and his eyes were wide open. Sam was weeping uncontrollably and as he dropped to his knees behind his son, the body snapped to the side and looked at him with fury.

'Fight.'

And then Sam had sat bolt upright. His body was slick with a cold sweat and he stumbled through to the bath-room and vomited into the toilet. As he wretched the final droplets of bile into the bowl, he hit the flush and then dropped back against the wall, a shaking and naked wreck. Carefully, he pulled himself up via the sink and then splashed water onto his face, snapping himself back into reality.

He stared into his own reflection, and Sam knew that the dream had been driven by the guilt of DS Vokes being laid up in the hospital. The last he knew, the detective was fighting for his life on the operating table and it was Sam who'd put him in the way of the bullet that had embedded in his stomach. It had triggered the memories of those he'd lost along the way, good people like Theo or Marsden, who'd laid down their life for the greater good.

People Sam felt he should have been able to save.

With his stomach settled and the shaking controlled, he eventually dressed and made himself a black coffee. He'd been out for a few hours, and as the clock approached lunchtime, he turned on the television to check the news.

Nothing.

There was a brief mention of a disturbance at the hospital, but by and large, it looked like the Met were doing their best to keep it quiet. Sam understood why, especially in the heat of the public backlash about the deaths of Harrington and Dyer. They needed to trick the public into thinking the situation was under control, even if it was anything but.

Sam had a shower and changed his bandage before he found himself restlessly pacing the apartment.

He had no weapon.

No leads.

No idea if Sutton and Vokes were still alive.

No way of stopping Silva, and those responsible for the chaos and the bloodshed.

He felt hopeless.

As he wrapped his thick parka coat around his beaten, muscular frame, he told himself he'd be more use out on the streets trying to rattle some cages than moping in the apartment and feeling sorry for himself.

He had to do something.

Then he heard the ping of a message and checked his phone.

Nothing.

As he patted down his pockets, he felt the solid object from the inside of his coat and pulled it out.

Sutton's phone.

It had over thirty per cent battery left, but more importantly, a message had appeared on the lock screen.

Vokes's Phone Location.

Although Sam couldn't unlock the phone, the security override of the app showed the location of the phone and instantly Sam knew that Sutton must have activated it.

Because it was moving.

Darting out into the howling wind and rain, Sam ran as fast as he could, hoping he could draw together a plan and that Sutton kept moving. It was unlikely they would get rid of her in transit, but the fact that she'd sent him her location told him she was in trouble.

And Sam wasn't ready to let another innocent person die because of him.

CHAPTER TWENTY-TWO

Sutton wasn't sure if it was the betrayal of DCI Hasan or Sam's inquisition into who'd sent Silva and his men to her apartment, but the last twenty-four hours had shifted her perception completely. Although Chief Inspector Dummett was nothing but concerned for her wellbeing, Sutton found herself being cagey around her superior officer. The two armed officers in the front of the car did little but peer menacingly out of their windows, as one of them guided the car through the streets of London to a nondescript safe house down a side street in Thornton Heath.

They'd driven for over half an hour, tackling the early morning London traffic with ease, and although Dummett asked the odd question, it was apparent to Sutton that she didn't want to discuss too much in front of the other officers.

The plan was to head to the safe house for a debrief, and then the commissioner herself would join them once she'd attended to the hurricane that Sutton, Sam and Silva had left in their wake. The media would have a field day, but then that was why Sarrett was paid the top salary.

She was a lightning rod for the criticism levied at the Met, and considering officers were dead, hospitals had been shot up and a large amount of gold had been stolen from the Bank of England in the past forty-eight hours, Sutton expected the conduction to be severe.

As they approached the house, Dummett's phone buzzed, and she looked at the number and tried to hide her dismay.

But Sutton saw it.

Suddenly, she found herself alert to everything, and every small detail seemed magnified. Dummett flashed a forced smile to Sutton and then turned on her seat, covering her mouth with her hand.

'I can't talk right now.'

The car pulled into a driveway on a normal-looking house, tucked between two others on one of the identikit streets that were part of the London fabric. Sutton looked up at the two officers in the front of the car, who glanced at Dummett in their rear-view mirror. Whoever she was talking to was clearly in control of the conversation.

'I'll see what I can do.' Dummett sighed and then nodded to the two officers. They obediently exited the car, and the passenger then opened Sutton's door, indicating for her to get out. Dummett nodded her encouragement and Sutton obliged, feeling the anxiety ripple through her body as she made her way into the house. It was cheaply furnished, but it had a few sofas and the usual mod-cons in the kitchen for someone to get by. As she entered the kitchen, she yawned and one of the officers suggested she rest as Sarrett would be a while. Sutton took him up on the offer, although her gut told her that she needed to lock the bedroom door.

Stretched out across the mattress, she fell asleep almost instantly.

She awoke sometime in the late morning as the throbbing in her skull intensified. She stumbled from her room to the bathroom, where Dummett had laid out a fresh towel, along with a new T-shirt. Sutton had a quick shower, slipped the T-shirt over her slight frame, and then carefully descended the stairs. When she reached the bottom step, Dummett called to her.

'In here, Detective.'

The voice came from the kitchen, and Sutton followed it towards the half-opened door. As she pushed it open, Dummett was sitting at the kitchen table, her hands around a fresh mug of tea. As steam rose from the top of the mug, Dummett smiled at Sutton, who froze in terror.

One of the armed officers had his gun in his hand.

'What the fuck is going on?'

'Sit.' Dummett indicated to the chair opposite her. Sutton, under the threat of the weapon, did as she was told. 'Tea?'

'I think a beer would be better.'

'Quite.' Dummett blew across the top of her drink and took a sip. 'I want you to know that I did everything within my remit to not let it come to this. I really did.'

'Then why did it?' Sutton spat, eyeballing the officer who made a small, threatening gesture with the gun.

'Because you wouldn't listen,' Dummett snapped. 'I told Karim to steer you away from that robbery, but you wouldn't listen. Then, when you had your little friend bring it to the table in the meeting, you gave us no choice. You both became loose ends.'

'I swear, if you do anything to Connor I will—'

'Oh, come on now. I'm not a monster,' Dummett said ironically as she took another sip. '*If* he pulls through with his recovery, we'll lean on him and his wife to take an early retirement based on the physical and mental injuries and will make sure their children have a good life. I wish it could be the same for you, Sutton, I really do. But based on what I saw at the hospital, you're never going to let this go.'

'What did you see exactly?' Sutton was surprised at her own resistance in the face of the situation.

'You helped Sam Pope,' Dummett said coldly. 'You fought for your life. Commendable, but it means we need to know you'll no longer be a problem.'

'We?' Sutton asked.

'Let's just say that there are some powerful people who need this whole thing to go off without any further hitches.'

'And then you get paid, huh?'

'I will be rewarded for my work.'

'For sending officers to die,' Sutton said in disgust. 'It was *you* who ordered Hasan to change the shifts, wasn't it? It was *you* who selected Harrington and Dyer. What did you do? Pull their names out of a fucking hat? For what? Money?'

Dummett scowled at Sutton and anxiously drummed her nails against the mug in her grip.

'Sutton, there is more going on here than just money. There are powerful people who want to change the very face of British politics. People who want to rebuild this broken system to improve our country. Improve the lives of all the people who are held down by the failures of this government. A sizable investment into their party will open the right doors, grease the right palms and bring about a change. This is bigger than a few dead coppers.'

As Dummett's explanation swirled around in her mind, Sutton could feel her muscles tremble with anger.

'A country built on the blood of people who'd sworn to protect it.' Sutton shook her head. 'Who is it? Henshaw?

He seems like the just the right kind of arsehole to put something like this into play.'

The twitch in the corner of Dummett's mouth gave it away, and she knew it. The twitch turned to a smile, and she finished her tea.

'Well, considering you did give your life for the information, yes. If you must know, Graham Henshaw will become the prime minister of this country within the next five years and sadly, you'll not be around to see the change it brings. I guess, well…you'll just be a puddle of blood we built it on.'

Dummett motioned to the two officers and the one without the gun pulled Sutton up from the chair by the elbow. The other jabbed the gun into her ribs and Sutton felt her knees buckle with fear.

'So that's it? You're just going to kill me here in cold blood?'

Dummett slid her arms into her coat and shook her head.

'Of course not.' Dummett smirked. 'We have paid killers to do that for us. Take her to the car.'

As Sutton was roughly shoved through the hallway and back out to the car, Dummett lifted her phone, desperate for Henshaw to answer the call. Despite Silva's threats, she still hadn't been able to get hold of the architect of the past few days and the clock was ticking.

In the back of the car, Sutton had pulled the phone out of her trouser pocket and quickly realised it wasn't hers. Then, with her mind doing its best to find a way to survive, the memory hit her like a bullet from a gun.

Sam had taken her phone.

As the two officers stood outside the car and spoke as one of them puffed on a vape, Sutton quickly tapped in Vokes's pass code and unlocked the phone. One of the officers noticed and just as he hauled open the door, she sent the phone tracker notification to herself.

She locked the phone and obediently handed it over and hoped Sam would realise that it was her final call for help.

———

As the car turned off the main road, Sutton looked out at the heavily wooded surroundings. The rain cutting through the army of trees that lined the secluded road was hammering the car, and in the distance, the roar of a plane engine rumbled through the sky like thunder. The late afternoon was already beginning to fade into an early evening, as the little sun that had managed to peek through the clouds had begun to set. They were close to Gatwick Airport, that much was obvious, but with all the attention purposefully taken away from the robbery by the clear execution of two police officers, it had meant Silva was able to hide in plain sight.

Dummett had taken the seat beside Sutton for the duration of the journey, making it very clear that if she tried anything, the armed officer ahead of them had strict orders to put a bullet through her shin bone. She didn't want to see Sutton's execution in person, but seemed more than happy to deliver the woman to the hangman. The tense car journey had been amplified by the constant attempts by Dummett to contact Henshaw, with the flustered chief inspector lifting the phone to her ear every few minutes, before muttering under her breath as the call failed to connect.

Something was wrong. Sutton could sense it, but whether that meant she had a stay of execution would remain to be seen. The only hope she had was that Sam had read her call for help and would try his best to intervene. The irony wasn't lost on her, and as she gazed out of the rain-soaked windows at the labyrinth of trees, she found herself smirking. She'd committed her life to upholding the law and had been fixated on bringing Sam Pope to justice. Yet here she was, being driven to her death by a superior officer, and her only hope was the vigilante she'd despised for so long. She understood why previous officers and the public had supported the man.

He may have been a criminal.

But he was one of the few genuinely good people in the world.

The abandoned warehouse soon loomed into view, shrouded behind the mist of the rain, and as they approached, Sutton peered into the open front of the rusty building. She could see four small transit vans parked in a uniform line, all with their back doors wide open as a line of obedient henchman passed gold bars to each other and stacked them neatly. Seeing such wealth in its physical form was a sight to behold, and as the car came to a stop, Sutton sensed everyone in the vehicle felt the same way.

That was a fortune worth killing for.

A rush of terror danced down Sutton's spine as a man emerged between two of the trucks, a smile on his face and his murderous hands clasped together. It was the same man who'd barged into the hospital the night before with a gun aimed directly at her head. Dummett quickly exited the car, followed by the armed officer from the passenger seat and she strode towards Silva and took his hand in a firm shake. The armed officer opened Sutton's door and gestured with his weapon for her to step out.

She did, and was blasted by the downpour, before they moved towards Silva and the shelter from the rain.

'Hello again,' Silva said to her with a grin. 'It is a shame we are meeting under such circumstances, eh?'

Although his accent was thick, Sutton could still sense the dishonesty in his voice.

'I've had worse first dates,' she barked back, drawing a genuine chuckle from Silva. Dummett frowned, clearly unimpressed.

'It's a shame you want me to kill her,' Silva said to Dummett. Then he turned to Sutton. 'Please know that for me, this is just business. She is the one giving the orders.'

'Enough.' Dummett scowled, already wracked with guilt. She refused to meet Sutton's eye. 'About your request…'

'Ah, my fee,' Silva said confidently. He waggled his eyebrows at Sutton.

'I haven't been able to get hold of him, so we'll need to negotiate that later.'

Silva looked amused, and Sutton could sense the power dynamic. Dummett had none, and it was clear to everyone.

'I don't work for free. You know this.' Silva took a step towards Dummett. 'Until he agrees that half of this is mine, then this fine lady here will live. In fact, I'll give her all the information that implicates you, your boss and everyone else and I'll fly out of here a very rich man. Do you understand?'

Behind Dummett, the armed officer agitated on the spot. Sutton noticed. Which meant Silva definitely did.

'Look, let's not be hasty and make threats.' Dummett tried to reason.

'It is not a threat, *mami*.' Silva's tone hardened. 'Perhaps you need to understand how fucking serious I am.'

Before anyone could register what was happening, Silva turned to the nearest henchman who was loading gold into one of the vans, pulled the Glock from the back of the man's jeans and realising Silva was now armed, the officer behind Dummett went to lift his gun.

It was an empty gesture.

Silva lifted the gun to the officer and squeezed the trigger twice, the gunshot echoing loudly enough to leave a shrill ring in Sutton's ear. The bullets ripped through the man's chest, lifting him off his feet and sending him sprawling backwards into the rain. As he hit the wet concrete, it instantly turned red as the blood spilt out of him, the rain washing it away just as quickly. The driver of the car stepped out, but Dummett lifted up a shaking hand.

Silva leant in and nodded firmly.

'Tell that *puta* to stay in the fucking car.' Silva's snarl was laced with menace. 'Otherwise, you'll have yet another dead police officer on your conscience.'

Silva then turned to Sutton and beckoned her forward with his finger. Tentatively, she took a few steps towards him, then looked back at the officer who was gurgling on his own blood as he clasped to the final moments of his life. By the time Silva had led her through the loading bay and to the steel steps, the officer was dead. Behind them, Dummett followed, the weight of another dead officer hanging heavily around her neck. As Sutton was led up the stairs, she cast a glance over the workshop below, recognising one of the men loading the gold into the trucks as the man who'd attacked her at the hospital.

Along with him and Silva, there were three other men, as well as the armed officer who'd now left his car and was kneeling over his dead colleague, covered by the ever-increasing darkness of the evening and the torrential downpour.

Seven armed men.

And she was relying on one.

One man with a reputation for fighting with everything he's got.

As Sutton took the last step and Silva ushered her

towards one of the uncomfortable-looking chairs, she took a deep breath and accepted the hard truth of the reality.

Even if Dummett couldn't come through for Silva, it was still unlikely the man would leave any loose ends.

This was where she was going to die.

And soon.

CHAPTER TWENTY-THREE

Having dumped the car after escaping the hospital that morning, Sam had braved the elements and marched through Greenwich and then followed the main roads up towards the o2 arena that loomed large and bright against the darkening London sky. The iconic building, which held numerous A-list music acts as well as some of the biggest events in the capital had been repurposed as an arena after its expensive and needless introduction at the start of the millennium. Surrounded by bars, restaurants and shops, it had become a tourist hot spot and a place where even the most wanted man in the country could effortlessly blend into the throng of excitable people who scurried around it. The arena was on the doorstep of North Greenwich Station, which had considerable links to the London Underground and Sam kept his head low as he traversed the security barriers and made his way to the platform.

The police would be on the lookout for him, and although it was unlikely, they would be watching every single CCTV camera in the city, it was still imperative he didn't get caught.

Sutton's life depended on it.

When the notification had pinged on Sutton's phone, Sam connected the dots instantly. Whoever had picked Sutton up to "protect her" after the incident at the hospital had made arrangements to ensure that whatever Sutton had discovered would stay dead and buried. The phone tracing app told him that the phone was on the move, heading out towards Gatwick, which was all Sam needed to know. The airport had been mentioned a few times, and if someone needed to get a truckload of gold out of the country, then posting up near the airport itself was a good start.

The only thing Sam didn't know was how much time he had.

Impatiently, he stood on the train as it began its stop start journey back into the city. With time to think, he contemplated the impact on his new identity, Ben Carter, which was now surely compromised due to the rental car. He scolded himself for being so sloppy, and once the Met traced the car on the CCTV and ran it through the necessary systems, they'd soon have his driver's licence and would be able to cut off a number of channels that he used so freely.

But he didn't have time to mull over it, and when the train stopped at Willesden Green Station, Sam stepped off and marched with purpose through the gates and out onto the rain-soaked streets. With his hands stuffed in his pockets, his hood pulled up and his head down, Sam stomped through the empty high street and veered off towards the estates where he'd been the day before. With the rain keeping everyone indoors, the streets were eerily quiet, and when Sam pushed open the door to the barbershop, the shrill chime of the bell seemed to catch the owners off guard. As Sam pulled back his hood, the burly barber rolled his eyes.

'The fuck you doing back here?' He snarled.

'Well, I haven't come for a haircut.'

The dad lifted himself from the chair at the back of the shop, stepping forward and putting a comforting hand on his son's shoulder. Reluctantly, the son backed down, and the man stepped forward and looked at Sam and the clear signs of battle across his face.

'You look like hell, son?' he finally said with a warm smile and extended his hand. 'Peter.'

'Sam.' He shook the hand firmly. 'And thanks...I feel a lot worse.'

'Yeah, well, this world will do that to you.' Peter chuckled. 'You keep knocking on doors looking for trouble. Eventually you'll find it.'

With a nod of agreement, Sam looked at the burly son who didn't seem too impressed. The other son was nowhere to be seen.

'As right as you are, Peter, I didn't come here for advice.' Sam took a breath. 'I came here for a gun.'

Immediately, the son leapt up, his eyes wide with anger as he stomped forward.

'What the hell you implying?'

Peter held an arm up and across his son's broad chest, furrowing his grey brow at his irate son.

'Calm the fuck down, Julien,' Peter snapped. After a few moments, his son did as he was told and turned and stomped to the back of the shop and disappeared through the door. Peter watched him go, shaking his head slightly before he turned back to Sam. 'Now, I might not share my son's rage, but I do share his sense of disrespect.'

'I didn't mean any,' Sam said earnestly. 'But I've got a situation and very little time.'

'And that needs a gun?'

'Yes, sir.' Sam nodded respectfully. 'I know you don't fully approve of who I am or what I stand for. But I also know you understand what this world is like. You know that the have-nots don't get the same opportunities as the haves, and that makes them easy targets. And right now, the people who threw that young police officer from that building are about to get away with the blood on their hands and they'll wash it with millions of pounds.'

'The fuck if I care if people steal some money?' Peter scoffed. 'Like the rich need to be that rich, anyway.'

'I agree. But they have a friend of mine. A detective. One of the good ones. And they might have already put a bullet in her, but I can't just sit by and let these bastards kill whoever they want and steal whatever they like. Now, I don't think you have a gun, sir. But like you told me yesterday, nothing goes on around here without you knowing. So…all I'm asking is for you to point me in the right direction.'

Peter regarded Sam carefully for a few moments, and Sam felt strangely anxious. The man held himself to a high standard, that much was clear, and he looked Sam up and down like a strict headmaster. After a few moments, he glanced out of the window at the rain and then reached for his coat that hung on the hooks near the door.

'Follow me.'

With authority, Peter hauled open the door and Sam followed, and quickly, the two men crossed the street and with their heads low, walked past the alleyway that still had a lingering police presence. Peter walked with a briskness that belied his years, and he turned swiftly down a small side road that led towards one of the many neglected estates that loomed over the city. The dreary building was littered with boarded-up windows, and the walls were covered with faded graffiti. As they approached the door to the stone staircase that clung to the side of the building, two young men were huddled inside it, their hoods up and their manner aggressive.

They saw Peter.

They stepped aside.

Sam followed, the two men making little effort to move for him as he wriggled between them and followed Peter who continued upwards until they reached the second floor. The older gentleman took a few steadying breaths before continuing, and as they walked along the balcony, Sam looked out over the grey city below. The rain added a misty sheen to the concrete landscape and as they approached the door up ahead, a few more men looked suitably annoyed by their presence.

'You lost?' One of them snapped, his eyes locked on Sam.

'He's with me,' Peter said. The man didn't seem to hear.

'Turn the fuck around, white boy.'

The other man squinted as he looked at Peter, and then he seemed to spring to life.

'Hey, yo…let them be,' he said to his friend. 'Sorry, sir.'

Peter nodded his thanks, and Sam was impressed by the authority with which the man seemed to carry himself. The obliging young man opened the door to one of the cramped, sparsely decorated apartments and let them in. As they stepped in from the rain, Peter pulled back his hood and smiled at Sam.

'I cut his hair. Have done for years.'

'Never mess with a barber, huh?' Sam joked and Peter led them through the dimly lit hallway, his coat leaving a trail of raindrops on the old, worn carpet. A thumping bass could be heard in one of the rooms, along with the offensive lyrics of a local hip-hop artist, and when Sam stepped through into the room behind Peter, he felt all eyes fall onto him. There were three men sitting across two beaten, leather sofas and a cloud of smoke that was heavy with the smell of marijuana. Peter made the gesture of batting it away, and one of the men took charge and stood up. With the joint hanging out of the side of his mouth, he clapped hands with the elderly barber before taking a long draw on his spliff and then blowing the smoke in Sam's direction.

'The fuck you bring me this guy for?' He chortled, handing the joint to one of the other men on the sofa. On the coffee table before them were packs of cocaine, stacks of money, and a few weapons that Sam wagered were loaded.

'He's a friend,' Peter said sternly.

'You cutting white boy hair now?' The man chuckled and then turned to Sam. 'The fuck you looking at?'

'I need a gun,' Sam said sternly. The man's eyes widened in shock, and he turned to his friends who all started laughing.

'The fuck you need a gun for? Fox hunting?' The man waved him away and took his seat once more. 'Yo, Peter... you messing with me?'

'No, Marcus,' Peter said sternly. 'The man needs a gun.'

Marcus sat back in his chair and looked at Sam with interest. The joint was handed back to him, and he took a long, thoughtful puff before he stubbed it out in the overflowing ashtray. As the smoke filtered out of his nose, his eyes sparkled with recognition.

'Holy fuck. This motherfucker is Sam Pope.' The other two snapped their head towards Sam, who pulled his own hood back as if to confirm it. Marcus stood and then casually reached down for one of the guns. 'I got a weapon for you.'

Marcus lifted the gun up and aimed it directly at Sam's forehead, the cold metal of the weapon a mere inch or two from Sam's skull. The move seemed to startle his friends, and Peter turned in annoyance.

'Marcus? What the hell...'

'It's okay, Peter,' Sam said calmly. He kept his eyes locked on Marcus.

'A lot of people round here don't like you. I put a bullet in you, and I become a her…'

Before anyone knew what was happening, Sam's hands shot up, one on the top of the gun, the other on the base of Marcus's wrist. As he twisted both to the side, he dug his finger into the pressure point below Marcus's wrist, loosening the grip. Smoothly, and within a second, Sam locked his grip on the gun, spun it, and aimed it back at the now terrified Marcus.

'Whoa. Whoa.' Marcus held his hands up. 'Let's chill the fuck out.'

'I'm not here for trouble,' Sam said calmly, the gun still locked on his target. 'But the people who killed that police officer the other day are going to do it again, and I need to stop them.'

'The fuck we care about a dead fed?' One of the other men piped up from the sofa.

'Because they'll blame it on you. The people who live in these estates. The people who have to break the law to survive. You're easy targets and it means those who keep the boot down on you will just do it with more pressure.' Sam lowered the gun slowly. 'That's why they chose to kill her in this estate. Because nobody would bat an eyelid. Because they knew they could blame it on the life they've pushed you into and that would be that.'

Marcus looked down at the other guns on the table and then back up at Sam.

'You don't just come into my house and jack me for my shit. You understand?'

Peter stepped forward.

'Maybe next time, don't point a gun at a trained killer, then?' Peter shrugged and then turned to Sam. 'One gun and we will never see you again.'

Sam nodded in agreement and then to Marcus.

'I'll look the other way. You guys go beyond what's on this table, then I'll knock the door down. Understand?'

Marcus mumbled something and gestured for the two of them to leave. Peter ushered for them to move quickly, and the duo swiftly left the apartment and headed back down the stairs. As they walked along the concourse, the man at the door called after Peter about a hair appointment, and Sam stuffed the weapon into his jacket. Sam half expected a bullet to hit him in the spine, but when they stepped out onto the streets below, he felt his muscles relax slightly. As they walked back towards the shop, Peter dipped his hands into his pockets and fished out his car keys.

'I'll report it stolen in the morning,' Peter said with a smile. 'Green Fiesta in the car park up there.'

Sam followed the man's pointed finger and then turned back to him.

'Seriously, you've done enough.'

'And you haven't. Not yet.' Peter patted him on the shoulder. 'You won't change things, Sam. Believe me. I've lived in this place for nearly seventy years, and it just gets worse.'

'Then why are you helping me?' Sam looked down at the keys and then back up at the helpful man.

Peter offered a hopeless smile.

'Because someone has to try.'

With that, Sam patted Peter on the arm and then broke out into a jog towards the car park. He found the Fiesta in one of the spaces, dropped in and started the engine. As the wipers began their relentless battle with the rain, and the heater burst into life, Sam opened up Sutton's phone and checked the tracing app.

Vokes's phone was no longer in transit.

Sam pulled out of the car park, turned onto the high street and headed towards the motorway.

He had a location.

He had a gun.

He just didn't know if he had enough time.

CHAPTER TWENTY-FOUR

There were no doubts in Sutton's mind that the balance of power had completely shifted. From what she'd ascertained, Silva had been hired by Henshaw to pull off one of the biggest heists in UK history and there had been a web of incriminated parties who'd all played their hand. Hasan, who'd paid for his inclusion with his life. Dummett, who was now locked in a meeting with Silva, and whose life was now also hanging in the balance. Henshaw had serious contacts, and the arrangements to shut down the airspace for an hour to allow Silva to get the gold out of the country would have been passed off with something as simple as a drone over the airport.

It should have gone off without a hitch.

The two unfortunate officers whose lives were killed due to greed masquerading as a political play would be immortalised as brave officers killed in the line of duty. Sarrett, who would never know that she'd been betrayed by her close allies, would rampage against the attacks on the Met and then Henshaw would use his newfound backing to make the right plays and the right connections to ascend to the top job in the country.

A prime minister who'd swept in on the blood of the innocent.

It was Sutton who'd been the fly in the ointment, and thankfully for her, so had Sam Pope. No one was supposed to look the other way when the Met was mourning the loss of their own, but she did, and now she'd likely pay for it with her life.

But the plan had been scuppered, and with the insertion of Sam Pope into proceedings, Silva had decided to take the reins himself. The man was a bloodthirsty mercenary, which he hid behind the veneer of his good looks and his charm. He could disappear into the far reaches of the world with the fortune and all of it would be for nothing.

That was what Dummett was protesting against, and although she couldn't see into the cramped meeting room that was sectioned off on the far corner of the floor, she could hear the muffled sound of raised voices. She was arguing the case for them to stick to the plan, whereas Silva was seemingly looking to change the arrangement.

It meant things were delayed.

Which meant there was still some hope.

Once Sutton had been led up the stairs, Silva motioned for her to take a seat and, moments later, Jay stomped up the metal steps to join them. He smirked at Sutton, a reminder of their altercation at the hospital, and he bound her to the chair with cable ties before returning to warehouse floor to oversee the final transfer of the gold into the four vans. The armed officer was finished grieving for his comrade, and after pulling his friend's corpse in from the cold and stuffing it in one of the common rooms, had taken to standing watch on the threshold of the open door, his gun in his hand. As the final bars were loaded in, Jay told the team to take a break before he lit a cigarette and began a slow march up the steps. As his head bobbed into view, he fixed Sutton with a nasty glare.

'Well, well, well,' he said with a sneer. 'Doesn't look good for you, does it?'

Sutton rolled her eyes.

'You're one to talk,' she finally said, and Jay chuckled as he stood before her, thrusting himself forward slightly in a disgusting show of male domination.

'What was that?' He snapped. Sutton refused to answer, and he reached down and snatched her jaw in his sweaty grip. 'Speak up, bitch.'

He let go, but didn't step back. His legs were pressed against hers, with his groin a few inches from her face.

'How do you think this ends for you?' Sutton asked. 'Do you really think that men like Silva, and corrupt people like Dummett will really keep someone like you safe? You'll either take the fall for it all, or better yet, end up in the fucking dirt.'

Jay regarded her for a few moments, tilting his head to the side as he took another drag. Then, unprovoked, he cracked her across the jaw with the back of his hand, snapping her head to the side.

'You've got a big mouth.' He blew out the smoke and then smirked evilly. 'A pretty one, too.'

As he crudely pressed himself against her, she lunged forward, driving her forehead into the man's crotch and crushing his genitals. Jay fell backwards, grunting in pain as he clutched his testicles and his cigarette spilt out of his mouth and into the room. Sutton tensed against her restraints, the plastic rubbing against her skin until it was red raw and she tried to maintain the adrenaline for what was to come next. The man was a menace, and despite the satisfying blow she'd just dealt, she was aware that she was no more than a sitting duck. She was in trouble, and as Jay composed himself, the spark of anger in his eye confirmed that for her.

Furiously, he scrambled to his feet, only for a voice to interrupt them.

'What's going on here, then?' Silva asked with a chuckle as he strode back into the room. With Jay holding his groin in some discomfort, and Sutton shaking with anger, Silva shrugged. 'Did you hit him in the *cojones*?'

'She fucking nutted me in the fucking bollocks.' Jay angrily confirmed.

'Good girl,' Silva said, before turning to an exasperated Jay. 'Maybe next time, you treat the ladies with a little respect, huh?'

Before Jay could respond, Dummett joined them, looking less crestfallen than before. Sutton felt her stomach flip, as it was clear an agreement had been reached which meant the final sands had tipped through her hourglass. Jay had also read the situation and smiled.

'At least let me fucking kill her.'

'Don't be a fool.' Dummett barked. She turned to Sutton with clearly forced sympathy. 'If it's any consolation, I'll make sure it's your death and your name Henshaw uses to facilitate the change. You'll be remembered.'

With her hands tied, Sutton's hatred for the woman manifested itself with a thick gob of saliva that splattered against Dummett's smug grin. In response, the chief inspector rocked Sutton with a violent open palmed slap across the face.

'Let's not make this personal now.' Silva cut in, stepping between Dummett and their hostage. 'Tell your boy to close the airspace down now. My guys will take the gold there. I'll handle this young lady, and then we can all fuck off in our separate ways. *Comprende?*'

Clearly flustered, Dummett wiped the spit from her face with her sleeve and tried to calm herself down. Jay was also champing at the bit to say something, and Sutton realised at that moment her life was about to end.

Then, the entire warehouse shook, and some of the fixtures broke free from the roof and clattered against the metal floor as the car that they'd arrived in exploded into a tremendous ball of flames. As it lit up the night sky, casting an orange glow against the torrential rain, Silva snapped into action.

Jay followed the orders like a lapdog as Dummett stumbled for cover in fear.

Sutton smiled.

There was still hope.

———

Six men in total.

Sam watched from the cover of the bushes that surrounded the warehouse, and for once, he was happy that the UK winter seemed to exist under an almost permanent rain cloud. The downpour added another layer of protection for what he had planned, but it also meant his own vision was slightly scuppered. When he'd pulled the car over on the dirt road a mile away from the warehouse, he'd once again checked the clip in his gun. All seventeen bullets were accounted for, but he wasn't sure it would be enough. As he slipped the low weight handgun into the back of his jeans, he'd then lifted the bag from the passenger seat and began to run, following the signal that still pulsed from the building somewhere in the forest ahead. The glass clinked together within, and the weight of four litres of vodka soon began to take its toll. As the dim lights of a warehouse loomed in the distance, Sam lowered his pace and stepped off the dirt path, pushing through the overgrowth with his shoulder. The slash across his tricep was still roaring with pain, as if someone was holding a red-hot poker to it.

But he ignored it.

He had to push on.

As he battled his way through the thick, overgrown woodlands and the sodden mud beneath him, he soon looked out upon the warehouse. Instantly, he was transported back fifteen years, to when he was part of a four-man squadron who'd laid siege to a derelict outpost in the heart of the Amazon. They'd found nothing but death, and Sam was the only one to walk away.

The ramifications of that fateful mission had materialised years later when Sam went to war with Pierre Ducard, the former head of the French Military, who now, thanks to Sam, was serving a life sentence in prison as opposed to running the country he'd murdered innocent people to protect.

And like that day, Sam knew he was going to have to fight like hell to make it out alive.

For years, his missions as a sniper had taught him the importance of patience and preparation. While time was of the essence, a full-scale assault on the building with his gun in hand would end in his bullet riddled body hitting the mud within seconds. Somewhere, Sutton was inside, and if Sam had any hope of getting her out and shutting down Silva's operation, he needed to know what he was up against.

Peering through the rain, he took stock of his surroundings.

A BMW was parked out the front of the warehouse, but the seats were empty. Standing idly by the side of the open entrance of the warehouse was a broad man who looked a little out of place. There was a gun in his hand, and Sam wagered he was a dirty cop or another mercenary. The four men who were loading the vans were nothing more than the usual garden variety petty criminal, lured into a 'big job' under the pretext of getting paid when in reality, they'd either take the fall or a bullet for their troubles. One of the men, a tall and lanky man with a beard, broke away from the others, and Sam recognised him as the one from the hospital. The man disappeared up a set of metal steps, most likely where Silva and Sutton were.

That left four men on the ground, and while all of them were likely armed, only one of them was trained.

Keeping low to the ground, Sam shuffled out of the bushes and raced as quickly as he could towards the parked BMW. In his hands was a long tablecloth and a bottle of lighter fluid. As he approached the vehicle, Sam ducked down behind it, then peered around the back.

Nobody had seen him.

Quickly, he opened the small flap at the back of the car and then unscrewed the petrol cap. In his hands, he rolled the tablecloth into a long, thin strip and then poured the lighter fluid up and down the fabric in long lines. Operating as fast as possible to counter the effects of the rain, Sam then carefully guided the rolled-up cloth into the petrol cap and began to feed it through. It disappeared quickly, making its way further into the car and into the petrol tank until only a foot or so was hanging out of the side of the car.

Another quick spray of lighter fluid, and then Sam flicked open the lighter and put the flame to it.

Then he ran like hell.

As his footsteps splashed against the sodden ground beneath him, he heard the first roar of the explosion pulse within the car, and as he leapt back through the bushes to his hiding place, the entire world shook as the car exploded into an awesome fireball, lifting the back two wheels off the ground before the car slammed back to earth in a mighty blaze.

Smoke billowed high into the sky.

Behind it, the warehouse was alive with panic.

Sam had announced his arrival, and somewhere beyond the fiery inferno he'd created, a team of men were locking and loading, ready to hunt him down.

He reached down and lifted two of the bottles of vodka from the bag, their fluid-soaked rags already flopping from their open tops. With a deep breath, his gun against his spine and the lighter in his hand, Sam stepped out of his hiding place and headed towards the warehouse. Beyond the crackle of fire, he could hear furious orders being hurled around inside the warehouse.

They were coming for him.

Sam clicked the lighter once more and lit the first bottle of vodka. He ran two paces and then hurled it as hard as he could over the fiery car and towards the vans that were lined behind it.

As the screams of panic and anguish echoed, he lit the other and tossed it. Then, with nowhere to go, and with the smoke clouding around him and the rain falling relentlessly, he pulled the gun from his spine, wrapped his expert hands around it and got ready to fight.

CHAPTER TWENTY-FIVE

With the warehouse rocking from the explosion, Silva angrily shoved Jay towards the staircase.

'Put *los hijo de puta* in the fucking ground.'

Jay nodded wildly, clearly a little dishevelled, and as he raced down the staircase, he began barking orders at the other three thugs who were all retrieving their weapons. Silva turned back to Sutton and shook his head.

'Whoops.' Sutton shrugged as much as her bindings would allow her. Angrily, Silva turned to Dummett.

'How did he find this place? You were supposed to keep the path clean.'

'I don't know.' Dummett looked terrified, and then turned to Sutton again. 'What the fuck did you do?'

Before anyone could respond, another large explosion erupted beneath them, as one of the vans housing over ten million pounds' worth of gold was suddenly engulfed in a ball of flames. The impact shook the warehouse once more, and was swiftly followed by the angry yells of revenge followed by errant gunshots.

It was all falling apart.

Sensing the plan was as up in smoke as the vehicles below, Silva spoke calmly.

'This is your problem now,' Silva said with a shake of the head, turning towards the table where his M16 was resting. 'Call your guy and tell him the plane is leaving in ten minutes.'

'That's not enough time to get the gold...' Dummett remonstrated, but Silva turned and grabbed her by the hair, yanking her head to the side. Whatever charm he once possessed had evaporated.

'I do not take orders from you.' He spat angrily. 'I will not give my life to this man, nor do I trust you have the power to keep me from prison. So, call him.'

As he yanked her hair once more, footsteps pounded at the top of the stairs, and an armed officer stepped out, his gun raised.

'Let her go,' the officer ordered. He made a motion with the gun that told Silva he wasn't joking. 'Right now.'

Without even taking his eyes off Dummett, Silva lifted the M16 with his other hand and pulled the trigger, sending a burst of bullets towards the officer. They followed the trajectory of the weapon and as the first bullet ripped through the officer's shin bone, the next two burrowed into his stomach. The last one to hit him caught him in the temple, blowing out the side of his skull and sending his dead body crumpling down the stairs to the chaos below. Dummett gasped in horror, and Silva headed towards the staircase, the assault rifle held upward in his expert hands.

'If you want her dead, you can do it yourself.' Silva shot a glance back at Sutton. 'It was a pleasure to have met.'

'Fuck you,' Sutton responded, drawing nothing but a smile from the *sicario*.

Another explosion rocked the floor below them, and

another one of the vans shook on its wheels as the petrol bomb exploded into it. A cry of anguish echoed beneath them, and Silva lifted the rifle and carefully made his way down the stairs, his vision clouded by the billowing, black smoke from the fires. Outside in the rain, he could hear gunshots, but without the line of sight, he couldn't even predict where his target would be.

All he knew was that the men who'd stepped outside to find Sam were dead.

Through the thickness of the smoke, he looked down at the bullet riddled body of the officer he'd killed, before the sound of coughing drew his attention to the third van. Leaning against the door, with his hand holding his own jacket over his face, was Jay. Silva crouched down low to the ground, beneath the damaging current of smoke, and he tapped Jay in the leg to join him. The commotion outside, along with the rumbling of the burning vehicles, meant Silva had to yell as loud as he could.

'Give me the keys,' he demanded. Without questioning, Jay fished them out of his pocket and handed them to him.

Outside, more gunshots.

'I'll drive.' Jay offered, reluctant to hand them over. In an instant, Silva's eyes flashed, and he pushed Jay back against the van and placed the barrel of the M16 under his chin.

'Give. Me. The. Keys,' Silva said through gritted teeth, and Jay dropped them into his hands. 'Take care of the two upstairs. Take care of Sam and then if you get to the hangar on time, you can come with me. *Comprende?*'

Jay nodded, still anxious at the gun pressed against his jawbone. Silva looked at him once more, then disappeared into the smoke and Jay heard the sound of the door being pulled open and then swiftly slamming shut. As he stumbled out of the way, the lights of the van burst through the smoke and Silva reversed the truck back towards the chaos surrounding the building. Like a magnet, it drew bullets, and as four or five bullets ripped through the side of the vehicle, the final two blew out the back windows.

Then it was gone. Screeching through the darkness to freedom.

With his place in the food chain resonating in his mind, Jay coughed and spluttered his way to the steps and then slowly began to climb them. The black smoke was beginning to rise to the floor above them, where the gaps in the old roof and the shoddily boarded windows were offering a few exits for it to filter through into the night. As the air became a little easier to breathe, Jay withdrew the gun from his jeans, climbed up towards the final step and promised himself he'd be on that plane.

Somewhere below, another gunshot rang out.

As soon as the first bottle crashed into the truck, Sam ducked down as near to the flaming car as the heat would allow him. Despite the bitter cold of the evening, and the relentless downpour, he could feel himself getting slick with sweat as the flames licked the air beside him. One of the trucks in the warehouse was now fully engulfed in flames, and he held his position and tried to peer through the smoke.

Two of the men had now stepped out into the rain, their guns hanging in their hands.

Untrained.

Unprepared.

Sam took a moment and blew out his cheeks, and his hand reached for the second bottle. As soon as it was lit, he'd need to hurl it, and then it would be a matter of who could shoot first. Through the smoke, he could see the two men scanning the area, both heading towards either side of the inferno that was providing his cover. With time very much against him, Sam lit the second cloth, stood, and hurled the bottle as hard as he could towards the warehouse. As it spun through the rain, the panicked voices of the men roared through the air and as Sam ducked back behind the inferno, bullets ripped into the body of the car.

They'd seen him.

The Molotov cocktail clattered against another one of the trucks, and the flames swept across the vehicle until they reached the petrol tank. Another ground-shaking explosion thundered beneath them as he took out another truck of blood money and then, through the smoke, he saw one of the men aimlessly stumbling through the smoke towards him.

Sam drew his gun and fired.

The bullet snapped the man's head back and then sent him sprawling limply to the concrete below. The gunshot itself drew more in his direction, and Sam ran towards the dead man and spun, rising up onto one knee and drawing the gun up to his eyeline. Through the smoke, he could see the legs of the second man closing in on the inferno, and Sam lifted his aim slightly.

He pulled the trigger.

The bullet hit the man in the shoulder, sending him spiralling off balance and onto the blazing vehicle that was lighting up the forecourt. Instantly, the night sky was awash with screams of anguish as the man's body became engulfed in the flames, and as he stumbled out into the rain, the terrifying flames flapped around his body like a flock of birds. Screaming for his life, the man smartly dropped to the wet ground beneath and rolled hysterically to extinguish them. As they began to die, the man's strength left him too, and gingerly, he tried to push himself back onto his knees with hands that were pink with blisters. The severity of the burns ran all the way up his arms, and underneath the T-shirt that had perished in the flames, his chest was pink and charred. Half of his hair had been roasted to the follicle, and he screamed in agony as he raised his horrifically burnt face into the bitterly cold rain.

Sam shut down the scream with another squeeze of the trigger, and the man hit the ground with a bullet in his forehead.

Two rear headlights burst through the smoke that was now billowing from the warehouse and Sam stood and watched as one of the vans reversed out and skidded as it turned. Behind the wheel was Silva, and as he threw the vehicle back into first, Sam lifted his gun. The wheels screeched like a howling wolf and the transit van sped off as Sam unloaded his gun at the moving target. The bullets embedded in the side of the van, ruining the plumbing signage that had been imprinted on its side. With his final two bullets, Sam blew out both of the windows on the back of the van before he lowered the weapon.

The van sped away, and as the lights shrunk into the darkness, Sam tossed the gun and turned back towards the warehouse. Two of the trucks were nothing more than kindling for the roaring fires they'd become and some-where within, he hoped he'd find Sutton. As he peered up to the second floor of the property, he could see the smoke filtering through the decayed building, offering enough ventilation for someone to survive.

But only just.

Through the smoke, he could see the final van still parked by the open entrance to the warehouse floor, and carefully, he edged towards it. Part of him thought about running to one of the two dead men out on the forecourt, but it was too risky. It would give away his position, and although he'd already sacrificed the element of surprise by blowing three vehicles and twenty-five million pounds to Kingdom Come, he still had the drop on whoever was left in the building. As he approached the back of the van, he heard the clunking of footsteps on the metal staircase, along with the laboured coughing of someone who was losing a battle with the smoke. Pressed against the back doors of the transit van, Sam peaked around the corner of the vehicle to see the lanky figure of the man from the hospital disappear through the smoke to the top of the stairwell. The man was clearly under orders, otherwise he'd have taken the vehicle providing Sam with cover and followed Silva.

Sutton.

The thought of Sutton at the mercy of the man blinded Sam for a split second, and he stepped out from behind the truck and into view.

A gunshot rang out.

The shooter clearly wasn't trained, otherwise it would have been Sam's final step, but the wayward shot still did as intended. The bullet ripped through the smoke and grazed the back of Sam's left calf, weakening him and wiping out his balance. Sam grunted through gritted teeth and as he hit the floor, his survival instincts rolled him back towards the cover of the van. From somewhere within the warehouse, the shooter stood and Sam breathed through the red-hot pain that was throbbing in his calf. With the vehicles beside him crackling under the flames, it was impossible to hear anything.

No footsteps.

No promises of violence.

Sam sat back against the bumper of the van and tried to assess the situation.

He tried to stand, but his leg buckled and he held his hand to the wound to try to stop the bleeding. Somewhere behind him, cloaked by the smoke and the sound of the world on fire, the gunman was approaching.

And Sam was a sitting duck.

CHAPTER TWENTY-SIX

As another explosion below them rocked the entire metal platform, Sutton's chair was tipped to the side, sending her crashing painfully onto her shoulder. Still strapped to the chair, Sutton struggled against her cable ties and the thin, sharp edges tore into her skin. As the blood began to seep from the wounds, it began to lubricate her wrist and with a scream of agony, she wrenched one of her hands free, ignoring the searing pain of the ripped skin that flapped from her forearm. The metal floor was warm, heating up from the flames that flickered below and as she tried to peer through the metal grating, all she saw was thick, black smoke that caused her to wretch. With her hand free, she hauled herself towards the nearby table, the weight of the chair causing her to grit her teeth and reach for strength she didn't know she had. Slowly, she inched across the floor, the scraping of her chair across the metal drowned out by the roaring fire below and the echo of gunshots.

Sam was fighting.

She knew she had to as well.

Once she reached the table, she reached up with her

free hand and felt around until her fingers knocked over a glass of water. She managed to push it with her fingertips, and the glass rolled to the edge and crashed onto the metal flooring beside her, shattering into a number of shards. As the smallest filtered through the gaps in the floor and disappeared into the smoke, she snatched a large shard and then hooked it underneath the other cable tie that kept her strapped to the chair. Trying her hardest not to touch her skin, she began to saw at the plastic, nicking herself slightly as she did.

The cable snapped open.

With both hands free, Sutton reached down and gripped the cable ties that had secured her ankles to the legs of the chair and cut through them as well.

More gunshots.

As she rolled free from the chair, Sutton lifted her T-shirt over her face and tried to catch her breath. The smoke was billowing up towards the roof, where it was escaping through the run-down ceiling and the glassless windows. As she coughed and stumbled to her feet, she could hear the sound of an engine through the commotion, and somewhere through the smoke, the brightness of headlights. As the van left the war zone, she heard a barrage of gunshots and the sound of shattered glass.

Then, the unmistakable voice of Chief Inspector Dummett.

'Help me.' The woman's voice was pain stricken, and Sutton stumbled further into the smoke, trying to peer through the thick haze. With each explosion, the dilapidated warehouse had shown its age, and as the roof had begun to collapse, a metal beam had tumbled from the roof to the metal grate that Sutton stood on. Underneath the beam was Dummett's clearly shattered leg and the treacherous senior officer was pinned to the ground.

Despite her betrayal, Dummett was still a person and Sutton's duty kicked in as she dropped to her knees beside her.

'Can you move it?' Sutton yelled through her T-shirt, which she'd hooked over her nose as she placed two hands under the beam.

'Just get me out of here!' Dummett yelled. The snapped bone had ripped through her trouser leg.

With a guttural roar, Sutton pushed all her power into her forearms and, as the blood trickled down them and the muscles tightened, she lifted the beam a few inches. With considerable pain and a scream that confirmed it, Dummett shimmied backwards, dragging her decimated leg free.

Sutton collapsed forward over the beam as she dropped it, trying to catch her breath in a room void of oxygen. Finally, she rocked back up onto her knees and stared at Dummett. The woman had also taken a bump to the side of the head, and blood trickled down her ear.

Apart from that and the horrific shin break, she was alive.

'Get me out of here,' Dummett ordered.

'You're not giving the orders anymore.' Sutton spat, but then sighed. 'But I can't leave you here to die.'

As Sutton lifted herself to her feet, she reached out a blood-soaked hand to Dummett, who took it eagerly. The elder woman screamed as Sutton eased her up, and unable to put any pressure on her shattered leg, Sutton hooked the woman's shoulder over her neck to support her. Dummett hopped to steady herself and then looked to the woman she'd tried to have executed.

'Thank you, Jess.' She tried to smile. 'I won't forget this.'

'Neither will I,' Sutton replied. The threat was clear.

Slowly, they turned and with careful steps, Sutton guided Dummett around the beam that had broken her leg, and then they shuffled back across the floor in the vague direction of the stairs. The temperature in the warehouse was rising dangerously, and although the smoke was finding its way into the night sky, it clawed at them both with its suffocating claws. Dummett whimpered with pain at every hop, as her left leg swung uselessly beneath her knee. Held together by the muscles and tendons, Sutton doubted the woman would ever walk properly again.

Throughout the ordeal, Sutton hadn't heard the footsteps that had made their way to the top of the stairs, and as they ventured towards them, a figure began to appear in the smoke.

Sam?

A few more steps, and Sutton had her answer. Jay caught her with a sickening right hook that sent her stumbling backwards and Dummett flailing to the ground with a shriek of agony. Sutton's legs clipped the chair she'd freed herself from, and she tumbled to the metal below. She spat blood onto the metal as she tried to get to her feet, and as she pushed herself onto all fours, she felt the merciless boot of Jay collide with her ribs and send her crashing into the table.

'Where's your big mouth now, bitch?' Jay spat angrily, as he stomped towards her through the smoke. Sutton tried her best to fight, but with the little air she'd left driven from her lungs by the man's boot, she felt his hands wrap around her throat and press down on her windpipe.

Feebly, she threw weak punches that slapped against his arms, and as the world began to blur, the last thing she remembered was the crazed look in the eyes of the man who killed her.

With the fire crackling from the vehicle beside him, Sam tried his best to focus his hearing. With his back pressed against the bumper of the van, he knew that soon the gunman would appear beside him with a bullet for him.

He had to act.

With his leg throbbing, Sam rolled himself onto his front and peered underneath the van. Through the thick smoke, he could see the black boots tentatively making their way around the side of the vehicle.

He had seconds.

Sam took a few deep breaths and envisaged all the people he was fighting for.

He thought of Sutton, somewhere on the floor above, hopefully still alive.

He thought of Vokes, a family man and a good detective, fighting for his life on an operating table.

He thought of the families of PC Melanie Dyer and PC James Harrington, no doubt filled with pride when they watched their children pass out as police officers and now, no doubt, broken to their core at their murders.

He thought of Jamie.

His sweet boy, who'd been taken from him.

Sam had to stand up.

He had to fight.

Sam slammed both hands onto the bumper and began to pull himself up, ignoring the pain as the skin on his tricep began to tear even wider. As the blood gushed down his arm, he grunted and shuffled onto his left foot, taking as much pressure off his right foot as possible. The back door to the transit van was still unlocked, and Sam popped it open and slid a hand through and wrapped his fingers around one of the weighty gold bars. As he lifted it, the man stepped around the van and Sam saw the panic in the man's eyes as he raised the gun.

Sam threw the door open.

It swung on its hinges and slammed into the man, knocking his arm to the side and as the gun loosened in his grip, Sam drove the gold block down onto the man's wrist, shattering it and sending the gun sprawling out of the warehouse and into the rain. The man howled with pain, but then turned and charged into Sam, sending them both crashing back into the van and the man drove his elbow down as hard as he could. Sam managed to lift his arm up to absorb the blow, and then swung the bar again, cracking the man across the jaw and sending him stumbling backwards. Dazed, the man threw a lazy punch, which Sam ducked and as he felt his leg buckle beneath him, Sam steadied himself and then drilled the man with an uppercut to the stomach. As the man hunched over, Sam grabbed the back of his head and drove him through the glass window of the van door. The man stumbled back from the shattered glass, his face lacerated with a number of cuts, and then Sam clobbered him once more with the gold bar that sent the man spinning to the ground.

He wasn't getting up.

Sam looked down at the gold bar, knowing how far people were willing to go to obtain it, and then casually tossed it into the flames of the other burning van. He bent down and pulled at the seams of the man's jacket sleeve, ripping it from his motionless arm, and then he wrapped it around his calf and pulled it as tight as possible then knotted it.

It was rudimentary, but it would work.

Sam peered around for the gun, but with the smoke and the darkness, he couldn't see it. The sound of a body crashing into something at the top of the stairs drew his attention and with a small grunt, he limped towards the stairwell, leaning against the handrail as he lifted himself up step by step. As he reached the top step, he peered through the smoke at the woman lying on the ground; her face covered from the smoke and the bone of her shin protruding through her trouser leg.

It wasn't Sutton.

Behind him, he heard the faint sound of a struggle and as he shuffled through the smoke, he soon saw Sutton pressed down against the ground and the man from the hospital straddled across her chest. His hands were wrapped around her throat, and her fists were feebly fighting for survival. Ignoring the pain in his calf, Sam stomped through the smoke and as he last footstep drew the man's attention, the wide-eyed look of shock on the man's face was obliterated by Sam's knee. The blow snapped the man's head into the side of the table, and as it rebounded back, blood pumped from the gash of the impact. Sam wrapped his hand around the side of the man's skull and drove it once more into the sharp edge of the wood, cracking it, before locking his other hand under the man's jaw and pulling his hands in different directions.

The velocity snapped Jay's neck, and the man slumped to the side. Dead.

Beneath his lifeless leg, Sutton gasped for breath and Sam reached down and helped her to a seated position.

'Hey.' Sam smiled and then extended a hand to pull her to her feet. 'Smart thinking with the phone.'

'Thank you.' Sutton stood, gently massaging her bruised throat. 'You saved my life.'

'Don't mention it.' Sam shrugged, and then as he turned, his leg buckled and he fell to a knee. Sutton went to help him, but he held a hand up. 'I'm okay. Get her out of here.'

Sam pointed towards Dummett, and Sutton begrudgingly marched across, hauled the chief inspector to her feet, and then helped her down the steps. Sam followed close behind, trying his best to find a weapon among the smoke and wreckage. Once they stepped out into the rain, Sutton dropped Dummett to the concrete, and the woman cried in pain once more. Feebly, Dummett turned and rested on her elbow, looking up at the bloodied and bruised detective.

'Let's call this in together, Jess.' Dummett pleaded. 'I can make sure this makes your career.'

Sutton leant down, her face contorted in a hateful scowl.

'Fuck you.' Sutton snarled. 'You'll go down for a long time for this.'

As Dummett began to weep at the inevitable future she faced, Sam stopped by the van where he'd retrieved the gold bar and opened the doors as wide as possible. There were another thirty or so bars that had been stacked, and lifting two at a time, he began to toss them into the fiery blaze of the van beside him. Dummett looked horrified, and Sutton stepped towards him.

'Sam? What are you doing? That's evidence.'

'Too many people have died for this,' Sam said grimly, tossing the final two blocks into the blaze. 'People can't kill for something they can't have.'

'That won't melt in there.' Sutton pointed to the flames that were now flapping over the gold bars. Sam shrugged.

'You never know.' He offered her a smile.

Turning with some difficulty, Sam limped towards Dummett and then took a knee beside her. The woman looked defeated, and the pain of her injuries was starting to turn to shock.

'Where can I find him?' Sam barked and Dummett woozily mumbled. 'Hey. What's the plan? Where's Silva?'

'Tell him and I'll say you cooperated,' Sutton offered, standing behind Sam with her arms crossed. After a few moments, Dummett told them about the window of opportunity they'd be granted on the airspace, and the hanger where the private plane was. Security would be mysteriously 'absent' for an hour on the back entrance to the runway, giving Silva enough time to load the vans and take off.

Sam stood as Dummett's head tipped backwards. Without a word, he turned and limped back towards the warehouse.

'Sam?' Sutton said with worry. 'Let me call it in.'

'There isn't time.' He turned to Sutton and smiled. 'Call this in and wait here for the police. Tell them everything. And if they get to the hangar and I'm still there, then so be it. That's my problem.'

'Sam…I can't just…'

'I need to finish this.'

With every perceived connotation she had of the man melting like the vans beside them, Sutton stepped in, wrapped her hands around Sam's neck and pulled him in for a hug. She squeezed him as tightly as she could, and Sam slowly rested his hands on her back. There was a war within him, Sutton could sense that, and she knew that there was no way for it to end other than for Sam to take the fight to Silva. After a few moments, she let go, and Sam gave her shoulder a gentle squeeze before he limped towards Silva's motorcycle that was parked underneath the stairwell. The keys were still in the ignition, and Sam wheeled it out into the rain and then swung his leg over it.

'You ever driven one of them before?' Sutton asked, raising her blood splattered eyebrow.

'No.' Sam revved the engine. 'But there's a first time for everything.'

He smiled at Sutton, who couldn't hide her worry.

'Be careful, Sam.'

He nodded, revved the engine and then burst forward

into the rain, leaving the flaming warehouse and the two police officers to deal with the fallout.

As the rain hammered against him, Sam followed his headlight through the winding roads towards the unmanned gated entrance to the Gatwick runway.

He just hoped he wasn't too late.

CHAPTER TWENTY-SEVEN

As the final bullet from Sam Pope's gun blew out the back window, Silva wrestled for control of the van, straightened up, and then thundered back down the stoney road. He laughed to himself, pleased to have escaped from Sam's ambush, but as he sped past the trees that lined the pitch-black road, that levity soon melted to rage. The headlights illuminated the raindrops ahead of him as he slammed his forearm against the steering wheel, loudly cursing at the plan gone wrong.

It was supposed to be the biggest payday of his life, but Pope had intervened and things had spiralled. As much as he loathed Pope, the true failure sat with the Metropolitan Police, who couldn't do the simple task of turning their own detectives off his scent. Detective Sutton was an impressive woman, and ultimately, she was just doing her job. But their inability to steer her away had put more officers in the firing line and Silva refused to put them on his conscience.

If he had one.

Now, with the chaos behind him, he mourned Sutton, knowing that Jay had been champing at the bit to end her life. The man had proved to be loyal and capable, and had things worked out smoothly, then Silva would have ensured he'd walked away with a reward. Now, he'd be left to the wrath of Sam Pope and if somehow, he evaded that, then he'd face a lifetime behind bars. Silva wouldn't shed any tears for the man, but it was an unfortunate return for the man's loyalty. Once he'd joined the main road again, Silva turned the van towards the airport, where the large flight tower loomed in the distance, lit up against the dark night sky. The air traffic control team would be subdued, and the security on the far west gate to the runway would be absent. Silva had forced Dummett to call through to Henshaw, who'd confirmed that the order had been placed.

Silva didn't need to know the details, nor did he care. If Henshaw had exaggerated his influence, then there would be more blood on his hands and no money to wipe them clean. They had threatened Silva's reputation and his freedom with their inadequacies, and Silva planned to disappear into the sky with the small fortune in the back of the van. He'd be able to pay for the pilot and crew's loyalty and then that would be it. Henshaw's political career would most likely lie in tatters, scattered among the ashes of the Metropolitan Police's credibility.

By the time the truth came out, Silva would be a ghost.

As he rounded the corner towards the gate, Silva could see the lone hangar at the back of the runway and the private jet parked outside of it. Beyond the warning lights across the runway, the rest of the airspace was in darkness, and miles into the distance, the commercial airlines and the terminals of Gatwick were alive with colour. Security had been told to stand down for the hour, which gave him more than enough time to load the gold, fix himself a drink, and take a comfortable seat. When the hour was up, he'd be thirty thousand feet in the air and miles away.

Strategically, Silva killed the headlights as he approached the gate, where the barrier had been lifted and the outpost deserted. Slowly, he guided the van across the dark tarmac, keeping his eyes on the dim light of the few spotlights that were peeking out from the hanger. The van slowed to a crawl, and he pulled it to a stop at the side of the hangar and got out.

Voices.

Silva lifted the M16 assault rifle from the passenger seat and marched around the side of the building, where he saw two men, backlit from one of the two spotlights in deep discussion. Both of them screamed military, with their broad physiques and cropped hair and to the side were a few suitcases.

'Gentleman,' Silva called out, snatching their attention. He kept the M16 hidden by his side, shielded by his leg. 'I wasn't expecting company.'

The first man turned with an arrogant smirk and rubbed his hands together.

'Mr Henshaw wanted a few assurances about his investment,' he said and then arched his head towards his colleague. 'We're just to ensure everything runs smoothly.'

'I see.' Silva nodded, then whipped up the M16 and squeezed the trigger. The first burst of bullets lit up the cocky man, sending him spiralling to his death. The second snapped into action, but before he could even move, Silva sent a flurry of bullets into his chest. The man stumbled backwards over his suitcase and dropped to the ground. Silva lowered his weapon and shrugged. 'Smooth for me.'

Panicked, the pilot and the two stewardesses emerged from the private jet, begging for their lives. Silva angrily remonstrated with them, promising them their lives as long as they had him up in the sky within the next fifteen minutes. Reluctantly, the pilot agreed, and Silva even ordered one of the cabin crew to fix him a drink for take-off. As the terrified crew disappeared into the plane, Silva approached the two corpses and patted them down.

They weren't armed, which Silva felt slightly insulted by.

He opened one of the dead men's suitcases and tipped out the mediocre clothing and then carried it around to the back of the van he'd parked in the darkness. He wrenched open the back doors, slammed the case onto the floor of the van and began loading it with gold.

In the distance, he heard the unmistakable roar of a motorcycle. Angrily, he zipped up the suitcase, leaving four of the bars that wouldn't fit into the small container, and then lowered it to the tarmac with considerable difficulty. The motorcycle's engine thundered through the gate, but the headlights quickly died as Sam killed the engine. Covered by darkness, he allowed the bike's momentum to roll through the shadows as Silva wildly emptied his assault rifle into the abyss. The sound of gunfire had obviously alerted the cabin crew, who'd drawn up the stairs to the private jet and slammed the door shut. Silva kept his finger on the trigger until the unmistakable click of an empty clip echoed and Sam stepped off the bike and let it drop to the ground. Silva's head snapped in his direction, and although Sam was a good hundred yards from the hanger, he could see the resignation on Silva's face.

There wasn't enough time to get away.

Not anymore.

As Sam hobbled through the darkness, he watched as Silva casually tossed the rifle into the shadows, reached down for the suitcase and then strode back beyond the wall of the hanger, lugging the gold behind him. A minute or two later, Sam emerged around the side of the hangar. As he limped into view, Silva slowly began to clap his hands.

'You are impressive, Sam,' Silva said as he sat on one of the trunks that lined the back of the hangar. With two floodlights positioned on either side of the hanger, their bulbs angled up to the curved roof of the building, the dim lighting gave Silva a sinister shadow across his face. 'Don't get me wrong, you are a pain in the ass. But impressive.'

Sam limped a few more steps into view. Silva noticed the effort it was taking.

'It's over, Dom.'

Silva chuckled.

'Look at us, eh? First name terms.' Silva patted his thighs. 'Can I ask you a question, *ese*? What's in this for you, huh?'

'Nothing,' Sam said firmly, shuffling a few more steps towards Silva. He glanced across to the two men who were lying in crumpled heaps in a steadily building pool of blood. When he looked back to Silva, the mercenary gave a playful shrug.

'Whoops. But seriously, what is in this for you? I'm interested to know, because all I know about you, Sam, is that you piss a lot of people off. Kovalenko. Vasquez. Many, many more. And for what? You get no glory from the people you protect. I see the news, man…you're public enemy number one in this country, *homes*.'

'Because someone has to do the right thing,' Sam said, grimacing slightly at the pain in his leg. Silva crumpled his face with disgust.

'Please. The right thing would be for you to hand yourself in. You think I'm a criminal, Sam? But we are the same. The difference is, I get paid to kill people. You do it, *vato*, because you *like* it. You love being this hero, this figure of fear. But to me, you're just a fool who doesn't know his own worth. Now me, I think we could do a lot more good if we worked together.'

'You think what you're doing is good?' Sam shook his head. 'You're a mercenary. You killed police officers.'

'Save me the speech, Sam. All of this, this was at the

word of your people. Your police force. Your politicians. I'm just a businessman. But together, *ese*, we could change things. We could overthrow governments, start revolutions. And get paid a lot of money to do it.' Silva swept his hand in a grand gesture. 'All of this was just a business transaction. Your political landscape wanted to make a change, so they needed the money to do so and also wanted enough chaos to make the people believe they wanted a change. I had my suggestions and then you stepped into the middle of it and discombobulated it all. Had you not…maybe there wouldn't be as much bloodshed? You ever think about that?'

Sam contemplated the words for a few seconds and then looked around the hangar. There was every chance that the full force of the Metropolitan Police were heading their way and there was every chance that when the time came, they'd throw him in with the likes of Silva.

He was a criminal.

He was a killer.

But Sam knew he wasn't a bad man.

'I wish I didn't have to do the things I do.' Sam confessed. 'But someone has to fight back. So how are we doing this?'

Silva sighed.

'That is a shame. Because there is a seat on that jet there…' Silva pointed to the private jet behind them. 'And I'm going to get up now. I'm going to take that suitcase and I'm going to get on that plane. Last chance to come with me, Sam. Do something for yourself for once.'

Sam rolled his shoulders.

'I know you're out of bullets,' Sam said dryly. 'I watched you waste them.'

Silva smiled cruelly.

'And I know you're not strapped, *vato*, otherwise we wouldn't be having this conversation.' He pointed to Sam's calf. 'That's a shame. I'd have preferred to kill you when it would have been a challenge.'

Sam bobbed his head, as if weighing up a decision. He cast a glance over his shoulder to the darkness beyond the plane. No sign of the police yet, and if what Dummett had confessed to him through her pain-stricken groans, nobody would be looking their way.

They were alone.

Just the two of them.

No back-up.

No weapons.

Sam reached down and tightened the knot around his makeshift tourniquet and then straightened up. Slowly, he slid his arms from his sodden jacket and tossed it to the side. He clenched his fists a few times, flexing his muscles to warm up, and he rolled his shoulders once more. Silva sighed, slapped his knee and pushed himself off the trunk. Like Sam, he tossed his jacket to the side, and stretched out his back with a few twists of the waist.

'I don't think we have a lot of time,' Sam said bluntly.

Silva smirked.

'Hard way it is then,' he said, relaying Sam's earlier threat back to him. In the dim glare of the floodlights, the two dangerous men approached each other, knowing full well that there was only one way to end this.

CHAPTER TWENTY-EIGHT

As Commissioner Sarrett followed the armed response unit down the country road, she could see the smoke rising through the rain to the clouds above. She'd been on high alert since the afternoon, when after not receiving a go ahead from Dummett, she'd taken it upon herself to venture to the safe house in Thornton Heath, which was the last known satellite signal for her phone. The phone had been in transit for a while after, but that was it.

Everyone had disappeared off the grid.

Since that moment, Sarratt had held an armed team on high alert and had stationed herself at the safe house in the event of Dummett returning. But something had felt off, and when the call came through to her phone, she'd been surprised when it was Sutton's voice at the other end of Dummett's phone. Sutton gave them loose directions but had told her to look out for the smoke.

Now it made perfect sense, and as her car rolled to a stop, she stepped out into the rain with her mouth open in shock. The warehouse was ablaze, with numerous vehicles crumbling under the flames that engulfed them. Littered around the outside of the warehouse were dead bodies, and sitting to the side, soaked through by the rain, was DS Jessica Sutton. The woman looked like hell, covered in cuts and bruises and a thick layer of soot and she'd removed her jacket and laid it over the prone body of Chief Inspector Dummett who was out cold beside her. As the armed response unit filtered out of the truck and began to sweep the area, Sarrett ignored their calls to stay back and rushed towards the detective.

'Is she…' Sarrett pointed to Dummett, and Sutton shook her head.

'She's alive. I think the pain finally got to her.' Sutton nodded to Dummett's leg, and Sarrett winced at the sickening sight of the protruding bone.

'Is it true?' Sarrett demanded, struggling to hide her betrayal. 'Was she behind all this?'

'Most of it,' Sutton said coldly. 'But Henshaw, he's the one behind it all. Some bullshit about a new political regime.'

'Jesus,' Sarrett said, mainly to herself. Sutton stood and stretched out the pain in her back.

'It was all for money. Fifty million in gold.'

'Where is it now?' Sarrett asked and then followed Sutton's finger, that pointed towards the blaze. 'Right. And Sam?'

'He's not here.'

'Where is he?' Sarrett demanded in an attempt to assert her authority.

'You know, I wanted to be a police officer because I always believed that whenever someone had one of these…' Sutton took out her warrant card and held it up to the rain. '…that they wanted to make this world a better place. Turns out, some people just use it as an excuse to do whatever the fuck they want.'

'Look, I know you've been through hell, Jess.' Sarrett

reached out and put a hand on her shoulder. 'But this isn't over. Not until we have everyone involved.'

'Trust me, Sam isn't involved. But he's gone after the other guy who is.'

'Who?'

'The one who murdered those officers. Silva. I think that's his name. He's the one who tried to kill me, and the one who killed Hasan, too.'

'He's working with Henshaw?' Sarrett began pulling up her radio. A fire engine burst through the darkness of the woods and raced towards the warehouse, followed by two ambulances. The entire place was becoming a beehive of activity.

'He's gone to the airport. Apparently, Henshaw pulled some favours to shut down the security to one of the hangars for an hour. Enough time for them to load up and get the hell out of dodge.'

'And Silva is there now?' Sarrett asked, and Sutton nodded. 'Right, let's go. Let's try to get to him before he does just that.'

As they marched back across the forecourt to Sarrett's car, the commissioner barked an order to the head of the armed response unit, telling them to follow her to Gatwick Airport. As the armed crew began to filter back towards their van, leaving the fire fighters to battle the blaze and the paramedics to tend to the wounded, Sarrett dropped into the driver's seat of the car and flicked on the heaters.

'Right. Warm yourself up. And let's go get this bastard,' Sarrett said with renewed conviction.

'Like I said. Pope has already gone after him.'

'Two for one, then,' Sarrett said, spinning the car around and shooting back down the country road, her eyes gleaming with anger as they thundered through the rain. Knowing she needed to buy Sam a little more time, Sutton made no effort to inform Sarrett or the following armed officers of the directions to the side gate of the runway.

They'd have to go through the front door, through all the bureaucracy needed to get to the runway, and by then, Sutton hoped Sam had done what he needed to do.

Otherwise, she couldn't save him.

If, of course, he was even still alive.

As the rain rattled against the metal roof above them and the bitter wind swirled through the hangar, Sam and Silva narrowed the distance between them. Roughly five feet from each other, they both slowed, raised their fists and tentatively approached, each man sizing up the other. Silva exploded forward first, drilling Sam with a few right jabs that he managed to block with a forearm before Silva swung his foot and booted Sam in the back of his injured calf. Sam grunted and fell to one knee, but dragged himself away from the following knee strike. Silva chuckled and mockingly hopped on the spot as Sam struggled back to his feet. As soon as Sam planted his foot down once more, Silva launched forward with a one, two combo, and as Sam deflected the first strike, the second breached his guard and caught him in the mouth. He stumbled backwards, dazed, and then spat a mouthful of blood onto the ground.

'Come on, *Ese.*' Silva goaded, beckoning Sam with both hands.

With a grimace, Sam stepped forward, and as he threw a right and a left, Silva weaved under both like a championship boxer, before he drilled Sam in stomach with a hard right, and as Sam hunched over, Silva caught him flush across the cheekbone with a pinpoint haymaker.

Sam hit the ground.

As quickly as he did, he rolled, dodging the stomp from Silva, but as he tried to roll to his feet, his leg gave out again, and as he faltered, Silva slammed his knee into the side of his skull, sending him sprawling backwards into the suitcase of one of the dead men. Sam groaned with pain, and Silva sighed, stretched out his back and looked up at the roof.

'This is disappointing,' he said with a rueful shake of the head. 'But I guess I do have a plane to catch.'

Silva took a step towards Sam, and as he drew up his foot to drive it down onto Sam's chest, Sam swung his right leg and swiped away Silva's standing foot. The mercenary dropped like he'd stepped on a banana peel, and as his back hit the concrete, the air was driven from his lungs. As Silva tried to push himself up onto his elbows, Sam hoisted the suitcase with all his might and swung it at his attacker. Silva got both hands up, but the impact still sent him snapping backwards and his head cracked against the concrete behind him.

He rolled to his feet, but then wobbled slightly. He pressed his hand to the back of his head and winced.

His fingers returned blood.

Sam stumbled back to his feet, and Silva showed him the blood and smiled, seemingly impressed. As the two men circled each other again, Silva made a few intimations of leaping forward, before he eventually did, hammering Sam with a flurry of body shots but then as he threw an uppercut, Sam weaved to the side, slid his arm over Silva's, then drilled his elbow into the Mexican's mouth. Silva fell back a step, his lip split, and Sam followed it up with a hard right that sent Silva sprawling against the trunk at the back of the hanger. Sam limped toward him, and as Silva threw a wild left hook, Sam ducked it, and as he rose, he caught Silva with a right hook of his own. Blood sprayed from Silva's mouth, painting the wall of the hangar, and as he fell backwards on the trunk, Silva jolted his foot out into Sam's stomach, halting his momentum. Nimbly, Silva pushed off from the trunk, ducked a blow from Sam, and then drove his foot into Sam's calf again. The pain was instant, and as it caused Sam to buckle forward onto one knee, Silva stomped on Sam's spine, sending him crashing face first into the metal trunk.

As Sam turned over and rested his back against it, the trunk was smeared with a bloodied face print, and Sam could feel the blood running from the gash across his forehead.

Silva took a breath, wiping the blood from his lip with the back of his hand before pointing his finger at Sam.

'You have some fight in you, *homes*. I'll give you that.' Silva reached down to the cuff of his trouser and pulled it up, revealing the small, six-inch Bowie knife that was strapped to his ankle. He pulled it from its case and spun it expertly in his hand before pointing it at Sam. 'But unlike you, Sam…I have something to fight for. And that…that always wins.'

As Sam pulled himself up via the blood splattered trunk, Silva charged and drove the knife towards Sam's stomach. Sam caught Silva's wrist, stopping the murderous blade a few inches from his abdomen, and Silva looked up at Sam in shock.

'I always have something to fight for.'

As Sam growled through gritted teeth, he caught Silva with a vicious headbutt, shattering the bridge of the man's nose and sending him stumbling backwards. With the pain shaking his skull and his eyes watering, Silva wildly slashed the knife in Sam's direction as he approached, but after the third unsuccessful swing, Sam caught Silva's arm, twisted it, and then drove the palm of his hand into Silva's locked elbow, snapping it upwards and causing the man to howl with pain. The knife clattered to the floor, and Sam swung

Silva by his useless limb and hurled him into the wall of the hanger. Silva, with his arm hanging limp by his side and his face covered with blood, roared angrily. He exploded like an Olympic sprinter towards Sam, who tried to move but Silva slammed his shoulder into Sam's stomach, and with his good arm, swept Sam's legs and took him off the ground, before driving him down to the concrete with a sickening thud.

Both men hit hard, and as Sam tried to draw in a breath, Silva viciously slammed his fist against the fresh bullet wound that had ripped through his calf. Sam threw out his other foot, catching Silva in the face, and as Silva rocked to the side, Sam reached out and wrapped his fingers around the handle of the discarded Bowie knife. As he got to his knees, Silva pushed himself to his feet and ran at him again, diving forward with a knee that was aimed for Sam's jaw.

Sam leant back, the blow missing by milliseconds, and as Silva landed in front of him, Sam rammed the knife as hard as he could into the man's heel.

Instantly, Silva dropped to the ground, screaming in pain as the blade obliterated his achilles. There was no coming back from it, and as Sam pulled himself to his feet, he limped the few feet towards Silva, and roughly removed the blade, drawing another guttural roar of agony from the man. For a moment, Sam stood, catching breath and doing his best to ignore the near unbearable pain of his calf. In the distance, he could hear the wailing of sirens, and he looked beyond the private jet to the North Terminal of the airport.

Blue flashing lights.

The cavalry was arriving.

Sam turned back to Silva, who, like Sam, had a face covered in blood. A monument to the hellacious battle they'd just shared.

'Just kill me, *vato*.' Silva almost begged, rolling onto his back. His arm was limp and useless, and blood was pooling around his decimated ankle. 'Just fucking kill me.'

Sam tightened his grip on the knife and took a step toward him.

'No.'

Silva frowned, and Sam tossed the knife into the shadows surrounding the hanger, and then back to Silva, who, despite the immense pain that had gripped him, began to chuckle.

'I like you, Sam,' Silva spoke in clear agony. 'This is a mistake. Because somewhere down the line, *Ese*, I will come back for you.'

'I'm looking forward to it,' Sam said grimly. 'Until then, this country needs to see the face of the man who killed those officers. They need to believe in the justice system again.'

With that, Sam limped past Silva, who made a feeble attempt to reach out to him. As Sam shuffled towards the edge of the hangar, he could hear Silva behind him.

'This is bullshit, Sam.' The man cackled, before chuckling to himself.

Sam stepped out into the cooling rain, which hammered against his broken body and began to wash away the blood. He stumbled towards the van that Silva had arrived in, which now had just a few loose gold bars strewn in the back. The sirens were getting louder, and as Sam disappeared into the shadows, he looked back to see the private jet bathed in a blue light, and he watched as Sutton and Sarrett emerged from one of the cars and rushed into the hangar.

There were three bodies on the ground.

Enough to keep them busy.

Sam ambled back through the darkness to the motorcycle, and with great difficulty, swung his leg over it, and leant forward across the bike. He looked back one more time to see the armed response unit scanning the edges of the hangar, throwing tactical hand signals to each other.

Sam revved the bike to life and shot off towards the gate, knowing that before the police had a chance to mobilise, he'd be long gone.

The bike sped through the darkness, sped through the rain, and Sam shot through the gate.

It was over.

CHAPTER TWENTY-NINE

There was nothing worse than an arrogant man.

Sutton could feel her blood boil as Graham Henshaw walked through the office of New Scotland Yard, his expensive three-piece suit a symbol of his wealth and power. The Minister of State knew that his reputation within the Met was tainted, and the decisions he'd made that had impacted the organisation were loathed, but he was bullish enough with his self-belief that people fell in line.

The man walked with an air of invincibility.

After the previous night's events, the national media were having a field day. The rumours of the gold theft had been blown up into public knowledge, and the reports of further deaths within the Met were being used once again to whip the country up into a panic. Every TV screen in the office was alive with images of Gatwick Airport, and angry passengers complaining about their inconvenience.

If only they knew.

Sutton didn't begrudge the public for not knowing what was going on behind the scenes, but she did find their irritation at their flight being delayed amusing. The bigger picture would never be shown to them, but the fact that senior police officers had aligned with dangerous mercenaries to murder and steal would make an extra few hours in an airport seem relatively quaint by comparison. Henshaw threw a few false greetings to some of the officers as he approached Commissioner Sarrett, who stood in the doorway to her office with a calm authority. Less than twelve hours before, she'd stood beside Sutton in the pouring rain, watching as they loaded a brutally beaten Dominik Silva into the back of an ambulance, his hand cuffed to the metal bar of the gurney. Now, she stood in her immaculate uniform, hands behind her back and a look of control across her face.

'Minister.' Sarrett shook Henshaw's hand. 'This way.'

'Let's get this mess sorted shall we?' Henshaw said rather accusingly, and he stepped into the officer. Sarrett turned and flashed a glance to Sutton, who she'd kept with her ever since they'd returned from Gatwick. She'd offered to take Sutton home so she could rest, but there was no stopping now.

Sutton needed to see this through to the end and Sarrett had admired it.

With some discomfort, Sutton eased herself off the chair behind the desk that Sarrett had assigned her, and she held up a hand to a fellow officer who looked on with concern. Her face was already beginning to bruise from the clubbing blow from Silva's murderous right-hand man, and her ribs were aching from the stiff kick he'd given her. The man had tried to strangle her, and although there would be no lasting physical damage, her throat burnt with every swallow of saliva.

She felt like hell.

She looked like hell.

But she was still standing.

As she opened the door to Sarrett's office, Henshaw

snapped his head back to look at her, his eyebrow raised with confusion as he lowered himself onto one of the plush, leather seats.

'Can we help you?'

'DS Jessica Sutton.' She introduced herself. There was no handshake. Henshaw looked to Sarrett for an answer.

'DS Sutton was involved in the arrest of Dominik Silva last night. She can help us get to the bottom of this.'

Sarrett was effortlessly becoming the commissioner that her predecessor had told her she was destined to be, and she gave Sutton a respectful nod. The detective took the seat beside her, and both women looked across the table at the slimy politician. Henshaw, feeling outnumbered, doubled down on his bravado.

'Well, good work, DS Sutton.' He drummed his fingers on the table. 'But I'm not too sure what more needs to be done? The man responsible for the robberies and the murders has been captured. Near ten million of the gold returned to the Bank of England.'

'Five officers. Dead,' Sarrett said coldly. 'Another four currently in the hospital with serious or life-threatening injuries. We are pretty far from done, Graham.'

The temperature felt lower, and Sutton looked at Sarrett in awe. The woman struck an authoritative figure, and as she interlinked her fingers and rested her hands on the table, Henshaw seemed to sense the shift, too.

'Well, of course there have been casualties. And believe you me, I will be working diligently to ensure that safer measures are put in place for our officers going forward.' He looked at the two women, who glared back at him. He adjusted his collar anxiously, searching for the right answer. 'And I will personally meet with every family of our fallen heroes to not only offer our sincerest apologies but to…'

'Will you have time for all that?' Sutton spat. She'd

heard enough, and Henshaw's eyes widened with anger at the interruption.

'Excuse me?'

'Will you have time for that? You know, with your new political plans and all the backpeddling you'll have to do.'

As his nostrils flared with rage, Henshaw turned to Sarrett for a response.

'Can we just let the adults in the room talk?'

'I think what DS Sutton means is we have considerable evidence, Graham, that you were not only the main bene-factor of the operation to steal the gold, but you in fact put the whole plan into motion yourself.'

'Oh, fuck off.' Henshaw laughed, rocking back in his chair as he adjusted his tie. 'You'll never find anything that sticks.'

Enraged by the man's arrogance, Sutton shot from her chair and marched around the table between them.

'Sutton…' Sarrett half-heartedly interjected.

As she stomped towards him, Henshaw's façade dropped, and as Sutton leant down into his personal space, a look of genuine panic spread across his face. She gripped both of arms of his chair, locking him in place. Her stare was unblinking, and her bruised eye was laced with hatred and her beaten face was twisted in a scowl.

'Because of you, my partner is clinging to his fucking life and his family are praying he pulls through. Because of you, good officers have died or had their heads turned by greed. All for what? Blood money?' Sutton shook her head in disgust. 'Chief Inspector Dummett has told us every-thing. Backed up everything. So you can sit here, in your fancy fucking suit, and act like you give a shit, but the only thing *you* need to worry about, is what happens to bent politicians in prison. And how much protection you think the guards will give you when they know what you've done.'

'That's enough.' Sarrett stated firmly, hammering home her order by dropping her fist on the table. Sutton stayed in Henshaw's face for a few more seconds before she stood and straightened her jacket. 'Thank you, DS Sutton.'

With that, Sutton nodded to the commissioner and marched out of the office, the glass door gently closing behind her. A few other officers, who'd seen her performance, looked at her in amazement as she once again took her seat. From her desk, she watched as Henshaw's body language morphed into that of a broken man, as Sarrett clearly and concisely laid out what they had on him. Two uniformed police officers, who'd shown Henshaw to the office soon appeared once again and a palpable excitement swept through the office with the same velocity as the rain-soaked wind outside.

Henshaw was cuffed, dropped his head, and was then escorted back through the office to face the severity of his crimes. Sarrett watched from the door of her office, and once the disgraced politician disappeared round the corner, the commissioner turned on her heel and approached Sutton, who'd watched Henshaw's walk of shame with a feeling of emptiness inside.

'Well, that was fun,' Sarrett said, trying to lighten the mood. She regarded Sutton for a few moments. 'Take a few days, get some rest.'

'I'm fine.'

'That wasn't a suggestion, sergeant.' Sarrett's tone hardened. 'With everything you've been through, I understand you're feeling betrayed. But the Met needs good people. So just think about it, okay?'

After a few seconds, Sutton nodded.

'Yes, ma'am.'

Sarrett reached down and squeezed Sutton's shoulder. As the head of the Met strode back to her office to deal with the carnage of the past few days, Sutton felt the

exhaustion begin to worm its way through her body. Everything ached, and her head was pounding too hard to think
about the decision she needed to make. She'd told Sarrett
on the journey back from Gatwick that she was done with
the Met and the broken system it represented and had
been met by resistance then.

The Commissioner of the Metropolitan Police didn't
want her to leave.

But with a grunt, Sutton pushed herself up from the
seat and headed for the exit, wondering if she'd ever step
back into New Scotland Yard again.

Before she headed back to her flat in Finsbury Park, Sutton
had taken the train across town to Charing Cross and then
braved the cold as she walked from the Tube station to the
police headquarters. It had felt like weeks since she'd last
been in the office, when in reality, it had been a few days.

The whole world felt like it had been tipped on its axis.

A few of the uniformed officers who she knew offered
her a few kind words about Vokes, and wished him well.

All she could do was force a smile and nod.

The saddest thing about the entire ordeal was she no
longer trusted anyone. For her whole career, she'd always
felt a connection to the ideal that everyone who put on the
uniform or carried a badge was sworn to a code of honesty
and purpose. To serve and protect, and while there were
officers who bent the rules or skirted a little too close to
edge, she'd never once come close to the undercurrent of
corruption that clung to the Met like a parasite.

It was always about money.

Money or power.

Those two commodities would always win out, and
although she felt a sense of justice at the broken shell of a

man that Henshaw was reduced to, she knew it wouldn't be long before another person took his place. Maybe not a politician, but there would always be a root of corruption embedded in the police service, and it made her sick to her stomach.

Finally, she made her way to her desk and, as she picked up a few of her belongings, her pocket vibrated and she pulled her phone out.

It was Laura.

Swiftly, Sutton accepted the call and lifted the phone to her ear.

'Laura?'

'He's going to be okay, Jess.' Laura Vokes sniffed through her tears. 'He's pulled through.'

Relief hit Sutton with such a velocity that she collapsed into her chair and tilted her head up to the ceiling.

'Thank fuck for that.' Sutton sighed. 'How are you? How are the boys?'

'They're fine. They're with my mum.' Laura sounded exhausted. 'I just wanted to you to know. They say it's a long road ahead as the bullet did some damage, but he should make a near full recovery.'

'Well, if there is anything you need…'

'You've already done so much.' Laura took a breath. 'He told me you saved his life…'

'Not exactly…' Sutton began.

'Thank you, Jess.'

Sutton felt the enormity of the past few days weighing heavily on her already throbbing skull and she nodded to herself and then said her goodbyes. After she disconnected the call, she sat in silence, her eyes focused on nothing in particular as her thoughts ran away with her.

There was so much to contemplate.

Too much to work through.

All she knew was that they found the bastards responsible for the deaths of innocent police officers, and the reasons why. She should have felt even a flicker of happiness, but all that clung to her was guilt.

Guilt that she couldn't do more.

Guilt that one of the few people she trusted in the world was facing a long road of pain, and the exhaustion that would fall upon his young family as he faced those struggles day by day. Although she should have been thrilled that it was her intuition along with her dogged determination that ultimately uncovered the web of deceit within the British government and the Met itself, all it had done was shatter lives.

Physically, Connor Vokes might never be the same again.

Mentally, she was broken.

Her faith in the institution had evaporated and her trust in good people was now waning. Commissioner Sarrett had tried to offer her another path, one that would see her working closer with the top brass at New Scotland Yard, but Sutton found herself questioning the validity of her words. It was a daunting prospect, to live the rest of her life in a permanent state of suspicion, but she'd found herself strapped to a chair and on the cusp of execution due to the actions of senior police officers.

There didn't seem like much of a way back from there.

As her eyes scanned the strewn papers, they fell upon a small white card that was placed on her desk at some point in time.

She couldn't remember when.

Detective Inspector Thomas Gayle.

Office of Professional Standards.

For a while, she held the card between her thumb and index finger, trying to place how or why the card had found its way to her desk.

But it had.

And as her fist clenched around it, crushing the card into a crumpled ball, she felt her hand begin to shake.

Something clicked within her, and she booted up her laptop. In the hours after returning from Gatwick, Sutton's adrenaline had denied her any notion of sleep, and she'd spent hours typing up her report of everything she could remember over the past few days. Everything pertaining to the orders given to her by the recently killed DCI Hasan, to every conversation with Sam Pope himself. She'd made no attempts to hide her collusion with Sam, who she made clear had saved both her and Vokes's life, and without whom, none of the truth would have come to light.

But there were a few other reports she'd read regarding the whole ordeal, and a few details she needed to amend.

It was the least she could do.

Her final act before everything about her life and career would change for good.

Then, she headed out of the door with a renewed purpose echoing through her shattered body.

She could still make a difference.

But most of all, she needed to sleep.

CHAPTER THIRTY

The week had been one of the most explosive in the recent history of the British political system. Once the news broke of Henshaw's involvement and arrest, the government had gone into overdrive to try to distance themselves from a prominent figure within their party. Henshaw had a number of supporters, and the man who'd once been clearly positioned as the next in line for the top job, was now the poster boy for political corruption and greed. The public, who'd long since lost faith in the government, were now baying for blood and Henshaw was the one who was hung out for them to bleed dry.

He was going to spend a long time in prison and the media were adding their usual sensationalistic touches to every story.

Dummett had also made the news, although her cooperation with the police had ensured that she'd at least see a little leniency. The fact that such corruption had existed so close to Commissioner Henrietta Sarrett had caused a number of Henshaw's backers to call for her head in retaliation, but a few endorsements by former commissioners Stout and McEwen soon poured water over that potential fire. It was all moving at the speed of light, and Sutton flicked through the endless articles about the crumbling state of the country and felt halfway responsible.

All she'd done was her job.

Sought the truth.

Fought for it.

Whatever the cost.

'You okay, hun?' the waitress asked, gesturing to the faded bruising around Sutton's eye. Sutton nodded, and the waitress shrugged and placed her coffee in front of her, and then went back to work. Sutton cradled it in her hand before adjusting the wool scarf that was scratching at her neck. It was either slight discomfort, or having everyone stare at the purple hand marks that still wrapped around her throat.

It had been a week since she'd spoken to Sarrett and confirmed to the commissioner her next step, and despite Sarrett's attempts to bring Sutton into her inner circle she soon realised that Sutton's mind had been made up.

Sutton had gratefully accepted the few days off to think it over, and she'd spent most of them at the hospital, where Vokes was now in full recovery. While he wasn't mobile, and would require some physio to get back to his best, it had been nice for her to sit with him, Laura and their boys and just feel somewhat safe.

Somewhere appreciated.

It would probably be a long time before she was as welcome in a room, or in a place where she was loved and respected.

But that was all part of the decision.

As she doom scrolled through her phone at the litany of articles predicting the downfall of the country, she felt the shadow of someone loom over her.

'This seat taken?'

Sam.

Without even thinking, Sutton dropped her phone onto the table and stood, launching herself into the man's arms. A few people turned and looked at the reunion, but for a full minute, she buried herself into his shoulder as he hugged her. She hadn't seen or heard from him since he'd driven away on the motorbike that fateful night at Gatwick, and she'd been sceptical about meeting with him. Despite everything, there was still the righteous cop residing inside her, and Sam was *still* the most wanted man in the country.

But without him, she'd be dead.

Vokes would have been dead.

Henshaw would have been on the road to victory.

The country owed the man a debt that they would never know, and the reason she'd agreed to meet with Sam was because he'd never ask them to pay up.

Sam didn't want anything from the country or the people he fought for.

Sam finally let go and looked her over.

'You're healing well.'

'Can't say the same.' She smirked and then took her seat. 'Where have you been?'

Sam gingerly lowered himself into the chair opposite and caught the eye of the waitress who smiled her acknowledgement. He turned back to Sutton and smiled to himself.

'About. Kind of hard to do too much after you stitch your own calf up.'

Sutton took a sip of her coffee and frowned.

'You know how to do that?'

'I had a good friend who was a medic,' Sam said warmly. 'He taught me a thing or two. How's Vokes?'

'He's okay. I mean, he's not, but as good as expected. He'll make it through.'

The waitress reappeared and looked sceptically at the

man who'd joined the table, clearly comparing the cuts and bruises on his face to the ones on Sutton's. Sam ordered a tea, and she shrugged, took the order and scrambled away. A silence sat between the two of them, and Sutton was a little perturbed at how comfortable it was. Eventually, she mustered up something to say.

'So, are you going to vanish again?'

'Vanish?'

'You know…head off into the sunset to fight another good fight.'

'If there is one.'

She smiled and shook her head.

'Why do you do it, Sam?' She leant across the table and rested her hand on his. 'None of what happened was anything to do with you. Don't get me wrong, I'm beyond grateful for what you did. But it wasn't your fight. So why?'

Sam's tea arrived, and he thanked the waitress and then took a sip. Everything was better with a cup of tea. He then fixed Sutton with a steely glance.

'Because someone *has* to. Sometimes, Sutton, you and the rest of the law are not enough. And that is why I fight. Because there are people who don't have a voice. Who can't fight back. And it's those people who are worth fighting for. *You* were worth fighting for.' Sam took another sip of his tea and loosened up. 'All that matters now is what you do next.'

'You think I'm crazy?' Sutton asked.

'I think one of the best people I've ever met in my life worked for the Office of Professional Standards. In a world where most people are only out for themselves, Adrian Pearce was the most honest man I'd ever met. The best of us. If you have a chance to follow in his footsteps, weed out the corrupt within the Met, then I'd say you were pretty far from crazy. I'd say you were one of the few who can see straight.'

Sutton blew out her cheeks and nodded. Her decision to take Detective Inspector Thomas Gayle up on his offer to bring her into OPS had been the easiest one to make, but she knew it would change her future drastically.

Nobody trusted OPS. Trying to catch out your own officers was seen as betrayal, and she knew that her life inside the Met would never be the same again.

'On the level, did Pearce help you?' Sutton asked bluntly, and Sam smiled. 'I just need to know.'

Sam took a sip of his tea before answering.

'Adrian saw what I saw. And somewhere along the line, he saw what was needed. Let's just leave it at that.'

'Is that why he left?'

Sam shrugged.

'You'll have to ask him yourself.' Sam reached into his pocket and handed her an envelope. 'You ever find your cause or your belief wavering, give him a call.'

Sutton frowned with confusion and lifted the envelope and tore it open. She pulled out a sheet of paper, which had Pearce's number on it. The implication was clear – she wasn't going to have many allies in the world, and having a direct line to a man that Sam Pope trusted wasn't the worst idea. She also pulled out a USB stick.

'What's this?'

'The truth,' Sam said as he stood. 'About Bakku. About Bloom, Hutchins and Grant. I told you I'd give you everything. Well, there it is.'

'I don't understand.'

'Look. This country is going to hell in a handbasket and the people who walk these streets need to believe in the Met. They need to see that no one is above the law. Now I could take that list, and I could take them down one by one. But they don't need me to do it.' He offered her a smile. 'Trust me, that list will make you a lot of enemies.'

Sutton stared at the stick for a few moments, twirling it between her fingers.

'Just so you know, I removed any mention of Ben Carter from the files about Gatwick and Henshaw.' She looked up at Sam.

'You didn't have to do that.'

'I know. I don't know why I did.'

Sam stepped around the table and placed his hand on her shoulder.

'Because it was the right thing to do.'

As his words hung in the air, Sutton tilted her head and rested it on her hand. They didn't need to speak their goodbyes, and a moment later, Sam released his grip and walked back across the coffee shop to the door. He pulled open the door, looking out to the rain and the busy city before him. He shot one glance back to Sutton, met her gaze with his own, and nodded.

She called out to him.

'Hey, Sam.' She smiled. 'The reports mentioned that twenty-one gold bars were recovered from the hangar. I could have sworn there were more in that van?'

Sam shrugged, pulled up his hood and then stepped out into the rain, heading off to wherever he was needed most.

Having the police visit the shop had often made Julien nervous, and his father, Peter, had told him to keep his mouth shut. They knew it would happen eventually, especially when his 'stolen' vehicle was recovered less than a mile from Gatwick where all the commotion had happened. The fact that one of the officers whose death had been a catalyst for all the chaos had happened across the road from their barbershop was too much of a coincidence, and Detective Finch, despite being a reasonably polite man, clearly didn't believe them when they said they had no clue about anything.

Peter said he hadn't reported his car stolen because he didn't have faith in the police, especially around their part of the city, and Finch had almost squirmed under the accusation that they didn't care. To be fair, Peter had a point, and although the estates of Willesden were hardly the wild west, they did feel lawless at times.

Finch had told them, in no uncertain terms, that he'd be back, and Julien chastised his own father for getting involved.

'It needed to be done, son.' Peter had said calmly and then given his son a few days off to clear his head.

The shop was never that busy during the wet, winter months, and early that morning, Peter had arrived by train to open up the shop. The morning Tube was a different beast entirely, and after navigating his way through the throng of commuters heading into the city for work, he walked through the rain-soaked streets from the station and sighed at the fresh graffiti across the metal shutter of his shop. The weather dictated that he wouldn't be out there scrubbing it clean, but in all honesty, it was a pointless task.

More would just appear the moment a fresh shutter was slammed shut.

After making himself a fresh coffee, he sat in one of the leather swivel chairs and gazed at himself in the mirror opposite. Despite his age, he still looked youthful, although the bags under his eyes told him his body was beginning to tire. Maybe it was time to hand the keys over to Julien and enjoy his later years?

Perhaps give back to a community that needed someone to wrap an arm around it?

His morning of reading the latest Richard Osman

mystery book was interrupted by one customer, a gentleman of a similar age who wanted his hair neatened and beard trimmed. It was a welcome interruption, and Peter found himself enjoying the walks down memory lane the customer took them on.

Then he thanked Peter, left a nice tip and went on with his day and Peter returned to his book.

He had no idea how much time had passed when the ring of the bell above the door drew his attention once more and a delivery driver stepped in, holding a heavily wrapped box that seemed to weigh the man down.

'Peter?' the driver asked, clearly relieved to be able to place the box on the counter.

'Yes, sir,' Peter said cheerfully, as he took off his reading glasses and stood. The man took a signature, and Peter raised his eyebrows. 'Who sent this?'

'I just deliver the stuff, mate.'

The driver left quickly, rushing back to his illegally parked van and Peter opened a pair of scissors and carefully guided it across the edge of the box, slicing the tape open. Inside was something wrapped in a thick, white cloth but on top was a folded piece of paper with his name on it.

Intrigued, Peter popped on his reading glasses once more and opened the note.

Peter.

Thank you for believing me. Like you said, I can't change things. But maybe you can. Do some good with this, trust me, the government won't miss it.

Sam.

. . .

With his grey brow furrowing with confusion, Peter pulled back the sheet to reveal four thick, gold bars. With a sigh of disbelief, Peter carefully recovered them, closed the box and then shifted the heavy delivery to the back of the shop. After concealing it safely within the stock room, Peter returned to his seat in the shop and looked out at the dreary streets. Ideas began to rush through his head, and a decision he'd been considering seemed to register with a lot more clarity.

He picked up his phone and sent a message to Julien, asking his son to stop by the shop for a chat.

It was time to hand over the keys.

It was time to give back.

As he watched a few cars zip down the road, his attention was drawn to a group of youths who were loitering at the entrance to one of the estates. They were just kids, with nowhere else to go, no means to get there if they did, and no one really looking out for them.

The world hadn't turned its back on them.

It had never known they were there in first place.

But as he watched them for a few minutes, the usual sadness didn't flood through him.

This time it was hope.

Because if men like Sam Pope existed, then the world couldn't be that bad of a place after all.

EPILOGUE

The most insulting thing about sitting in the private hospital bed wasn't the lack of privacy that had been afforded to Piers Bloom. It was the police presence outside the door. After having his collarbone decimated by a well-placed bullet by Sam Pope, he'd have thought the country would have offered their sympathies that one of their most influential engineers and businessmen had been assaulted by a known vigilante.

Instead, they'd placed him under arrest.

It was Hutchins who'd made a deal, the little rat, and Bloom wasn't surprised when he was told. Despite being seen as a 'crypto king', Hutchins was a man who was ill-equipped to handle such power and Bloom had always protested that he should never have been brought into *Poslednyaya Nadezhda*. But Balikov had insisted that they needed inroads into the crypto market.

Now, everything had crumbled, along with Hutchins's resolve.

For a week, Bloom had sat in discomfort, snapping at the nurses who facilitated his expensive private health care. With no visitors allowed, Bloom let his attention drift to the flat screen television that was built into the wall of his private room.

The news cycle was relentless.

The murders of two police officers were soon linked to the death of a detective and a murderous mercenary with a grudge against the Met. It was like watching a conspiracy thriller played out in real life, and when the connections were made to the biggest gold heist in the UK's history, Bloom was thrilled that the attention would be drawn away from him.

The headline of corruption within the Met was more tantalising for the public than 'rich man breaks the law'.

The name Sam Pope was bandied about by a few panels, erupting into arguments about whether he was in the right for bringing down criminals or whether he was a menace who undermined the authority of the justice system. Bloom knew where he sat on that particular debate, and with hefty prison sentences being suggested for himself, Grant and Hutchins, he knew he'd have support.

Something needed to be done about Sam.

Something permanent.

It was why he'd made the necessary call, and why, when the door to his room opened, he wasn't surprised to see his old friend march into the room with his usual air of authority.

'Piers.' The man said in his well-spoken manner. 'You're looking well all things considered.'

'Fuck off.' Piers snapped. A man of unscrupulous habits, Bloom had found the denial of his daily exercise routine, high calibre chefs and his weekly beard trim to be excruciating. 'So...you have a plan?'

'We have something in the works.'

'In the works?' Bloom's eyes bulged. 'Look at me, Nick. I might not have a fully functional arm again, so when I'm in prison giving out fucking hand jobs for cigarettes, I'm going to be royally fucked.'

'That's a little dramatic.' The man took a seat next to the bed.

'Is it? Easy for you to say. It's not your name and reputation being dragged through the mud, is it? You're not the one with a twenty-year prison sentence hanging over your head.' Bloom drew his jaw tight. 'But you could be.'

The man smiled politely.

'Is that a threat?'

The words were softly spoken, but Bloom understood the threat they were laced with.

'I'm just saying your name would be on whatever list Pope has. You were in those meetings just as much as I was, and you believed in *Poslednyaya Nadezhda*. It could have been you sitting in this bed right now.'

'But it wasn't, was it? Because I'm a very careful man, Piers. And you would do well to remember that.'

As the man stood, Bloom felt his own authority neutered by the imposing figure of Admiral Nicholas Wainwright. As the Chief of Defence Staff for the United Kingdom loomed over him, Bloom was reminded how powerful the man was. Not only was he a respected, long-serving soldier within the armed forces, he was also a powerful, political ally to a number of leaders across the globe. The man held considerable sway, and there were rumours he'd even orchestrated the removal of the last police commissioner. As Wainwright stood before him in his immaculate suit, Bloom sheepishly looked up at him, realising that any idea of threatening Wainwright into action would be met with brute force.

The man may not have been Ervin Wallace.

But he was just as fearsome as the previous incumbent of his role.

'So…what is the plan, then?'

Wainwright smiled; his wrinkled face insincere.

'Like I said, we have something in the works.' Wainwright took one step closer and snarled. 'But believe me, we will end this Sam Pope problem once and for all.'

With that, Wainwright turned on his heels and marched with the authority that his position commanded and left the hospital. Bloom collapsed back against his propped-up pillow and let out a sigh of relief.

Even if it meant prison time, he was comforted by one thing.

Sam Pope was as good as dead.

GET EXCLUSIVE ROBERT ENRIGHT MATERIAL

Hey there,

I really hope you enjoyed the book and hopefully, you will want to continue following Sam Pope's war on crime. If so, then why not sign up to my reader group? I send out regular updates, polls and special offers as well as some cool free stuff. Sound good?

Well, if you do sign up to the reader group I'll send you FREE copies of THE RIGHT REASON and RAIN-FALL, two thrilling Sam Pope prequel novellas. (RRP: 1.99)

You can get your FREE books by signing up at www.robertenright.co.uk

SAM POPE NOVELS

For more information about the Sam Pope series and other
books by Robert Enright, please visit:

www.robertenright.co.uk

ABOUT THE AUTHOR

Robert lives in Buckinghamshire with his family, writing books and dreaming of getting a dog.

For more information:
www.robertenright.co.uk
robert@robertenright.co.uk

You can also connect with Robert on Social Media:

facebook.com/robenrightauthor

instagram.com/robenrightauthor

Printed in Great Britain
by Amazon